BLIND HOUSE
A CHILLING HAUNTED HOUSE THRILLER

JAIMIE LEE BROOKE

First published in 2022 by SpellBound Books
Copyright © Jaimie Lee Brooke

The moral right of the author to be identified as the owner of this Work has been asserted by them in accordance with the Copyright, Designs and Patents Act, 1988.

All rights reserved. No part of this publication may be reproduced, stored in a retrieval system, or transmitted, in any form or by any means, electronic, mechanical, photocopying, recording or otherwise, without the prior permission of the publisher.
This is a work of fiction. All names, characters, places, locations and events in this publication, other than those clearly in the public domain, are fictitious, and any resemblance to actual persons, living or dead, or any actual places, business establishments, locations or events is purely coincidental.

'For Liam and Lewis.'

For Liam and Lewis

CHAPTER 1
BLIND HOUSE 1878

'Why are you doing this? Do they know you're-'

The Doctor struck her hard across the head, 'From now on you are known as patient Number One, and I'm the Doctor. Say either of our actual names and you will meet more than my scalpel. Do you understand?'

Pain spiralled up Patient Number One's legs, up and up towards the pain burning down her arms from the scalpel wounds. Random cuts to cleanse her body and mind. The Doctor put on a white coat then proceeded to make notes, detailing the scale of fear in the woman's eyes and then on to drawing up a treatment plan.

'First to get you in the appropriate attire. And this needs to come off.' The Doctor grabbed a handful of the woman's lengthy blonde hair.

The cuffs chained to her wrists bit into her flesh as she squirmed away from the scissors. Chunk by chunk her hair fell to the dirty stone flooring. Her tears fell to meet them. More notes were made before the Doctor produced the nightgown- plain and white and full in length.

'Keep still.' The Doctor unlocked the cuffs.

She allowed her blouse to be removed and the gown to be placed over her head, the long sleeves rapidly absorbing the blood from her bleeding arms. She screamed out, pulling away her own skirt. Moving her legs was excruciating. If she could take the opportunity to kick the Doctor in front of her now she would. She'd lash out, she'd fight, she would claw off that smug expression. But her legs were broken.

The cuffs were locked back into place; the Doctor knew that restraining her legs was unnecessary. Number One trembled as she watched the Doctor rummage through a box of equipment and then pulled out a hessian sack. It was the look on the Doctor's face that told her things were going to get much worse. Her sobs became uncontrollable as she begged to be left alone.

'Please, I don't know what I've done, please don't. I'm sorry, whatever I did, please I need to go home, just let me- I promise I won't tell...'

The Doctor ignored her and then placed the sack over her head before tying it securely with twine. Number One started to hyperventilate. She fractured her arm once; she'd fallen from a horse and spent some time recuperating at her parent's house. It doesn't matter how old you get, sometimes you just need your parents- and their dog. Speckles, their spaniel with her soft wavy ears. Dogs know don't they when you're hurt? When you're sad. Speckles knew. She'd snuggle into her bandaged arm as if her soft fur and brown eyes could fix it. No one was here to fix this now. She needed her mother and father and she needed their dog. But they weren't coming for her; they wouldn't even know she was missing. No one would be looking.

'This drowning technique is one method in ridding you of this lunacy.' The Doctor pushed her to the floor and dragged a bucket of water over, before gradually tipping it onto the woman's sack-covered face.

Number One gasped as she writhed about on the floor, desperately she tried to hold her breath, but sick filled her mouth. The sack was ripped from her head, and she spat out her mouth's contents, gasping and heaving.

'Disgusting creature.' The Doctor grabbed her shoulders and dragged her to the cage which sat against the wall.

Number One's cuffs were removed before being pushed inside the cage, its door locked. Her neck bent as she tried to sit up, the low roof restricting her movement.

'Treatment will continue tomorrow. I fear you may be here a long time. Play your part well and we shall consider an early release for you.' The Doctor removed the white coat and packed up the equipment before heading out of the door.

Heavy bolts sliding across the door were the last thing the woman heard before all went silent. She pressed her face into the straw bedded floor and sobbed. If it wasn't for the stinging cuts and the sickening breaks from her legs sending shooting pains ripping through her, she'd have thought that none of this was real. None of this was possible. This just couldn't have happened. Sleep did take hold as exhaustion set in, but before it did, her last thought was, *did he know?*

CHAPTER 2

MONDAY 3RD SEPTEMBER 2018

Ghosts aren't real, Megan reminded herself again. Christina would have proved otherwise by now. Christina would have revealed herself and said, 'I told you so.' Megan scanned the Victorian style mansion before her, wondering why people live in these houses and then complain that they think they are haunted. Visually it's terrifying. It's all that you expect an alleged haunted house to be with its grey stucco and stone facade and high pitched roof. There are even gargoyles. Ugly creatures which scream haunted house.

Megan reluctantly left the safe zone that was her car. She crunched across the vast gravelled driveway. *Blind House.* The house name adorned a decorative floral plaque on the impressive wooden door; a small bit of beauty on such a bleak exterior. Even the name was grim. If Christina could see her now she would be laughing. *I need you,* Megan breathed in wishing her friend was here. It should be the two of them. It was their new business venture. It wasn't meant to be just Megan. Christina was the one who believed, the one who could have pulled this all off. Now Megan, who doesn't feel remotely sensitive to ghosts and spirits felt like a massive fraud as she knocked on the door. She remembered how much she was being paid. *I have to do this. I can do this.*

Instead of Lurch from the Addams Family opening the door as Megan feared, she was relieved to be greeted by a less threatening appearance- a man, good looking but red in the face, complemented by a layer of sweat. Most importantly he did not have bolts in his head and he smiled warmly.

'Hi there, Megan is it?' The man held out his hand, 'Excuse me, I've just finished a workout. I'm Marc, I work for Ross. Come in.'

Megan greeted him and stepped through into the reception area.

'So, paranormal investigator?' Marc eyed her up and down. 'You're not what I imagined a ghost detective to look like.'

'Is Ross Huston here?'

'Yeah, he's just cleaning up from his workout; I'll let him know you're here.'

Megan sucked in the air as Marc left the room. She hugged herself quickly, steadying her nerves. She looked around the room admiring the high ceiling and modern furnishings- surprising as it's not what she imagined from the outside. When Ross Huston contacted her, requesting her services, she had to smile and shake off the idea that he was *the* Ross Huston. As if Ross Huston the movie star would be phoning her. It must be irritating for those people who share the same name as the famous. Looking around at the expensive decor now, and the fact that Ross had staff; Megan started to think it could actually be him after all. She grinned, shook her head and started to relax. Be confident, it's your first job, don't screw it up, she reminded herself.

It's him. Shit, it's actually him. Megan clammed up and was unable to compute how to move as *the* actual Ross Huston strode towards her with his hand out. It took embarrassingly too long for Megan to return the handshake.

'Megan Forrest? Ross Huston. Please come through to the living room.' He gently guided her through the arched doorway.

Megan had often heard people refer to celebrities that they have met as being much shorter in real life or different in appearance in some other way, but Ross was just as tall and muscular as his screen presence depicted- and as beautiful. Christina would probably have passed out at this point. Her stomach lurched at yet another painful reminder that she was doing this well and truly on her own. Now would not be a good time to cry.

'Pleased to meet you Mr Huston, sorry if I was a little startled, I didn't expe-'

'You may call me Ross. We need to discuss terms before we begin, please sit.'

Megan perched on the end of the plush sofa, terrified of actually creasing it. The immaculate and well-presented white and cream furnishings suggested that children definitely didn't live here- it just wasn't possible.

'I hope you understand Miss Forrest-'

'Megan.'

'The importance here of confidentiality. Our dealings here must remain private.'

'Of course, I completely underst-'

'Ghosts, I mean… look, as briefly discussed over the phone, some strange things have been happening. I have a reputation and none of this can get out to the press. I'm doing this for my wife to put her at ease.' Ross handed Megan some paperwork.

'And where is Mrs Huston?' Megan leafed through the documents.

'She left yesterday for London; she needed a break from this... she was getting scared. I promised to sort it, get someone in. Please sign the document.'

Megan spent a few moments reading through it. She wouldn't have thought of running to the press in any event. The thought of attracting fame and attention made her feel uncomfortable. She paused over the section explaining that she would be required to hand over her mobile phone whilst inside the property. Any photos or video footage taken with a camera would remain with Mr and Mrs Huston and not to be shared externally. All footage was to be deleted before any cameras were taken off the property on finishing the investigation. Likewise, any usual and personal day to day activity from within the household must not be reported to the press. If Megan needed to explore the grounds outside then she must consult the security guard, Marc Thorne, first in order for him to ensure no paparazzi were outside and then he will accompany her at all times. Any breach of these terms will result in legal action.

Megan scribbled her signature, despite feeling uneasy. She didn't feel completely ready for this job in the first place, let alone this level of intensity. She swallowed the acid forming in her throat. Thinking of the alternative documents that had turned up at her home for unpaid debts, she handed the paperwork over to Ross. Not that it was her home anymore, not since she ran from it, but she wondered if everything would catch up with her. *I need this job.*

'Now that's out the way, let me fill you in.' Ross shouted over to Marc to fetch them some tea. 'This house actually belongs to Deborah, my wife. It was handed over to her about two years ago by her parents who have relocated to Australia. It dates back to the mid nineteenth century. With the help of Deborah's Uncle Ian, they researched the house's history and discovered that in its early years it was used as a private residence for the mentally insane. Deborah is convinced that the ghosts here are that of those patients. There is no evidence elsewhere to suggest any other deaths under this roof over the years.'

'So you know that these patients died?'

'Deborah spoke with a local historian who said that records were scarce, when it came to private residences for the insane. Often the families of the ill wished for it to remain a private matter. Other evidence suggests though, that the mentally ill of those times often lived out their days and died where they resided.'

'And what do you believe?'

'I believe that my wife is genuinely terrified. It's true that strange things have happened, but I like to think I'm rational... ghosts? No, but I'll do what it takes to keep the Mrs happy.'

Megan pulled out her notepad and pen and gratefully accepted the tea Marc had offered. She took the smallest of sips- the danger of spillage was high.

'So run through some of the unusual activity that you've both witnessed.'

Ross sat back in his armchair and gestured with his eyes for Marc to leave the room.

'Like I said, I'm a rational guy, so much of it I'm sure there could be an explanation, but for me, the weirdest thing has to be the sounds of women crying- muffled cries- distant. Every day for the past week, I'd say. Deborah never heard it so I assumed that part was just in my head.'

'And what about Marc? Does he spend a lot of time here? Has he heard these cries? Anyone else living here?'

'No, it's just me and Deborah. Yes, Marc is here a lot. He's in charge of our security and a good mate. He lives in, as and when required. I recall that once he said that he thought he could hear a woman crying but shrugged it off as it was so faint.'

'And what else?'

'Things being moved, sudden bangs, thuds and knocks in the night, pictures falling off the wall and ending up on the other side of the room, glasses falling off the counter and smashing. You know the usual stuff you hear about... I mean it's an old house, it's gonna creak and bang right?'

'What about any CCTV footage, you must have security cameras? Caught anything on tape?'

'Yes, Marc went through some footage and did spot the odd thing being moved, including one of the glasses that fell off the kitchen counter. There is also one dodgy image of a possible white misty figure moving upstairs. I'm not convinced by it. I'll get him to show you the footage later.'

'Yes please. I'd like to take a look around the house now if that's okay? Then I'll get my equipment from the car and get started.'

'I'll just fetch Marc to show you round.'

Megan swallowed down her remaining tea and breathed in deeply. She hadn't realised how lightheaded she had become; did she forget to breathe from the moment she entered the house? Crying women: she shuddered, rubbing each of her arms. I just need to set up my equipment, pretend to talk to dead people and declare that there are no ghosts here, she reassured herself. Simple. It wouldn't be to Christina's standards but Christina knew that she was the sceptical one, so what else would she expect?

Megan flinched as Marc burst through the door. She cringed and hoped it wasn't obvious.

'Bit jumpy Miss Forrest?' he grinned, holding the door open, gesturing her over.

She got to the doorway but Marc blocked her path. He was now wearing a suit and it hadn't escaped her notice how handsome he looked. She blushed at their close proximity and she could smell his subtle aftershave. He held out the palm of his hand.

'Your phone, please Miss.'

'Yes of course... yes sorry.' She fumbled for her phone from her back pocket and handed it over. As she followed him out into the hallway, it hit her how unsafe she felt in a strangers home- despite how famous he was. Without her phone, she suddenly felt cut off- vulnerable even. This was definitely a bad idea but she knew that there was no going back now.

CHAPTER
THREE

Megan gasped at the view of the impressive formal-looking garden through the large double patio doors at the far end of the kitchen. Daylight was just beginning to fade and a few scattered solar lights twinkled like something from a fairy tale. She looked around the large kitchen with its deluxe fuel range cooker. Imagine baking in this kitchen with that view, she marvelled- she wouldn't even mind doing the washing up either. She traced her finger over the marble-topped kitchen island.

'So, Ross said that a glass fell off by itself?'

'Yes,' Marc moved next to her, 'right where your hand is actually. Caught it on camera.'

'But Ross doesn't believe it was a ghost?'

Marc smirked, shaking his head, 'Ross is scared alright. If he's told you any different, then he's lying. The man is terrified. Yes, he thinks this house is haunted.'

'Oh, and you?'

'Well I shall reserve judgement until the expert confirms it.'

He winked at Megan. The inside of Marc's suit jacket started to vibrate. He pulled out Megan's phone and held the screen up to her. 'Scott wants you. Take it. It's okay if I can hear your conversation.'

Megan shook her head. 'Shall we move on?'

They both entered a second sitting room. This one had a less sterile feel to it than the other one. Plush sofas covered in throws, original beams, a fireplace and rugs on the wooden floor felt more in character to the house. A striking oriental vase next to the fireplace looked a little out of place Megan thought but then what did she know of interior design? She thought back to her sparse little flat. It may not have been much but now she didn't even have that. She was never going back. Ever.

'Do you know how Ross found me? Surely there are well known celebrity paranormal investigators he could have called on?'

'Just scrolling online for someone, Ross doesn't always like the celeb scene. He gets his kicks out of dealing with the ordinary folk.'

'Well I'm flattered then... I think.'

'So are you picking up on anything yet Miss Ghost Detective?'

'I need to see the whole house.'

'You know your phone is going off again. Scott is persistent. Boyfriend?'

'Just turn it off. Can we carry on?'

Marc raised his eyebrows and gestured his hand towards the door. They look around the rest of the ground floor- a small study, a laundry room, a cloak room and a small gym. As they head upstairs, Marc mentioned the ghostly shadow he caught on camera. Megan looked up and around.

'Where are the cameras?'

'There aren't any inside the house. I set them up temporarily in an attempt to capture some footage before we contacted you.'

'Sounds like you have this in hand on your own then.'

'Ah but I don't claim to talk to ghosts like you do. I can't ask them what they want. That is where you come in Miss Ghost Detective.'

Megan thought that if he called her that one more time, she may have to punch him in his sarcastic mouth. At the top of the stairs, the door facing them opened and Ross stepped out, closing the door behind him.

'I would prefer it if you didn't come in this room at any time,' Ross said, 'this is my room and to be honest there has been no activity in here anyway… paranormal activity. The rest of the house is all yours.'

'No problem,' Megan replied. She looked along the landing, it was dimly lit and it looked to branch off in different directions. The walls were lined with mahogany panelling and the door frames were crooked; a deep maroon rug ran along the wooden floors length. Unlike downstairs, it was dark and unwelcoming. Megan felt that she would prefer not to enter any of the rooms in fact.

'Excuse me; I have to take a video call with my agent. I'll catch up with you shortly,' Ross said, retreating back into his room.

'This way,' Marc headed across the landing and stopped outside a door further along. 'I assume you've heard that Ross is in the running to be the new Inspector Dark? They are finalising talks now. If he takes the part, then he'll be off to Ireland for a year or so. He has a house there too and one in the States. Yet this is the place he calls home and it doesn't even belong to him.'

'No I didn't... I don't actually follow celebrity news, to be honest I haven't seen any of the Inspector Dark films.'

'Now there's a novelty,' Marc grinned and opened the bedroom door.

The room was large with an imposing four poster bed. Small windows revealed the rapidly fading light. Tapestries hung from the wall; the whole room had a musty feel to it.

'Such a contrast to downstairs,' Megan said. She suddenly thought had she already said too much, was that rude? Should she have lied and said that she knew all about Ross and his acting career?

'Deborah loves all this olde-worlde stuff. Ross likes it modern, hence the difference downstairs. It was a condition of him moving in. He likes to impress his guests; he likes to entertain.'

'Sorry, it's not my business really. So what kind of paranormal activity happens up here?'

'Bangs in the night, the sounds of thumping on the walls and the floorboards creaking.'

Megan pressed her foot firmly into the carpet and released it to hear it creak. She looked over at the tapestry and met with the eyes of a soldier in battle with his gaping mouth and bloodied eyes. At his feet was a large black dog, twisted and bearing its sharp teeth. Megan smoothed the gooseflesh on the back of her neck and for a moment she felt lost. She had seen a similar dog before.

Marc broke her thoughts, 'There are five further bedrooms all similar to this one, I'll show you mine.'

They turned left at the end of the landing and entered the first room to the left. As Marc had said, the room was similar in style to the other one. This room though had large windows, overlooking the gardens and woodland. A large plasma TV complete with an X-Box and PlayStation sat adjacent to a large desk supporting three PC monitors and a keyboard. Marc approached the desk and flicked on the screens. The monitors displayed the area to the front of the house, either side of the house and the gardens out the back.

'Here you go, my office slash room.'

Megan looked closer at the screens, 'I'm surprised there is no CCTV inside of the house, you have the outside well covered.'

'Ross and Deborah enjoy their privacy. Ross always says he has enough of being surrounded by cameras at work.'

'Is Deborah an actress too?'

'You really don't know your celeb gossip do you?'

'I'm not really... I don't-'

'Deborah is a makeup artist for stage and screen. She's quite famous for it, done makeup for all of the big names, won awards and stuff. It's how she and Ross met. I reckon, Deborah would like more time in front of the camera, she's had a few failed attempts at breaking into the acting world.'

Megan broke eye contact and scanned the room. She felt a twinge of inadequacy again- embarrassed that she didn't know this stuff and began to panic that she wasn't making a good impression.

'So have you experienced any activity in this room?' Megan changed the subject, this is what she was here for, she told herself not to care what Marc, or Ross for that matter, thought of her. She had her own little world to rebuild, far removed from this one. She needed to focus.

'Paranormal activity you mean?' Marc's eyes twinkled, 'Well I've heard thumps on the wall in here and the lights have been known to flicker. Oh and once, I swear the wardrobe door opened by itself.'

Megan moved over to the wardrobe and stroked her hand across the double doors.

'I think I may be picking up on something in here. I think I'll set my equipment up in here first, if that's okay?'

'Sure. Shall we finish checking the remaining rooms and I'll help get your kit.'

Megan noted that Marc didn't look at all alarmed at the suggestion of a presence in his room. He looked amused if anything. Self-doubt crept in again, not that it had completely left her. *I have nothing left to lose* Megan reminded herself. *Literally nothing.*

'Lead the way then,' she smiled. Fatigue had already set in and putting up this pretence was probably going to mentally finish her off, but she would do it with a smile on her face. She would do it for Christina.

CHAPTER 4
TWO WEEKS AGO

'So?' Christina started the ignition, pulling away from the Old Needle Works and Mill.

'What?' Megan smiled sheepishly.

'One last Ghost hunt. One last practice. Can we please now hit the go live button on our website? We are so ready, you were brilliant tonight and that whole dog thing...' Christina flicked on the main beams, illuminating the lane before them.

'I did see a bloody dog. Great big black thing, like a Black German Shepherd- huge ears. I can't believe no one else did.'

'I never told you the legend of the black dog, did I? So, if you see the black dog it means you're going to die.' Christina let out a mocking evil laugh.

'Jeez not helping. It definitely passed by the window during the séance, it-'

'Anyway so?'

Megan smiled at Christina who was raising her eyebrows and grinning wildly. Shaking her head she agreed, 'Yes, yes okay. Hit the live button when we get back. We are in business.'

'No need, I already did it.'

'What?'

'Look, I already did it. Thought it would take a few days for word to get around and stuff, so I just went for it.'

'Why am I not surpris- oh watch that branch!'

Christina yanked the steering wheel to the right, swerving around the branch jutting out across the road. 'Whoa, think I'm more tired than I thought,' she gasped.

Megan pulled out her mobile and checked the time. Three-Twenty a.m. She stared out of the window for a moment as the shadows of the trees flickered by, allowing a twinge of excitement to fill her chest. Never did she think that she would be running her own business. Advertising, accounts and tax were all things that kept putting her off, the feeling clueless, not knowing the first thing. She did manage to do a short online course to get a basic overview of setting up a business, that and her best friend's knowledge and enthusiasm were enough for her to bite the bullet. Christina must have clocked that Megan had zoned out, deep in thought and placed a hand on her shoulder.

'We need this; this is such a good move for us. Tomorrow night let's celebrate. We are going to be ace business partn-'

'Okay hand back on the steering wheel Chrissy.'

'I can't wait to wave bye bye to ST Style,' Christina scoffed.

'Amen to that. Oh, did you hear another branch closed? Manchester?'

'We def need out before our store collapses too. Not bleeding surprised, the management are shite.'

Christina was right; it was the right time and the right move for both of them. Her confidence and positivity left little room for Megan's self-doubt to creep in, no matter how hard she tried to feel negative. It was just in her nature to not feel worthy or capable of more, but Christina had a way of smashing those thoughts and encouraging her to believe in herself. No one else did that for her, not even Scott- especially not Scott.

'I do love you, you know Chrissy. You had faith in me even when-'

'Hun, listen, don't thank me. You're my rock too. You can thank me by leaving that idiot of a boy-'

Bang. Christina grappled with the steering wheel as the Fiat spun away from the hidden pothole over the brow of the hill. The tyre burst, she lost control, veering off the side of the road. Megan tried to grab the wheel to help regain it, but it happened so fast and with an almighty crash they ploughed head on into a tree. Megan screamed as the impact tried to force her forwards but the seatbelt held her back. She fumbled to release it, unsure if she had banged her head on the window, her ears were ringing and her coordination was off.

'Chrissy, Chrissy. Shit.' With a pounding heart, Megan realised that her friend was motionless, she reached over and felt her head, withdrew her hand and inspected the blood. She shook her gently but there was no movement. Scrambling out of the car, Megan hurried around to the driver's side, but the door wouldn't open. The driver's side of the bonnet had felt the full force of the impact and had crumpled in, crushing Christina's legs. Megan clutched her chest as intense pain shot through her, she cried out loud and with shaking hands she pulled out her mobile and punched in 999.

'Ambulance please.'

Megan got through the call despite the pain in her throat from her sobs. She scurried back around to the passenger side and slid back in next to Christina. Stroking her hair, she reassured her friend that help was coming. That's when she glanced out of the window to see the black outline of a large dog. Megan held her breath and shone the light from her phone in its direction. The black hound sat there motionless, head held high, staring. Then it was gone. Megan shone the light to her left then to her right. *Where did it go?* She gently took Christina's hand, fear consumed her as she held back her tears to try and be brave for her best friend. She needed to hold it together.

'Please Chrissy, wake up, you're gonna be okay, wake up.'

She heard the sirens first and then saw the blue flashes. She lifted Christina's hand and softly kissed it. Help was close; she had to be okay she just had to be. There was no holding the tears back, she let them fall and allowed herself to crumble.

CHAPTER 5
MONDAY 3RD SEPTEMBER 2018

THE REMAINING SUN LIGHT WAS ALL BUT DIMINISHED AS MEGAN closed the curtains in Marc's bedroom. Ross entered the room, joining herself and Marc as she unfolded the flimsy, compact wooden table- its surface a Ouija board.

'Can't say I've done one of these before. Can't say I've ever wanted to either,' Ross tentatively ran a finger across some of the letters.

'Me neither mate but we are in the hands of a pro, she will keep you safe.' Marc winked at him then focused his attention on Ross's hand, he had clocked it was shaking.

'Piss off Marc, I'm not scared. Let's lay these ghosts to rest so Deborah can come home.'

'That's a more frightening thought right there,' Marc joked, dodging the punch Ross aimed at him, 'she's only been gone one night.'

'Remind me why I employ you again?'

Breaking the banter, Megan held up a couple of colourful plastic balls, explaining that they were used as toys for cats.

When a cat plays with them, the balls flash multi coloured lights. Any energy from spirits present can set them off flashing too. She pulled out more of them from her bag, then scattered them around the room.

'All very high tech I see,' Marc said, 'I was expecting proton packs and all that.'

'It's all that's needed... for now.' Megan smiled.

Rummaging through her rucksack had bought her a few more moments to regulate her breathing and to think. Looking at the spirit voice box, she decided to save that one until later. She pulled out a K2 EMF Meter device and examined it for longer than was necessary. Being in the house with an actor- a hugely famous one at that had sparked distant memories of how she used to aspire to being an actress. Her nine year old self brimming with confidence, dancing and twirling on stage in her first lead role in the school production of the Golden Goose. That was the moment her shyness melted away and her imagination ignited, her confidence had blossomed. School productions eased the torment that school could inflict on her, it was her escapism. Six years on and the land of make believe she surrounded herself in collapsed. Her last performance went on to change everything- her confidence, her self-esteem, everything.

I forgive myself. Megan stood up. Christina taught her to forgive herself, so it was time for her to act once more. She allowed her survival instincts to kick in. This is what this was to her now- survival. She placed the K2 EMF Meter down and explained that the lights would flash on it if it picked up on supernatural energy. She turned out the lights.

'Right, if you both rub your hands together, get the energy flowing and place one finger each on the glass. This usually works better with more people as the more energy the better, hopefully we will be enough,' Megan instructed.

'Don't you have a partner?' Ross questioned, 'Your website profiled you as partners, we could have used her pair of hands then.'

'Yes, my business partner Christina... she no longer...she died. Recently.'

Abrupt laughter came from the inky outline of Marc stood opposite her.

'So actually, she is probably very much here with us right now then. Got ourselves some help on the inside or the other side-'

'Jesus Christ,' Ross elbowed Marc in the ribs.

'What?' Marc protested, 'Okay I'm sorry. Truly.'

'If we could just put our fingers on the glass now.' She decided that as she couldn't see Marc's face right now then it wasn't worth punching.

Megan directed the glass across the board to the words 'yes' and 'no' at opposite ends. She called out to the spirits instructing them on where these words were and how to use them before returning the glass to the centre.

'So if we have any spirits with us tonight, please let us know that you are here. Use our energy to push the glass. Let us know how we can help you?' Megan called out then let the room stand silent for a few moments. 'Do we have a spirit with us who was a patient here long ago, a patient who has suffered? Use the glass to answer yes or no.'

A few more moments of silence passed. Megan's eyes had started to adjust a little to the darkness but it seemed to go much darker again.

'Do either of you think it's gone darker?'

Marc disagreed but Ross agreed, convinced that it had.

'I think that you are here with us spirit. What is your name? Please spell your name out for us, use the letters on the board.'

Still no movement from the glass. Repeating her questions a few more times with no luck, Megan left the table and cautiously made her way over to flick the light on.

'No joy from the cat balls either,' she said. 'It's still fairly early and we have to be patient with these things. It's true that spirits are most active in the middle of the night and it's when our senses are most heightened. Let's take a break and I'll do some meditating to clear my thoughts.'

'Right you are,' Ross agreed, 'I'm going to knock us up some supper then, are you hungry Megan?'

'Yes, that would be lovely, thank you.' Megan had forgotten how hungry she was. Nerves had masked her hunger pains for most of the day but now she realised she was starving. She had enough change to scrape together to buy a packet of crisps at the services on the way here but she'd had nothing else since sometime yesterday.

'I'll get on it then.' Ross beckoned to Marc to give him a hand, 'Looks like it's gonna be a long night.'

'Yes, as long as it takes,' Megan replied as they left her in peace.

She sat on the chair, resting her head onto her folded arms on the desk. If she closed her eyes for a second, she feared she'd be asleep. The last twenty four hours had been nothing short of exhausting, crazy, everything. When she woke up yesterday morning, the very last thing that she had expected to be doing now was this, doing a Ouija board with *the* Ross Huston. Life does throw some bizarre situations at you doesn't it? Megan wondered what kind of person Marc was to make such an insensitive joke about Christina. But then she thought back to some of the ghost hunts she had been on and some of the unkind thoughts she had about some of the other guests who claimed to be mediums. It is a joke to those who are sceptical. To be fair if Christina was on the "other side", watching, then she would be laughing at that joke, and at her. She could really use some of Christina's energy now and some advice on how to wing the rest of the night wouldn't go amiss either. She lifted her head and rubbed her eyes. Things would improve once she'd eaten, she just needed food. She also needed to be away from Scott and she was, and that was all that mattered.

CHAPTER 6

YESTERDAY

MEGAN PICKED HER WAY ALONG THE NARROWING CLIFFTOP FOOTPATH until her sanctuary came into view- a cluster of rocks known as the dragon's back. Perching herself on her favourite rock she allowed herself to cry. Her hoodie pulled around her tightly, was just enough to stave off the late evening breeze. She hadn't been to this spot for a number of years, but it had never ceased to be her favourite place. It signified happier times, family holidays before she had ruined everything. As a playful youngster with her ever evolving imagination, she would climb across the dragon's back which had been frozen in time. The dragon would breathe into life and lift her off to carry her into battle over the fearsome waves.

The waves were no longer fearsome but a distraction she needed. Megan's tears flowed freely as she watched the waves crash against the rocks below. She ignored her phone vibrating in her pocket. She was here now and she was never going back. She never wanted to see Scott again. The three and a half hours journey here to Mortehoe was a complete blur, it's like her instincts had just taken over and put her into auto drive. Rummaging through her rucksack, she pulled out some small change. The cash she had managed to snatch from Scott's jacket pocket bought her petrol and a phone top-up. Not much left for food. She knew her bank card wouldn't offer anything more. Right now though, she felt safe and free with all the crap left far behind in Worcestershire.

It was the morning's text that Megan had received from her line manager that was to set off the chain of events. ST Style had collapsed and she was unemployed with immediate effect. The news hadn't gone down well with Scott. They had already sold all but the clothes off their own backs to try and pay off mounting debts- debts that Scott accumulated through gambling and a fondness for weed. Not working himself, Scott controlled Megan's wages, insisting he needed it to keep the drug dealers and other heavies away as his life was in danger- yet there never seemed an end to it and the rent continued to remain at the bottom of the dog pile.

Megan didn't have the brain space to fight with Scott over the sudden lack of income- it was Christina's funeral just a couple of days ago and she was still grieving. One of the last things that her best friend had said to her before the crash was that she should leave Scott and she had already decided that it was over. Putting up with it for so long was easy because she felt that she didn't deserve better. Her best friend had worked hard on her, encouraging her to forgive herself and that she was worth loving- and now she was gone. Images of the crash haunted Megan, not least the image of the black dog which sat at the roadside- watching. She had seen the same creature during the ghost hunt that night. Did it take Christina? Was it watching, ready to take her? Megan had done some research online about old folktales about black dogs who guide spirits to the other side. Christina had joked that if you see a black dog, you die. But she hadn't seen it. Only Megan had and she'd convinced herself that she was next.

Since the funeral, Megan quickly realised that she wasn't going to get the support she craved from Scott- far from it. After that text, he turned on her in a flash. It was her fault and she had to get out there immediately to get another job, but in the meantime, he had a solution.

'Look,' he said, 'there's a geezer I still owe a bit of cash to. It'll be one less debt cleared if you could just do him a favour, you know, sort him out, you know...'

'You've lost me.'

'A quick shag okay, we gotta get some cash. Just shag him then the debts gone.'

'Jesus fucking Christ, my best friend is dead. I just can't belie-'

Scott blocked her walking off and pushed her against the wall, squeezing his hand around her throat. He didn't win any award for being the best boyfriend by any means but he hadn't ever been physical with her, well a few times maybe. Relaxing his grip he paced up and down the small hallway.

'Look, I gotta make a call. We gotta sort this shit.' He kicked the wall and stormed off to the kitchen.

Megan peeled herself from the wall, shaking and not really thinking. She grappled with his jacket which was slung on the floor, found the cash, about thirty-five pounds and ran into her room. She stuffed what little amount of clothes and toiletries she had into a rucksack and grabbed her holdall of ghost hunting equipment before she bolted out of the front door. Not thinking, she started the car and drove, looking back to see Scott chasing her on foot. She floored the accelerator until he gave up and was out of sight.

Sitting on the rocks now, Megan let the waves below clear her thoughts. She didn't know what she was going to do but she wasn't going back, she knew that much. Going hungry and sleeping in the car was a much better option. Tomorrow she would ask around the local shops in nearby Woolacombe and Ilfracombe if they had any jobs going. With daylight fading, and it getting rapidly cooler, Megan lifted herself from the rock but was startled to hear a sudden growling. Looking down at her feet, she saw a little terrier, tail clamped down and teeth on full show.

'Sorry, sorry there,' an out of breath voice of a lady in about her late seventies appeared from behind. 'I must say he's not usually this grumpy.' The lady bent down and re-attached the terrier's lead.

'It's fine,' Megan replied.

The lady looked quite spritely for her age wearing a bright sky blue headscarf and clashing colourful mac and welly boots. She looked striking amidst the overcast late afternoon.

'You know,' the old lady continued, 'I don't think he likes your dog. Maybe you should learn to control it.' The old lady didn't wait for a reply. She tugged on the lead and marched away.

'But I don't have a dog,' Megan's reply trailed off and she once more found herself alone.

Just when she thought her day just couldn't get any stranger, her phone rang. She looked at the screen not recognising the number. Not that she had many contacts on her phone. She resisted answering it for a moment in case it was Scott, but then she did; she figured at least she knew how to hang up if it was him. It wasn't. It was a Ross Huston requesting her ghost hunting services. *Shit.* She had forgotten about the business. It had been a couple of weeks since

Christina had created the website and it went live and no one had been in touch. She wasn't surprised as Christina had suddenly died and Megan did nothing to promote or advertise the business.

Megan tried to halt Ross Huston mid flow to say that she wasn't available, but he was persistent and got his request across instantly and then mentioned payment. Money. Megan listened on. Before she really knew what hit her, she was hanging up after leaving instructions for him to text his address. It was Charlington in the Cotswolds, so it was only back up the M5. She was to be there early tomorrow evening. Sod it, she thought, she really had absolutely nothing left to lose.

She made her way back to her car to try and warm up a bit. She was kicking herself that she didn't grab a blanket from home too. It was fortunate that it was just out of season and she could park in this roadside spot overnight for free. The car's heating could be turned on and off sparingly which would offer some relief. The only thing she didn't have was food. Crying wasn't doing her any good, so she tried to think positively. It's just a night in the car; she'd be earning some money tomorrow working for Ross Huston. She laughed to herself imagining that it was the actor- *as if*, then she could come back and not rest until someone gave her a job. It would all come together, she had to believe it would. How much longer would life punish her for?

CHAPTER 7
MONDAY 3RD SEPTEMBER 2018

Megan wasn't sure if she should be waiting in Marc's room until she was called down or not. Half an hour had passed and the hunger pains were making her feel sick. The only plan she could formulate during this time was to perform a vigil in each room throughout the night and simply wing it. Opening the door, she hesitantly walked along the landing. She stopped, turned and went back to the bedroom doorway. She turned again. Why did everything have to feel so awkward all of the time? No, she decided she was too hungry now to contemplate her insecurities. She marched to the top of the stairs and skipped down them, momentarily stopping at the bottom to admire the high ceiling, the decor and how surreal this all was. Then the waft of the smell of cooking filled her senses.

It was the raised voices from the kitchen, which halted Megan from walking straight in. She gently listened in from the door which was only slightly ajar.

'Cut the crap,' Marc growled, 'something more must have gone on that night. Sarah hasn't spoken to me since. It's been over a week now. Must be some reason she wants nothing more to do with me.'

'Mate, I'm telling you like it is, yes I went to kiss her but she backed off. I was sorry, she was fine, how many times... Christ, get over it, you what? Went on like two dates?' Ross replied.

'Not the point though is it,' Marc snapped back, 'I was really keen on her. She was special. After Michelle... well I can't believe you'd do it to me again.'

Megan pushed through the door; she didn't want to be discovered eavesdropping even though she was intrigued as to why Ross would be trying to kiss Marc's girlfriend. There was a quick awkward silence. Ross broke it by placing serving plates onto the table.

'Please join us,' he grinned. He dished up some leafy green salad and topped each dish with slices of grilled chicken.

Megan perched on one of the stools as Marc passed her some herby lemon dressing. Salad had never looked so tempting. There were even scattered pieces of fruit and chunky croutons. Wasting no time cutting into the chicken, she took a big fork full savouring the explosion of char-grilled flavour in her mouth. Anything would have felt like an explosion of flavour after not eating properly for twenty four hours.

'This is delicious, thank you.'

'You're welcome,' Ross answered looking a little bemused.

Megan was suddenly aware that she was eating a little too greedily so slowed down. She thought it best to discuss the night's plans to break up stuffing her face.

'So I was thinking, in order for me to try and get through to a spirit, it might help if I have a little more to go on. So we think that mentally ill patients from the 19th century are haunting the property, but is there any more specific details you know of? Exactly how one of them may have died? Anything?'

'Nothing,' Ross answered. 'Admittedly I haven't sought to investigate the history of the house. I left that to Deborah. She got the little info she has from her Uncle Ian. He's the one into all that history stuff. Her parents left her the house when they moved to Perth a couple of years ago. She maintains that they only gave her the house as an incentive to stay here and not move with them.'

Marc coughed as he tried to swallow some water.

'Anyway,' Ross continued, 'her parents were of no help. When they bought the house, they had no interest in its history. They were new into money and just wanted to buy the first grand house that took their fancy.'

'So what we have to go on, is what history tells us in general about how the mentally insane were treated at that time. From the little I know from watching TV dramas and stuff is that treatment of patients could be brutal,' Megan offered.

'Yeah, tortured and killed. Maybe right even where you're sitting ey Ross,' Marc mocked.

Ross put his fork down as if he'd just gone right off his food, 'Not helpful...anyway no, no one was tortured and killed in my kitchen. There's no such thing as ghosts, I'm not buying it.'

'But that's where the glass fell off by itself, right there next to your hand,' Marc winked.

Ross stood abruptly and started to clear away the plates. Megan swallowed her last mouthful and refused to hand her plate over, insisting to help clear away. She stood and carried her plate to the sink area.

'Dishwasher's over there,' Ross pointed.

As Megan looked over, a shadow caught her eye from the window above the sink. She froze. She continued to look out into the darkness and there it was again. The moonlight illuminated briefly, the shadowy outline of a large hound. The plate nearly slipped from her fingers.

'Do you have a dog?' Megan blurted out.

'No,' Ross answered.

'I just thought I saw-' Megan decided to not bother with continuing to say what she thought she saw. If they didn't have a dog then they didn't have a dog. It was ludicrous for her to think it was the black dog again. The chances of being the only one to see some random black hound again was moving into the realms of being too weird. *If you see a black hound you die.* Megan couldn't forget Christina's words, she knew she was joking and besides, she didn't die, Christina did. A shrill buzzer rang out, breaking Megan's thoughts.

'Who on earth is that then,' Ross looked over at Marc for the answer.

Marc shrugged his shoulders and slid from his chair. He answered the telecom then pushed the button. Hanging up the receiver, he said 'It's the police. They're at the gates.'

CHAPTER EIGHT

Marc led the two police officers into the kitchen. They introduced themselves as Detective Brian Page and PC Steve Turner. Megan noticed how neither man seemed phased by being in the presence of Ross Huston. How professional.

'Shall I leave the-' Megan started.

'No, please stay. We need to question you all,' Detective Page said. He stepped forward and held up a photo of an attractive woman, late thirties with an abundance of long dark curly hair. 'Do you recognise this woman?' He showed it to Ross first.

'Yes,' Ross said, 'Her name is Kerry...her surname is escaping me now... Beck. Yes, Kerry Beck. Why?'

The detective showed the picture to Marc who also knew her. Megan simply shook her head as the picture was passed to her.

'Kerry is missing,' Page said, 'since the night of Saturday 1st September. Two nights ago. We have reason to believe that her last known whereabouts was here, Mr Huston. In your house.'

Ross ran his hand through his hair, his jaw tightened. He

relaxed his face and looked thoughtful for a few moments.

'Yes,' Ross confirmed, 'she certainly was here Saturday night. I had a small dinner party. She was my guest. It was in her honour for all of her recent charitable fundraising for Childhood cancer... the charity I'm patron of. I recognised her efforts. And she's not been seen since?'

'Her husband reported her missing early this morning,' Page explained, 'the whole family are worried. Very out of character for her not to contact her husband or her mother. She has a son too. Her last known whereabouts only just came to our attention. A friend of Kerry's made contact with us to disclose that Kerry had been here Saturday night. According to this friend, no one knew she was here except for her. Not even her husband. Said that you had got Kerry to sign some papers to consent to strict confidentiality. This friend felt obliged to stay quiet, initially thinking that Kerry was just spending some extra time here and was scared of getting Kerry into trouble. But now she has come forward.'

Ross was clearly looking confused. He pulled a chair up and sat down, inviting the officers to sit also. Megan continued to lean back on the kitchen counter, too afraid to look out of the window and too uncomfortable to look at the police. She focused on her scuffed trainers and the grey porcelain floor.

'Despite my fame-' Ross started to explain.

'Yes, I've seen you in *The Death of The First*,' piped up PC Turner, 'good film that was.' Turner quickly remembered himself after Page shot him a look. 'So can you run through the events of Saturday night?'

Ross continued, 'I'm not big on media attention. I treat many people from my charitable organisations and I don't do it for publicity. Hence the contracts. Saturday night was all straightforward really. Kerry arrived about Seven pm,' he looked over at Marc who nodded, 'we ate dinner by about eightish, then we sat around chatting, ooh, until I guess around eleven-thirty pm?' again he looked over at Marc for confirmation.

'Yeah, that's about it,' Marc agreed, 'Ian, that's Mrs Huston's Uncle, drove her home around that time.'

'So who was present that night?' Page asked.

Marc answered, 'Well there was Ian, then just me, Ross and his wife Deborah here.'

'And where is Mrs Huston now?' PC Turner pressed on.

'She's visiting friends in London for a few days. Left yesterday to have a break from work,' Ross confirmed.

'And you are?' Page directed the question to Megan.

It took Megan too long to realise she was being spoken to. She looked up with a start and apologised.

'I'm...' Megan noted the look Ross quickly flashed her, 'I'm Megan, just a family friend.'

'We'll need the contact details for Ian then. If he drove her home, it would appear he may be the last one to see her. We'll need to confirm his movements,' Page said.

'We have CCTV,' Mark offered. 'Would probably show Kerry leaving with Ian?'

Detective Page and PC Turner agreed and asked Marc to lead the way. They all headed upstairs. Megan discreetly folded up the Ouija board table and moved it to one side as the others gathered around the computer monitors. Marc's fingertips swiftly tapped away at the keyboard, quickly bringing up footage from the date and time in question. Nothing at 23.30 or shortly after, so he rewound it back a bit and there it was. 23.22 showed a dark, grainy image of two figures walking from the front door a few steps across the driveway and then getting into a silver SUV.

Marc rewound and replayed the few moments of footage a few times and then paused it. Both figures had their backs to the cameras the whole time but both Ross and Marc confirmed that the man was Ian and that it was Ian's vehicle and that the woman was Kerry. Page held up the photograph of Kerry and asked Marc to zoom in on the image. Sure enough, the image on the screen showed the woman to be of similar height and build and she had lengthy thick curly locks.

'We'll need a copy of this footage,' Page said. 'And we'll need to speak to Ian to confirm what happened after they drove off.' He handed Ross a card with contact details.

'Give me a moment,' Marc said fast forwarding the footage. 'There.'

Marc stopped and let it play on. The SUV had returned to the house at 23.45. Ian got out of the car alone and walked to the front door.

'That'd be about right then,' Ross said. 'Kerry only lived in the next village. It wouldn't have taken Ian long to drop her off, about twenty minutes. He came in and we stayed up drinking for a bit. He kipped over.'

'We'll still need to interview him,' Page said sternly. 'And Mrs Huston. If she could be encouraged home at her earliest convenience, it would greatly help our enquiries.'

Ross agreed to help fully with anything that they needed. He led the way back down the stairs. Opening the front door, he halted.

'Look,' Ross said in a hushed tone before allowing the officers out, 'will this remain private? I mean, this can't be leaked to the press, right? I'm awaiting news on a big acting role, and this could-'

'It's for the new Inspector Dark movie isn't it, I'm right aren't I?' Turner butted in.

'We have no intention at this stage to make anything public,' Page snapped, 'we are early on in our investigation and your status will not be a barrier should that matter need to change. Good night to you Mr Huston.'

Ross closed the door behind them and took a deep breath. Megan and Marc had joined him at the foot of the stairs. Megan had heard what PC Turner had said and thought it amusing that he was not so professional in front of a famous actor after all. To think that even the focus of something as serious as a missing woman could be lost so quickly when in the presence of a celebrity. At least Detective Page kept it together. *A missing woman though.* She felt the prickle of gooseflesh, suddenly feeling more awkward and a little alarmed. It was a big reality check that she was in a complete stranger's home. She was alone with two men that she didn't know at all. It didn't matter that they were in the public eye. If a detective says that a woman is missing and was not seen since a night here then that would make anyone feel uneasy.

Marc must have clocked her troubled expression, 'Don't worry Megan, Ian dropped her home in one piece. We'll do all that we can to help find her, right Ross?'

Ross rubbed his face, 'Yes of course. What the bloody hell's happened to her? I best call Ian, find out what happened after he dropped her home. Get Megan a drink then I'm going to need my lawyer's number for advice. I best call Deborah too.'

Marc grimaced at Deborah's name, 'Oh she's not going to be happy.'

'No she isn't, Christ. Get me a drink too.'

Megan made her way back up to Marc's room, leaving the men to talk. Little did she know that a black hound followed her all the way. Unseen and unheard.

Chapter Nine

Megan took the opportunity of being alone for a few moments to collapse onto Marc's bed. She hung over the edge so she was upside-down. She felt the soothing pressure of the blood rushing to her head. It calmed her. It was a technique she used when anxiety started to get the better of her. This was one of those times. She realised she was probably going to have to leave now. Things had a taken an unexpected turn and everything felt tense. She'll go back to Mortehoe she decided. Just drive straight back there, despite how late it was. Then she could sleep. The car had been uncomfortable the previous night but she was so tired, she could sleep anywhere.

A deep thumping sound drummed in her inner ear. Thump, thump, thump. She massaged her ears and sat up. She was aware that this would not be a good look if Marc walked in on her. The thumping continued low and unnerving. She pressed her palms against her ears. Marc entered the room and the thumping stopped.

'You okay?' he asked.

'Yes. I was just about to get my stuff together. Best I leave you to it,' she said.

'No need, stay and finish the job. Ross has insisted. We are worried about Kerry but it'll all be taken care of. Ross is on the phone to Deborah now, she'll be coming home tomorrow so it'll help if we can surprise her and say that we've banished some ghosts.'

Megan noticed how Marc's tone had changed- less cocky. His face looked a bit strained. She didn't know whether to feel relieved about staying longer now or not. Driving all the way back down south in the dark wasn't that appealing. But then neither was spending the rest of the night looking for ghosts in a house where a woman spent her last night before going missing. No, like they said, Kerry was dropped home in one piece. This was work and she continued to remind herself, she needed the money.

'Okay then if you're sure, I think I'd like to set up a vigil in the first guest room that you showed me down the landing,' Megan said, starting to gather her equipment.

Marc helped her and then led the way. He left her to set up, saying that he would join her shortly. She turned on a couple of K2 EMF Meter devices and placed them at opposite ends of the room. Then she scattered the cat balls around the floor. She began to unfold the Ouija board table and as it clicked into place, the thumping returned to her ears. A sudden thump much louder came from behind her. She spun round to face the wall but there was nothing to see. Just the tapestry. She edged towards it and looked closer at the battle scene before her. She focused on the black hound that had caught her eye earlier. A disfigured man with the whites of his eyes flooded with blood lay at its feet. Soldiers cowered on their knees in a circle; nothing on their faces except terror, leaving Megan feeling momentarily lost again.

The door flung open and Marc entered holding out a bottle of wine and a couple of glasses. She nearly jumped out of her skin.

'Please tell me that drinking on the job is allowed?' Marc said, his eyebrows arched and hopeful.

Megan smoothed the gooseflesh on her arms and simply said 'Yes, yes it is.'

Since yesterday Megan had said her final goodbyes to her best friend, lost her job, left her abusive boyfriend and her home. Lost everything. She was sure that she was being stalked by the hound of death and now she was in a famous actor's house searching for ghosts of dead lunatics. She wasn't a big drinker, not anymore, but she took a big glug of wine.

'So how do these work?' Marc said picking up one of the K2 EMF meters.

'They pick up electromagnetic frequencies. If there is anything paranormal here, they will light up.'

'You know, I want to reassure you again to not be alarmed about the missing woman,' Marc said. 'Sorry you got caught up in this.'

'Honestly, it's fine.' Megan thought that Marc sounded a little like he was slurring his words.

'I was seeing this woman… Sarah, she had dinner with us a week ago and I've not seen her since. Now Kerry isn't seen after a night here either. The company and the cooking here must be terrible. I shouldn't joke.'

'Is Sarah reported missing too then?' Megan recalled the argument she overheard in the kitchen and wondered if Marc was aware that she had listened in.

'Nah. Wouldn't know I don't think. The number she gave

me is out of action. I never got round to getting her exact address. We'd only been out a few times. She was meant to have spent the week in a hotel nearby so that we could spend more time together, get to know each other but she never checked in. Must have gone back home. And get this, she's not even on social media. She's not calling me; I can't find her.

'You could call the police, see if she's been reported missing?'

'Maybe. Nah, I don't know. She just lost interest in me, I guess. Who the hell isn't on social media nowadays anyway?'

'I'm not.'

'You must have something to hide too.' Marc grinned and topped up their glasses.

Megan was grateful for the wine but she was conscious of needing to remain in control. She was tired and had very little in her stomach. It didn't feel like the best recipe. From the argument she overheard, she knew that Sarah didn't just lose interest in Marc. It had something to do with Ross. But that was none of her business and she felt a little uncomfortable with Marc opening up to her, he'd clearly had a bit too much to drink.

'What the hell did you do in the kitchen?' Ross burst through the door breathless.

'What?' Marc asked shrugging his shoulders.

'Come and see,' Ross urged, 'seriously not funny Marc. You can be a dick sometimes.'

Marc shook his head and he and Megan followed him down the stairs through to the kitchen. Megan gasped. The drawers were all open. The cupboard doors were all open. The bar stools were lying on the floor.

'Well it wasn't me,' Marc protested. 'I came in, grabbed wine and left. Must have been you Ross.'

'Like I said, you're a dick,' Ross snapped.

'It wasn't me,' Marc replied raising his voice. He stormed around the kitchen closing all of the drawers and doors. 'We need to set up cameras.'

'Fine,' Ross said. He rubbed his temples and looked at Megan. 'Thoughts?'

'Well, emotions have been heightened this evening. Our emotions radiate energy. Energy is what spirits feed on... it gives them the energy they need to communicate... to move things,' she answered.

Megan felt in danger of actually sounding like she knew what she was on about. Winging it was definitely her mantra. She had been on a number of organised ghost hunts with Christina. It was their hobby. Christina believed in spirits. She could sense them and had experienced things. Nothing visible, just touches and sounds. Megan never felt anything. Not once. Neither had she seen anything like this. This was the stuff of poltergeist movies. Had they seen this, would they have wanted to rush into starting up a ghost hunting business? Even Christina? She wasn't sure any of this was possible and something weird was going on but what she was sure of though, was the colour draining from her face.

CHAPTER TEN

Megan and Ross gave Marc the space and time to set about rigging up some cameras in most of the rooms. He said that it wouldn't take him long, they were only throw-up ones, the type people use to check on their pets. Ross invited her to sit with him in the main lounge and offered her a glass of single malt whisky. Megan declined, firstly thinking that it wouldn't sit well with the wine that she had but also the fear of spilling anything on the plush sofa was still all too real. Ross began filling Megan in a little over his acting career, how he'd moved to the States to make it big, never actually thinking it would happen.

Ross went on to explain how he was missing his home in the States. He picked up his iPad and nestled on the sofa next to Megan. Her insides fluttered as Ross's leg and arm brushed against hers. Turning on the iPad, he swiped through some photos of his Beverly Hills mansion. It was stunning. Jaw dropping Megan thought. The house she was sat in now was an impressive size but what she was seeing now was something else- like something straight out of a glossy magazine.

'When will you be returning there?' Megan asked.

'Could be another year or so yet. Been here in the UK for eleven months, filming. That's done but now I'm waiting on the go-ahead for Inspector Dark then it's off to Ireland for a year.'

'And does Mrs Huston travel with you?'

'Depends on her work schedule but yes when she can.'

'Has she always been a makeup artist for stage and screen?' Megan asked keen to make conversation whilst ignoring her stomach knots.

'She was your average beauty therapist. Got drafted in through some local agency when we were short of help on a filming project. Not gonna lie it was love at first sight. I continued to request her services and that had a lot to do with boosting her career.'

Ross paused over a photo of his wife and gently stroked the screen.

'It's a lovely story, and good luck then with the Inspector Dark thing,' she said.

Ross asked which of the Inspector Dark films she liked the best and she had to admit that she hadn't seen any.

'So what kinda films do you like then?' Ross asked looking amused.

'I don't know... I don't really watch a lot of-'

Megan jumped as Marc entered the room. She stood quickly.

'So are we all ready?' she asked.

'Yes, good to go,' Marc replied.

Megan suggested starting in the kitchen as there had been obvious activity. Marc agreed but Ross hesitated and said that he would sit it out and go up to his room.

'I strongly suggest you join us,' Megan said. 'We will get this done quicker with more of us, we need your energy.'

Ross reluctantly nodded but made his way over to the far end of the lounge to pour himself another drink first. Marc stepped close to Megan and with a lowered voice said, 'Be careful with him. You're just his type you know.'

Megan couldn't speak she just stepped past him and out of the door. That sounded like a warning she thought. A ridiculous one at that. Megan didn't think she was anyone's type. She wondered how many more glasses of wine Marc had had whilst he was putting up the cameras. She didn't have time for these childish remarks. She was about to face the dead.

Marc led them through to the kitchen and pointed out the camera to the far right corner of the ceiling. He opened up his phone and showed Megan on his app the camera footage. He swiped across and showed images from the other rooms.

'Do you have that footage that you captured on the stairs? Can I see?' Megan asked.

Marc scrolled for a moment and handed her the phone. She pressed play and looked closely. Sure enough a white mist hung around on the stairs. It rose tall, almost human shaped. Faint but visible. Handing back the phone, Megan looked impressed.

'That's incredible,' she said.

'It's dust though, right?' Ross scoffed. 'Lighting... dust... something like that?'

Megan agreed but the human shape it made was fairly defined. It definitely cast an uncertainty. Ross rubbed and squeezed his wrist.

'Don't you get scared?' he asked Megan.

'Let's see what the ghosts want shall we,' she replied. It was a question she didn't want to give an honest answer to. 'Marc, can you turn off the lights?'

The kitchen fell into blackness. Megan prompted each of them to hold hands in a small circle. She called out to the spirits, introducing herself and the two men. She reassured the spirits that they meant no harm and that they just wanted to help. They fell silent. They listened. Not a droplet from a tap or the ticking of a clock could be heard. Silence. Then scrape. Sharp fingernails kind of scrape across the windowpanes of the patio doors. The group jumped back, breaking the circle. Ross smacked the light switch back on.

'What the fuck was that?' Ross gasped.

Marc was already at the patio doors with his face pressed against the window trying to peer out. He shook his head then went to unlatch the lock.

'No don't,' Megan blurted out. She was scared that she knew what was in the garden. She didn't want to believe a black hound was following her, she tried telling herself that it was ridiculous, but she had seen it through the window. She knew she wasn't crazy. It could still be out there. It had taken Christina and now it was coming for her. After witnessing poltergeist activity, she was sure of it.

'She does get scared then,' Marc smirked, answering Ross's previous question.

'We just need to contain the spirits in this room,' Megan said, swallowing down the rising acid. She was beginning to feel sick.

Ross turned the lights back off and made his way back carefully to the others. The second their hands touched again; a shattering smash echoed beside them. Ross ran back to the light switch, this time knocking a stool flying on the way. Megan couldn't hide her fear this time. She clutched Marc's arm and they both backed away from that side of the room. Marc squeezed Megan's hand and gently removed it from his arm. Ross pointed to the cupboards, his hand visibly shaking. Marc slowly edged towards the cupboards, reaching his hand out to open one of the units. Carefully he clasped the handle but then swung it open. Backing up quickly, the three of them observed the carnage. Every single glass inside was broken and smashed.

'Holy Shit,' Marc said.

Ross put his hand inside and retrieved a broken fragment. The piece bit into his flesh, drawing a little blood.

'Okay. I'm outta here. This isn't fu-' Ross took a breath and looked at Megan. 'You get rid of these ghosts... these... and I'll pay you double. Anything. I can't do this.'

Ross attempted to march from the kitchen but Marc blocked his path.

'It's best we stick together, don't you think? You don't wanna be on your own right now. Right?' Marc said.

Ross nudged Marc away from him, 'I'll lock myself in my room. Christ, this is what I pay you for.' He turned to leave but froze as a carving knife slid swiftly from its holder, clattering at his feet. The colour drained from his face and he bolted for the stairs.

'See, told you he was really scared. Making out this was all nothing,' Marc sneered.

'He had a goddamn knife thrown at him,' Megan snapped. She was beyond trying to wing this whole thing. This was a whole new level. Tears scorched her eyes.

Marc put his arm around her, 'We should get out of here. I don't want to stick around either,' he said.

Megan pulled away from him and made for the door. Marc, hot on her heels, guided her to the second lounge. They sat in silence for a few moments. This time they kept the lights on. Megan needed time to process everything. What on earth was going on she thought? Neither Ross nor Marc had described activity that intense when she first arrived at the house. It's not possible. None of this is possible. *Is it?* And what the hell is with the black hound?

'What next ghost detective?' Marc asked.

Megan shot him a look.

'We're out of our depth aren't we,' he continued. 'I'm gonna guess, you haven't actually done this before have you?'

Megan got up and went to the window, not that she could see out of it. She scanned the cosiness of the room. Definitely more homely than the main lounge. She steadied her shaking arms.

'Do you have a gun?' she asked.

Marc raised his eyebrows. 'Ross has a shotgun. Yes. Not usually used for ghost hunting though.'

'We need to patrol outside. I think there's some sort of demon stalking the house. Causing this.' Megan said. She felt all common sense leave her and at her most vulnerable and scared, she had nothing else to lose. She needed to go with her gut feeling, even if that meant she was crazy. What they had all just witnessed was crazy enough.

'Well I don't know, what does a demon have to do with dead lunatics?' Marc asked.

'It's a black hound. This hound it- I think it's some sort of guide to the dead. It takes souls. I've seen it a few times. It's here.'

'And a shotgun will kill it?' Marc asked.

Megan simply shrugged her shoulders then slumped back on the sofa with her head in her hands.

'I'll get the gun,' Marc said and jogged out of the room.

Megan felt the thumping in her ears. This time a bit louder. Quicker. It stopped. Crying. She could definitely hear a woman crying. It was more of an echo. Is that what Ross had described to her? She ran a hand over one of the walls. *What had gone on inside these walls?* When you have nothing to lose you become fearless, right? Marc returned, shotgun in hand. Shoulders back, head held high and with direct eye contact Megan said, 'Let's go.'

CHAPTER
ELEVEN

Megan pulled her hood up to guard against the night's breeze. She shone the torch as they stepped out into the formal garden.

'You know this is nuts right?' Marc said.

'You were right what you said back there,' Megan said. 'I haven't done this before. I've done many organised ghost hunts but this is my first solo job. Christina was the gifted one but I think even she would think we were out of our depth.'

A few of the scattered fairy lights were still shining brightly as they stepped cautiously along the pathway. Megan shone the torch towards the sound of trickling water. There, stood a stone figure of a Roman woman pouring water from her stone jug. She looked angry- sinister even. Perhaps she felt the unrest in this place too? Megan thought.

'She's actually quite beautiful in the daylight,' Marc said, sensing Megan's thoughts.

'Most things are.'

'You know, I don't actually have a licence to fire this thing,' Marc said nodding to the gun he was carrying.

'Let's hope it doesn't come to that then,' Megan said in truthfulness.

'What do your family think of what you do?' Marc asked.

'Shhh, what was that?'

Megan flashed the torch around. Plants and leaves swayed and rustled in the breeze. The fairy lights dimmed and diminished one by one. Megan couldn't swallow. She prayed that she wouldn't see the hound and she prayed that Marc would stop asking her questions.

'The garden leads out to a small orchard and then along to the lake. It circles back to the house. Let's keep moving,' Marc said, guiding her forwards.

They continued in silence, listening out, paying attention to every rustle and every movement until they reached the arched gateway to the orchard. It was impressive. Megan admired the stone wall and marvelled at the gate. She only wished she could enjoy it during the daylight and in less terrifying circumstances. It was the stuff of secret gardens, magic and imagination. The stuff she could only dream about. The stuff that would forever be out of her reach. Marc unlatched the gate and Megan shone the torch around the trees- the trees which also looked angry. The thud of an apple falling at her feet startled Megan. She shone the torch surveying the scattered browning apples along the ground. Leaves gently fluttered down to join them. The apple tree knew it would soon be stripped bare.

Megan hugged and rubbed her arms. The cold was beginning to infiltrate her bones. They picked up the pace along the wider path running through the centre of the orchard.

'We can turn back,' Marc suggested.

'No, let's keep-'

'Shit,' Marc cursed as he stumbled and collapsed in a heap on the ground.

'Did you just trip over an apple?'

'Bloody ankle,' Marc gasped, lying the gun down and clutching his injury.

'Here,' Megan said holding out her hand.

Marc refused the offer and heaved himself up. A sudden shadow ran from behind the tree, darted towards them. Marc grappled for the gun as Megan froze. Her heart pounding she shone the torch at the creature. Marc pointed the gun. With her free hand, Megan pushed the shotgun aside.

'Wait,' she gasped.

It was a fox. Just a fox. A fox that nearly scared her to death.

'Holy shit,' Marc laughed.

Megan allowed Marc to link her arm. Earlier on this evening, she would have been quick to repel him. She'd had her fill of cocky and arrogant men, but right now she was shaking. Through the cold and fear, she was shaking and was grateful that he was with her. They carried on with Marc slightly limping.

The pathway turned to the right and ended at another gateway. The still darkness of the lake now lay before them.

'So the Huston's own all of this. This lake?' Megan asked.

'Yes, it's all part of the grounds, their property.'

Marc gently guided her away from the edge of the water. He laughed and warned her that if she slipped and fell in, he would not go in after her. The odd splash sounded out as if weighty stones were being plopped into the water. Megan shone her torch across the lake but couldn't see anything.

'Fish?' she asked.

'Yeah, they've been known to jump out of the water.'

'It's incredible that Mrs Huston was left all of this,' Megan said.

'Isn't it just,' Marc replied. 'To think, Ross didn't know

anything about her family's wealth when he met her and not even when he proposed to her. It was only shortly after their engagement that he was introduced to her parents. Not long after, her folks announced their move to Australia, leaving all of this in her name. They are loaded.'

'I bet Ross was made up. But he loved her when he thought she had nothing,' Megan said. 'True love.'

'You'd think so,' Marc scoffed.

Megan didn't have time to question what he meant. Another disturbance came from the bushes ahead of them. Marc carefully raised the shotgun.

'Hello?' Megan softly called out. 'If it's you hound. Show yourself. We aren't afraid.'

More rustling and then a screeching sound.

'What do you want?' Megan called again.

They both edged closer. Slowly closer. Megan was fully aware that she was trembling. Marc pointed the shotgun ahead.

'Damn it,' Marc growled as the fox bolted from the bushes, carrying a dead rabbit in its jaws. He kept the gun aimed at the fox. 'I'm going to shoot the little bast-'

'Oh no you're not. You're not killing the fox... I'm going to,' Megan shouted and playfully tried to wrestle the gun from him.

Megan relaxed her grip and stepped away from him. She took a few slow deep breaths.

'That fox will be the death of me,' she sighed.

'C'mon,' Marc said, 'just over there is a small woodland area. It brings you back through to the garden.'

Megan was relieved to get back to the garden and outside the house. She shone the torch towards the kitchen doors. She didn't, however, want to go back inside. The hound was waiting somewhere for her. She knew it was. It was just biding its time. Waiting. She sat herself down on the patio area surrounding the Roman statue. Crossed-legged, she placed the torch on her lap and closed her eyes.

'If you can hear me, let me know you are here. I know you are following me hound,' she called out.

'Megan, there is no hound of death. Like I said, this is nuts. There is no-'

'Nuts?' Megan scrambled back up, 'What? More nuts than what happened in that kitchen?' She shouted, waving her arm over to the doors. 'You saw what went on in there. Anything is possible now, right?'

Marc raised his hands up in surrender. Megan sat back down and he joined her.

'If you can hear me spirits. If you can hear me black dog. Please leave. You're not welcome here. Please leave this place in peace,' Megan called out. 'Just go and leave us. You don't belong here. Not anymore. Not now.'

They both sat in silence for several moments, shivering. Listening and watching. Nothing. Just the sound of the trickling water from the stone jug.

'You know, it could have been the fox... that you saw from the window,' Marc spoke up.

'It was a black dog. A big one,' Megan protested. 'It was there a couple of weeks ago, at a ghost hunt I was on. The same one I'm sure of it. It then sat and watched as Christina died. I saw it... staring. Now, I've seen it here. It's following me.'

'I'm sorry about your friend. I am. But cut yourself some slack. There is no dog here,' Marc said as he stood up. 'We should go back in and deal with the ghosts we know about.'

Megan knew he was probably right and she felt like an idiot. She didn't know if she could face anymore back inside the house. It was too much. Too much for the little confidence and self-esteem that she had. Her nerves couldn't take it. Acting brave was wearing thin.

'I'm not sure we are safe here,' Megan said. 'You saw what happened. We need to leave the house. I think Ross should get a priest in. Someone more experienced. We are in danger. I can't do this.'

Marc helped Megan up.

'Ross isn't going to want the attention,' he said. 'Please give it one more shot. We'll go into that kitchen, tell those ghosts to leave and see what happens. I'll be with you. If it gets too much, we'll leave then alright?'

'Fine, I guess, but I think you should check on Ross first. Make sure he's okay, if he hasn't gone to sleep yet?'

'Oh he won't be asleep. He's bricking it. He's far too scared to sleep.'

'Why don't you go sit with him? This is what I'm here for… getting paid for. I'll do it alone. If you're scared too?'

'Now what kind of a man would that make me?' Marc said in all seriousness.

Megan wondered if that was a dig at Ross. There were clearly some issues between them. Some issues over women perhaps. Ross was a married man though, so why would he be trying it on with Marc's girlfriends? At least that's what the argument sounded like that she had overheard earlier on. Perhaps Marc lives under Ross's shadow of fame. Maybe Marc has a jealous streak; he does seem to be taking enjoyment out of Ross's suffering. Figuring out this fame and fortune lifestyle was something Megan didn't think she'd be able to get her head around. It was as foreign to her as figuring out ghosts and spirits.

Marc marched towards the kitchen doors. Megan followed.

CHAPTER
TWELVE

'Go, honestly, I'll be fine for a few minutes,' Megan insisted.

'Okay, I'll be straight back,' Marc said almost jogging from the kitchen. He went to lock the gun away and to check on Ross.

Megan spotted the knife still lying on the floor. She picked it up, examining it closely. Placing it on the counter, she carefully pushed it back and forth. *How did it slide off by itself?* The kitchen clock said it was nearly three-thirty am. Her adrenaline was working hard, doing its thing. Tiredness seemed to have left her. She surveyed the smashed glasses in the cupboard again. There was a small pantry room, just off the kitchen, she headed inside and found a bin liner and dustpan and brush. She gingerly picked up the pieces of glass and placed them in the bag then she swept out the small fragments.

Hurry up Marc, she thought as she tied a knot in the bin bag. Of course she didn't mean that she would be fine on her own for a bit, how could any of this be fine? She looked at her finger and realised there was a trickle of blood.

'Damn it,' she scolded, heading for the tap.

The cold water drenched the minor cut. It was small but stung. Tears filled her eyes. She wished Christina were here with her. She had no warmth of a hug from a loved one, no one worrying about her. Not one person she could run to. Big or small, she had to patch her own wounds. She mapped out her own future the moment she lied to her family and she had to live with it. The cold water started to burn.

'Help me,' a loud whisper echoed behind her.

Spinning round Megan met with an empty room.

'Hello?' She called out, 'Marc?'

Nothing. Her body froze. Frantic whispers circled her. She turned left then right then behind her.

'Help me, help me,' the whispers rushed around her.

It went silent. Megan steadied herself against the island. She wanted to run for it but her legs felt heavy. She had to make this stop.

'What do you want?' she managed to call out, her voice shaky. 'Tell me how to help you?'

Oh God, hurry up Marc. Megan pleaded to herself.

'I will help you. Just tell me how?' Megan jumped as the wind rattled at the window. 'Show me then, help me to feel your pain?'

Megan lifted her wounded finger to see blood pumping down her hand. It ran down her arm as she gripped her wrist. So much blood. She let out a sob and backed up to the sink. She couldn't breathe. No, she really couldn't. Her throat was being squeezed. She felt the pressure tighten around her windpipe. Clutching at her throat, she gasped and heaved but there was nothing that she could feel to fight against. Feeling dizzy, she fumbled to turn the tap on, splashing at her face. She started to cough as the choking subsided. She gasped and panted, rinsing away the blood from her arm and hand. As the bloodied water swirled away, her finger revealed the same tiny cut that was there before.

'What the hell?' she gasped.

'You okay?' Marc appeared in the doorway.

'Something attacked me... tried to strangle me.'

'What?' Marc rushed to her side.

Megan felt her throat and checked all over her arm.

'I was bleeding- this cut... but there was so much blood. Then I was choking,' Megan showed him her finger. 'I heard a voice saying *help me*. We need to leave this house.'

Megan felt frustrated that Marc appeared to be looking at her confused- disbelief even in his eyes. He rubbed his chin.

'I'm here now. Let's ask again what they want. Anything else happens, we'll get out of here. Ross is up there still bricking it and he's offering you a hell of a lot of money,' Marc said. He took a step closer to Megan and wiped away a smear of blood from her right cheek.

'I can't-' Megan tried to say.

'You can. You have a gift. I have faith in you, ghost detective.'

Megan resisted kicking him in the shins. She felt weak with fear.

'Okay,' Megan sighed. 'But we are keeping the lights on.' She clasped Marc's hands and took a few deep breaths. 'Hello?' she called out again. 'Thank you for showing me your suffering. We mean you no harm. You must have suffered terribly. Were you treated cruelly as a patient here? Did they hurt you, when they should have been caring for you? We are sad for you.'

Megan remained silent for a bit, waiting for some kind of response. She opened her eyes to see Marc with his eyes still shut. He looked to be taking it seriously.

'You try,' Megan said, squeezing his hands. 'Call out to them.'

Marc looked at her bemused.

'Okay,' he said. 'Can anyone hear me? Like Megan said, we mean no harm. Erm...just leave? Do one?'

Megan nudged him.

'What? I feel stupid,' he said.

'Spirits, I know you're angry at the injustice you must have suffered,' Megan continued, 'but now is the time to move on and find peace. We aren't to blame for what happened to you. May you forever rest in eternal peace.'

They both remained silent. Megan felt that kindness was the best approach. Isn't that what all hurt people want? A little compassion? She resolved to see if she could do a little digging of her own about the history of the house. She wouldn't know where to start but she couldn't deny that she was curious now. Chances were that she wouldn't step foot back in this building once it was daylight and she was done but she needed to know what happened to the patients of this house. However it was all too late for any kind of justice.

Marc pulled his hands away first. He was starting to feel clammy. They sat down at the island in silence for a bit longer. Marc looked like he was growing weary- tiredness taking hold. He rested his forehead down on the table for a moment then lifted his head up yawning. Time ticked away for another hour as they sat and waited. The silence felt uncomfortable but Megan wanted to pay full attention to the surroundings. Still nothing else happened. It was approaching five a.m.

'Coffee?' Marc piped up.

'Yes.' Megan let out a defeated sigh. It felt over, a relief yes but she wasn't certain. She wanted to be sure there was no more danger. Ross had a knife thrown at him and she had been strangled.

Marc put the kettle on.

'I think you did it,' he said. 'Feels calm now, don't you think?'

Megan could only shrug, fatigue was definitely setting in. She wasn't convinced it was that easy.

'Where are you from?' Marc suddenly asked.

'Redditch, an hour or so away maybe.'

'I know it, has an infamous ring road, right?'

Megan smirked in acknowledgement, willing him to hurry up with the coffee.

'You know, you can get some sleep before you go home. You can use the guest room. It's the least we can do.'

Megan gratefully wrapped her hands around the mug that Marc had passed her. Sleep. She had hardly slept for two nights now and her body longed for it. She only had the car to go back to anyway. She could feel her heavy limbs begging her not to drive. Look what happened to Christina. Normally her wish to not be an inconvenience would win but she was done with feeling awkward.

'Yes please. I'd be really grateful actually.' Megan smiled thankfully and took a gulp of soothing coffee.

'I'll grab you something of Deborah's to wear and you can use her toiletries in the bathroom. She's generous, she won't mind at all,' Marc offered.

'I actually have a bag with my stuff in so it's fine,' Megan said suddenly hesitating.

'Do ghost detectives always carry changes of clothes and toiletries with them?'

'Please stop calling me that,' Megan shook her head. 'I

happened to be returning from a few days away when Ross called me. I came straight here. So yes, I have some stuff.'

She looked up at the ceiling. Of course the camera, she thought. Before she went to sleep, she needed to be sure.

'Actually, can we look back at some footage? Can we see the moment I was alone and felt like I was being strangled?' Megan asked.

'Anything for you ghost detective,' Marc said winking at her.

He pulled out his phone and opened the app. A few moments later they both looked at the images of Megan wrestling with herself, with her hands to her throat. She was hoping to see some figure attacking her but there was nothing. No blood could be seen pouring from her finger down her arm either.

'You know, you could have been just having a panic attack? It's been a crazy night.' Marc said softly.

'Perhaps,' Megan sighed. Knowing full well it was more than that. She drained her coffee and asked if Marc would escort her to the car to get her rucksack.

∼

Marc showed Megan to the guest room. She wasn't convinced she wanted to be in the room with the brutal tapestry but she was too grateful to speak up.

'I'll leave you too it,' Marc said, 'Get some sleep, you've earned it. I'll just pop in to see Ross and fill him in on everything calming down for now. Let him know you're kipping here for a bit... as long as you need.'

'Thanks,' Megan replied coyly, feeling a little vulnerable.

Marc smiled and gave a friendly nod before closing the

door. Megan crawled onto the bed and face-planted the plush pillow. She was suddenly aware that her whole body ached with fatigue. Stretching out, she allowed her body to relax and sink into the deep mattress. What a contrast to the cramped car she slept in the night before- seemed such a long time ago now. Her heavy eyelids closed and within moments she fell into a deep sleep. Little did she know the shadow of a black hound sat in the corner of the room, watching her.

CHAPTER 13
BLIND HOUSE 1878

WAS IT WEDNESDAY? PATIENT NUMBER ONE BELIEVED IT WAS. Difficult to tell, no windows, no way to measure time. The doctor had attended her at different times throughout the day and night since Saturday- since she was locked up in this hell. Yesterday nothing though, had she been forgotten? Number One clutched her growling stomach. Was the doctor coming back? It was unusual not to be locked in her cage during the night. She massaged around the iron cuff, which was digging into her ankle, her skin rubbed raw. The chains were long, allowing her movement around the room, she could shuffle over to the trough for food and water. The trough hadn't been replenished though- not for hours. Had it been hours?

Why? Saturday night Number One was dining with the family- she had been invited. They were eating and laughing. It was friendly, informal, normal. Then here. What did she do wrong? Why was she targeted? The same questions were sending her mad, over and over, going round and round in circles. *Did he know? Did he do this to her? Why hasn't he come for her?* Number One winced at the open sores and lacerations scattered along the length of each of her arms. The one near her left wrist looked infected- oozing yellow fluid and radiating heat. Every inch of her hurt, at least one of her legs was broken, she was sure of that. She had to get out. She wanted her mother; she wanted her hugs, her care, her roast dinners. She didn't even know if her parents were aware that she was missing. *Was anyone looking for her?*

The sound of the bolts sliding across made her jump. The doctor was back. Number One shuffled backwards and held herself tight as her whole body began to shake. The door swung open.

'Ah Patient Number One, you'll be pleased to know that I have new treatments to try out on you.' The doctor was carrying a bucket and raised it for the patient to see.

Number One felt like throwing up as she watched the doctor go through the routine of putting on the white coat and gloves and setting up the equipment. She didn't think that she could survive anymore of this.

'Please don't, please just let me go, please. I'm sorry, please...' Number One sobbed as the doctor knelt before her with the bucket.

'But you're not cured yet.'

The doctor stood back up leaving the bucket in front of her. The stench suddenly hit Number One's nostrils and she gagged. The doctor walked over to the far wall to retrieve the bucket used as the toilet. Returning, the doctor poured the contents into the other bucket, topping up the liquid that was already in there.

'That is plenty now.' The doctor grinned. 'Your piss, mixed with mine... a marvellous antioxidant for the mind and spirit.'

Number One gagged. She dare not be sick. She was sick

before and was forced to lick some off the floor. The doctor paced behind her and stroked her greasy blonde hair, then grabbed a hand full of it

'It's another drowning technique,' with that the doctor pushed Number One's head forwards, plunging it into the bucket.

Number One grabbed the sides of the bucket, after a few moments the doctor pulled her head back up and as she retched and gasped for breath, she threw the bucket over, the contents spilling across the filthy floor. The doctor slapped her hard across the face. She frantically tried to wipe away the wetness from her eyes and face, coughing, gagging, not feeling the stinging of her cheek.

'Well perhaps that was enough,' the doctor mellowed. 'I have one more thing to try.'

Number One struggled but it was fruitless as the doctor clamped chains on to her wrists. Raw pain from the infected sore burned her flesh as the metal dug into it. She was then pushed down on to her back.

'Resist and I'll be forced to start removing pieces from you,' the doctor pointed a knife to Number One's left breast. 'Look at all these wounds,' the doctor admired the gashes up each of her arms and the black bruises spanning both of her legs. 'These wounds drain out your poison, strengthen your mind and teach you humility. Yet, the effects aren't evident yet are they? There is one area, we are yet to try.'

The doctor fetched the tool bag and took out a white candle, struck a match then lit it. Number One begged for the doctor to stop as her gown was pushed up exposing her naked lower half. Her thighs trembled violently as the doctor lowered the lit candle to her privates.

'What are you doing? Please I'll be good, please stop...'

The doctor didn't listen. Number One screamed.

'That concludes tonight's treatment,' the doctor dragged Number One over to her cage, unchained her and pushed her inside. 'See you tomorrow.'

The bolts slid back across the door and the room fell silent once more. Number One curled up in her cramped space, clutching the pain. She didn't know how to stay strong. She tried to think of her mother and father but that just hurt more. The pain and cold engulfed her and she gently banged her head against the wooden bars. Thump, thump, thump.

CHAPTER
FOURTEEN

Thump, thump, thump echoed around Megan. She lay in an empty room in complete darkness, the air felt heavy, musty, claustrophobic. She covered her mouth, the stale air consuming her senses. She felt around her with her other arm, was something there? A hand grabbed hers, digging its nails in, pulling her. Megan tried to pull back, she turned away but another hand grabbed her other one, pulling her in the opposite direction. Two figures either side of her pulled at her arms, clawing up their lengths until their breath was in her ears.

'Help us,' one whispered.

The two figures lay over her, wrapping their legs and arms around her, pinning her to the floor. Megan grasped at long, thick, matted hair, but they lay firmly entwined around her, sobbing into her neck. She could feel the wetness of their tears flood down her throat to her breasts. She tried to scream but the air was suffocating. The room lit up and the women were gone. Megan sat up, panting, scanning the empty room. She didn't know where she was. The air was still dank. She inspected the scratches and nail marks on her arms.

'Help us,' a voice sobbed.

Megan tightly closed her eyes. Opened them to a woman stood before her, blood leaking from the corner of her mouth, thick dark curls matted against her forehead. Blood soaked through her ragged night gown as she clutched at the gaping wound in her throat. The woman screamed, loud, piercing.

Megan shot awake. Quickly scanning her surroundings and registering that she was in the room she fell asleep in. The four poster bed, the tapestry- everything as normal. *Jesus that felt real*, Megan padded over to the en-suite and splashed her face. Her watch said ten thirty-five a.m. Still shaking, Megan turned on the shower. She looked her arms up and down and they were fine. It was time to get out of here. It was time to go and start her new life. As luxurious as this house was, she couldn't wait to see the back of it.

∽

Megan put on a pair of jeans and a sweatshirt. They were a bit crumpled, but not surprising after they had been shoved in a bag at speed. She wondered how much money was "a lot of money." Ross had said he was offering her a lot of money. She wasn't sure if she'd done enough to earn a lot of money, but she was hoping it was enough to get a new outfit or two- something nice to help get her a new job, to make that fresh start. She carried on towel drying her hair, her thoughts interrupted by the sound of raised voices downstairs.

Creeping to the top of the stairs, Megan listened in. A woman sounded angry. Must be Deborah, she thought.

'Christ, you've just walked through the do-' Ross protested.

'It was bloody humiliating, 'Deborah shouted. 'You really don't want me to succeed do you? I mean after the first time, you said that you wouldn't interfere again, but then I find out you've done it again. Do you think your bloody agent is loyal to you? Did you expect him to keep quiet? No he didn't. Once again, you clicked your little fingers and made sure I didn't get the role. Am I really that embarrassing to you? Am I so bad? I find this out on top of the fact I need to be interviewed over a missing woman. I mean I just… I really… and who the hell is she?'

Megan gently stepped down the stairs to be met with Deborah's icy glare. Ross rubbed his forehead, exasperated.

'This is Megan Forrest,' Ross breathed. 'Just hear me out okay, she's a paranormal investigator. I thought, whilst you were away, I'd get someone in. I said I'd sort it. She's been up all night working and I said she could sleep before heading home. Megan, this is Deborah, my wife.'

It took an uncomfortable few moments but Deborah relaxed her shoulders, dropped her bag and extended her hand to Megan.

'I'm so sorry, Megan. I've had a hellish journey from London and with so much going on I… I'm sorry. It really is lovely to meet you. You'll have to fill me in on everything.'

'Lovely to meet you too,' Megan said, returning the handshake.

'Let's grab a coffee. Ian is on his way to pick me up. A Detective Page is expecting us at the station,' Deborah said.

'You know, he had a PC Turner with him, when they came round. Page… Turner,' Marc laughed.

Megan jumped, not realising Marc had joined them and was stood behind her.

'Only you could find that funny, Marc,' Deborah puffed. 'C'mon,' she ushered Ross towards the kitchen.

Marc gently held Megan back, 'Don't worry about Deb, she blows hot and cold but she really is lovely. Sleep okay?'

'Yes,' Megan lied, thinking back to that nightmare.

They both followed through to the kitchen and the kettle was already steaming away. They gathered, seated around the island. Ross filled Deborah in on last night's events, with Marc and Megan filling in some details. Ross looked genuinely apprehensive over Deborah's reactions, on hearing what went on. She sat with her hand clasped to her mouth in disbelief.

'But we only had the odd bang and the odd thing being moved,' Deborah gasped. 'Nothing like knives being thrown and cupboard doors opening and things smashing.'

'We think it's stopped though,' Marc quickly piped up. 'Megan did her thing and then it went quiet. Nothing since.'

The buzzer to the front gates rang out making everyone jump.

'Jesus, that'll be Ian.' Deborah said. 'I'm not going anywhere though until I've had my coffee.'

Ross actioned the opening of the gates then made up the coffee, whilst Marc went to greet Ian at the door. Megan studied Deborah for a moment. She was stunning. She couldn't help but feel a bit intimidated in her presence. Her own jeans and sweatshirt suddenly felt like bin bags next to Deborah's designer dress, her glossy blonde up-do and radiant complexion. Megan thought back to the argument that Ross and Marc had. It did sound like Ross had tried it on with or had stolen one of Marc's girlfriends. Why on earth would he cheat on Deborah? Megan concluded that she'd never understand men.

Deborah rushed over to hug her uncle, then quickly introduced him to Megan.

'I still can't believe all this,' Deborah said, 'I know it's all perfectly innocent but I feel like such a criminal... going into a police station to give a statement. Surely we can't actually be suspected of anything?'

'How do you think I feel? I was the last one to see her. I dropped her home. If only I'd bloody hung on and watched her enter her house. But no I just dropped her at the junction and left,' Ian sighed.

'Did she seem okay to you?' Ross chipped in.

'Yes, perfectly,' Ian said.

'Well you absolutely mustn't blame yourself Uncle,' Deborah said to him. 'God I hope Kerry turns up. I mean where on earth did she go? Such a lovely woman.'

'She is,' Ross said. 'She works incredibly hard for the trust.'

'And amazing hair. Fabulous dark curly locks,' Deborah added.

'Trust you to make someone all about their hair,' Marc said, fluttering his eyes sarcastically at Deborah.

'Sod off Marc,' Deborah scowled back at him. 'Right Ian, let's get this nightmare over with.'

'It'll be fine, the police have the CCTV remember,' Ross said.

'Megan, are you sticking around for a bit?' Deborah asked her, 'I'm sure this won't take too long. Let's go for lunch when I get back, I want to hear all of your ghost stories.'

Megan wanted to say no, she wanted out of this house. She wanted to find her normality. Ross flashed his Hollywood actor smile at her though and insisted she stayed too.

'Okay, that'd be lovely, thank you,' Megan heard herself say.

As the front door closed behind Deborah and Ian, Megan suddenly felt lightheaded. She propped herself against the wall, steadying her shaking legs. *Dark curly locks.* The sudden realisation hit hard. Kerry. Her dream. The woman clutching her bleeding throat. She knew what Kerry looked like from the photo the police showed her. The dream was so vivid, so real. Why was she having a nightmare about Kerry?

CHAPTER FIFTEEN

Megan marvelled at the floral decor of the quaint tearoom. Fresh flowers filled every available space, that and the aroma of fresh coffee and baked goods created a heavenly mix, satisfying all of her senses. Deborah collapsed into her seat.

'Gorgeous little place, isn't it?' Deborah said. 'Gosh I'm exhausted. It's been a long day already, but I just don't think I can be in the house with Ross at the moment. I'm still mad at him.'

'Did all go okay at the station?' Megan asked.

She didn't think she could offer any opinions on the argument between Deborah and Ross. She didn't know them well enough and had no idea what it was all about really. She felt a change of subject was best- hoping it wasn't too intrusive but she couldn't get the image of Kerry out of her head.

'Yes all good,' Deborah replied. 'It's just worrying. The police are concerned because Kerry hasn't used her cards over the last few days and none of her clothes are missing. She has a son and it's very unlike her not to get in touch, so they are treating her disappearance seriously.'

A waitress came over to take their order. Deborah ordered the crab salad and Megan asked for the bacon and brie toastie. She couldn't compare herself to Deborah in the slightest so she wasn't going to attempt to match her food choices. If she didn't have any stodgy food, she felt she might pass out with hunger.

'What gets me though,' Deborah said, 'is Kerry never actually told her husband where she was that night- that she was at my house. But she told her best friend- she confided in her best friend but not her husband. Her friend even kept her confidence for a couple of days even after Kerry was first discovered as missing. That's loyalty isn't it? True friendship...' Deborah's voice cracked a little, 'I had a feeling these confidentiality waivers would come back to bite Ross on the arse one day. I suppose Ross got you to sign one too?'

'Yes he did,' Megan replied.

'Anyway so you're a paranormal investigator? I want to hear everything. How did you get into it? You must have the best stories to tell.'

Megan felt her cheeks grow hot. She hadn't really got the best stories at all. The waitress approached, placing their food in front of them. Megan was glad at the distraction, giving her time to organise her thoughts. The best story she had yet, had taken place last night in Deborah's own house. Terrifying things, unexplainable things. Things which had put her off being in the business completely. She started off by telling how it became a hobby of hers and her best friends- her only friend. Megan didn't have much else in her life such as lots of hobbies or more to the point the money for lots of hobbies. She wasn't well travelled and was cut off from her family and no friendship circle to speak of.

Ghost hunting became an adventure- something exciting. It got her adrenaline up, spending nights at creepy venues pretending to be something out of Scooby Doo. It felt magical to her, a kind of escapism from reality. Career choices were limited, as Megan hadn't finished school- couldn't sit her exams. With the support of her social worker- for which she'd forever be grateful, she got a job at ST Style. *It's not what you know it's who you know*, she was once advised. She didn't have either. That was until Christina suggested setting up business together, doing the thing they loved. She then felt like she had everything. And then Christina died.

'I can see why he hired you. Why he homed in on you. You're just his type you know,' Deborah said with a thoughtful smile. She placed her cutlery down and sat back in her chair.

'What?' Megan said uncomfortably, quickly remembering that Marc had said the same thing to her last night.

Deborah laughed, 'Let me explain. Ross likes to think he lives in the real world. That he was once a struggling actor out of pocket, trying to make his way in the world. Well he never was. His rich Mummy and daddy funded all of his travelling to the States. He stayed in the top hotels and never once went without. He bought his way into the industry, networking at the right parties until he landed his first break. As you said it's not what you know but who you know and you can add how much money you have to that too. Ross loves to massage his ego... gets off on it. Literally. Let's just say that we have an open relationship going on. He loves nothing more than to seduce women who are of a much lower class. Poor, little prospects that kind of thing. Makes him feel powerful. Dominating.'

Megan struggled to swallow down the last bite of her toastie. 'It's not really my business and honestly it's not at all like that-'

'It's okay. Really. He invites women round for dinner parties, seduces them and they usually say yes. Of course they would. It's Ross Huston. Except Kerry. She politely declined him. Huh.'

'And you're okay with all of this?' Megan said, her nerves on high alert.

'Oh yes. I expect his devotion and loyalty to be mine first when required at all times. I am his wife and that's what sets me above the rest. Oh Megan, I'm so worried he is losing interest in me though. He loved me when he thought I had nothing then things felt different after we were married and he found out how wealthy I really was. It's like I stopped *doing it* for him. He holds my career back when I want more. I don't think he expected me to become as successful as I have and now I want to break into acting, he puts a stop to it.'

Megan could see Deborah's eyes beginning to shine. She didn't see this coming at all and she thought her own relationship had been a messed up one. How the other half live is not so different. This is not something that Megan wanted to get caught up in. Angry spirits, missing woman, sexual fetishes. She wanted money to start a new life, she wasn't prepared to put up with all of this though. Once more, she longed for the sanctuary of her car and the open road. Ross had not once made her feel uncomfortable or that he had any intention of seducing her. The idea was completely laughable to her. She just wasn't interested.

'Forgive me,' Deborah continued. 'Kerry's close friendship with her best friend has got me missing someone to confide in. Probably a good job you did sign that confidentiality waiver.' Deborah laughed and stood up, gathering her jacket and handbag, ready to settle the bill.

Megan was lost for words and only just about managed an

awkward smile. They both left the cafe and made their way back through the village for the short walk back to the house.

'I'm not sure if I've played it down a bit,' Deborah said after a few moments of silence. 'I really am scared of going back into my house. After what I've been told about what happened last night I don't think my nerves can take it.'

'Well I'm hopeful the spirits have left now. I can't be sure but it definitely all went quiet.'

'Please stay another night, I would-'

'No, I couldn't possibly, it's too-'

'No please, I absolutely insist. Whatever Ross agreed to pay you, I will match it.' Deborah stopped in her tracks and looked pleadingly into Megan's eyes. 'Please, I'm actually terrified. Just one more night, just to be certain my house is no longer haunted. I'd feel so much braver with you here.'

Megan felt like screaming. More money had never been more tempting but she didn't think her nerves could take it either. The petrol left in her car probably wouldn't make it back to Devon anyway. Perhaps one more night wouldn't be too bad. Extra cash may mean a new outfit and did she dare hope for a night or two in a B&B also? Oh and decent food. How she longed for fish and chips, sitting on the dragon's back, away from people- people who seemed to be getting stranger to her by the minute.

'Yes,' she said. 'I'd be happy too.'

'Oh I can't tell you what a relief that is,' Deborah beamed.

They approached the gates to Blind House where Marc ran out to greet them. Deborah walked ahead as Marc requested a quick word with Megan. He leaned into her and held his phone up for her to see. She looked closely and when she realised what the words were saying on the screen, her stomach sank.

'So,' Marc said, 'Want to explain why you are a missing person?'

CHAPTER
SIXTEEN

Marc ushered Megan into his room and they both perched on his bed.

'So I know Redditch because I have a friend of a friend who lives there. I'm scrolling on Facebook to see that this mate has shared a post from the *What's Happening Redditch?* page. That's you isn't it? The picture. Missing since yesterday afternoon by all accounts. The comments are the best bit,' Marc explains, handing Megan his phone so that she can examine the post herself.

Megan takes her time reading through everything. She hands the phone back and holds her head in her hands.

'Well?' Marc asked, 'I don't think Ross needs another missing person scandal, do you?'

Megan shakes her head, 'I'm not missing. I left my stupid boyfriend that's all. I packed my stuff and left him. I can't believe he did this. To find me. He knows damn well I'm fine. Look he has even put that the police aren't concerned yet because I took my things and my car. He's just desperate to find me, he's dangerous and I'm not getting in touch with him.'

'Well I think you're gonna have to call him. Just once at least. He'll continue to post stuff if he's desperate like you say he is. We need to put a stop to it before it gets out of hand. And what do you mean he's dangerous?'

'He's abusive, he's a druggy... look I don't want to go into it... this is so embarrassing.'

Marc held out her phone to her, 'Please, call him. I'm here.'

Megan took her phone and switched it on. She rubbed her throat remembering how Scott had squeezed it tight after threatening to pimp her out to his dealer. That was a whole new low for her. She had never expected much out of life anymore but she no longer wanted to be that doormat. She wanted and needed better. Christina had broken through to her; she was worth so much more and was finally ready to cut the strings from her past. She hit dial on Scott's number.

'Finally, Megs, I've been worried sick,' Scott blurted out.

'Scott, you need to remove that fb post. I'm not missing. I'm fine. I'm staying with a friend.'

'What friend? Megs, I need you back.'

'I'm not coming back. What you did... said. I've had enough-'

'Whoa, we're in this shit together. Yes it got heated but I need you right? You can't leave me in the shit like this. Alright, I'll get evicted.'

'I'm not coming back. Delete the post. Goodbye Scott.'

'No wait, you fucking owe me, please-'

Megan hung up the phone. Turning it back off, she handed it to Marc willing herself not to cry.

'You had all your stuff on you didn't you? You actually have nowhere to stay do you?' Marc said sensitively.

Megan shook her head in defeat, 'No, I don't but it's okay. I'm just trying to work, earn some cash and get back on my feet. To be honest, I've never felt more positive.'

'I take it there's no love lost between you and your family? Who's Sammie Forrest? Her comment on that post was a bit harsh.'

'My sister... she's my sister.'

'Well she reckons you're an attention seeking little bitch and no one should be worried. But hang on though, someone then puts, "surely you wouldn't wish her dead though, what if the worst has happened, isn't it time you made peace?" and then Sammie replies, "Perhaps. It has been on my mind and of course, I wouldn't want harm to come to her. I'm not getting into it on here."

'We fell out years ago... eleven years ago, I was fifteen. We haven't spoken since.' Megan said quietly.

'And these comments off Rich and Stevie Hall? Both say along the lines of that you're not worth finding. I mean who says things like that on a missing person's post?'

Megan couldn't hold the tears back any longer, 'They are members of my step-dad's family.'

Megan sobbed into her hands, genuinely upset over the angst from her family. It had been eleven years since they fell out and Megan had maintained a low profile, accepted all of the hardships that followed and worked hard. She often wondered what her sister thought of her now- if she thought of her at all. Now she knew and it cut her heart open.

'Sounds like you've screwed up once or twice,' Marc said. 'I'm not great with girls crying, is there anything I can do? Get you?'

'No I'm fine. None of this should be a surprise to me.

Honestly, it's fine. I'm so embarrassed.' Megan wiped her eyes and took a deep breath.

Marc carried on looking at his phone, 'Just checking out your sister's fb profile. Look she's a massive Ross Huston fan.'

Megan took a closer look at Sammie's wall and sure enough it was filled with giffs, memes and pictures of Ross. One photo showed him topless sat astride a black horse. Sammie's words below read, "What I'd do to him given the chance," followed by numerous heart emojis.

Marc sat in thought for a few moments, 'Invite her here... tonight?'

'What? No that's crazy.' Megan stood from the bed, hugging herself and paced the room.

'Seriously, Deborah would be all over the whole reuniting sisters thing. She's soppy like that. Ross wouldn't mind at all.'

Megan thought back to what Deborah had said about Ross using the underprivileged as his playthings. It's not something that she wanted to be part of. Her and her sister's troubles were not entertainment value to give Ross and Deborah boosted power trips.

'It's been eleven years. Sammie isn't going to want to see me now, not ever.'

'Yeah right, like she'd turn down the opportunity to have dinner at Ross Huston's house. There is no way she'd say no. Call her to reassure her you're safe, tell her where you are and ask her to come. Simple.'

Megan allowed herself to think about it. The palms of her hands became clammy and her chest tightened. She'd love nothing more than to see her sister but her guilt felt so raw still. Not one of her family members had reached out to her over the years. Not even on the night that she couldn't take the hurt anymore and had taken an overdose. She struggled to swallow as she remembered her stomach being pumped followed by shedding tears into the hospital bed pillow as she lay there alone. The hatred must run deep. Megan didn't think she could face that. She was too ashamed.

'No,' Megan said.

'Well the offer's there, Sammie did say that it was on her mind to make peace with you,' Marc replied almost looking disappointed.

Deborah popped her head round the door and asked if they were both alright. 'I'm off for a lie down, I'm simply shattered. Ian's coming for dinner later, help take his mind off things. I'd feel happier with more people in the house to be honest, keep me safe from these ghosts,' she said. 'Do you need anything Megan?'

Megan thought that Deborah looked a little strained, not fresh faced as earlier. Had she been crying? Also the mention again of ghosts brought Megan back to the present. She had a job to do and willed tonight to go well. It's awful not feeling safe in your own home.

'No, I'm fine than-' Megan tried to answer.

'Debs,' Marc interrupted, 'Megan was telling me that she hasn't seen her sister in a while and is missing her. Can we invite her for dinner tonight too?'

'Definitely.' Deborah replied, 'Like I said, the more the merrier. Is she into ghost hunting also?'

'Well I... it's not necess- she's-'

'She looks fit is what she is,' Marc interrupted again, laughing and winking at Megan.

'Jesus,' Deborah said, 'Have you ever wondered why you can't keep a girlfriend Marc? What was the last one's name? Sarah?'

For a moment Marc's jaw tightened but then he relaxed, 'Her loss is definitely Megan's sister's gain.'

Deborah shook her head in defeat and backed out of the room. Marc looked at the expression of disbelief on Megan's face.

'Oh, I'm kidding.' He reassured her. 'Told you she wouldn't mind though. Well?'

'No. Look I'm not putting you all out. It's good of you and everything but there really is no need for your help. It's asking too much. Really.'

'You heard Deb; she'd like more people-'

'No, anyway I don't think Sammie will appreciate me inviting her to a haunted house. I'm not putting her in danger. She hates me enough as it is.'

'She can stay for dinner and then we can send her home before it gets late and you start work. C'mon she's not gonna turn down Ross Huston. I know his fans. C'mon, I've been alone in the past, I'm just being a helpful kinda guy. Call her.'

Megan stepped over to the window and looked out to the woods, wondering for a moment where the fox that half scared her to death was hiding out. It really is the most magical property. She wondered if she could go and look around the grounds again whilst it was still daylight. She imagined sharing this experience with Sammie. That she would throw her arms around her sobbing how much she'd missed her. She imagined the look on Sammie's face as she was introduced to Ross. Maybe this was a good opportunity to get in touch with her. Surely Sammie would be over the moon. Isn't it the least Megan could try and do for her?

'I don't have her number,' Megan said hesitantly.

'Call her on Messenger. I'll message her first and hopefully she'll respond and not think I'm some crazy dude and then you can call her.'

Megan squeezed her wrists and heard herself say, 'Okay.'

What's the worst that can happen, Megan thought, that Sammie would just say no. Or was it she'd say yes?

CHAPTER 17
BLIND HOUSE 1878

PATIENT NUMBER ONE SCREECHED AS SHE RIPPED THE LEECHES FROM her arms. That was her treat. It was Saturday morning and the Doctor was in a good mood. Number One had apparently been good the previous day because she didn't vomit up the pig's heart she had been force-fed; this pleased the Doctor. So a morning of leeches to aid healing her wounds was the treat. Number One pressed against her arms to try and stem some of the bleeding. Perhaps it was a treat. There wasn't more than an inch of skin between wounds anywhere on her body.

Saturday. A whole week. She believed she would die here. The Doctor announced before leaving her with the leeches, that there would be a surprise for her tonight. It was Saturday and she deserved treats and a surprise. She wanted to laugh and she did a little but everywhere hurt. She was actually going mad. Saturdays were for dancing, good food, relaxing and… him. *Is he part of this? Did he do this?*

The trough had been replenished with bread too. She dragged herself over to it and examined the chunks of crusty loaf. Covered in dirt as usual but after wiping it down, it was merely replaced by streaks of blood. It tasted of pigs heart. Each dry mouthful turned to the reminder of the rubbery muscle full of blood. She gagged. She longed for her Mum to bathe her wounds and feed her back up with home cooked food and snuggled in a blanket. How could she have been such an idiot? Naivety and stupidity landed her here, she knew it. But she had no reason to not trust them, no reason at all. Why would she?

What was her surprise? If leeches were a treat, then what was the surprise? Number One couldn't help laughing again. Every possible piece of her hurt. She was going mad and she would die here. She knew it for sure.

CHAPTER EIGHTEEN

Megan ran out of the front gates and down the lane until the high street opened up before her. Stopping, she gasped for breath and clutched her hip to ease the stitch. *Were the buildings swaying? Why was there two of everyone?* She recognised that she was having a panic attack and doubled herself over, reaching for her toes. The blood sent its soothing pressure to her head. She slowly stretched up, breathing in for five and out for three. *My sister is coming tonight.* Sammie had agreed.

Megan had wanted the opportunity to explore this town a little more when she had clapped eyes on it earlier after eating out with Deborah. The shops, restaurants and cafes were beautiful with their Cotswold stone walls and the street lined with hanging baskets still in full bloom. It was a far cry from the rough council estate where she lived. It was a struggle for her to appreciate it now though and take it all in. Her sister was coming. Not for a second did Megan actually think that she would. She felt dizzy. Sammie was curious enough to take the call and listened as Megan explained that she wasn't missing and quickly glossed over leaving her ex and that she was simply working away. Sammie refused to speak to Megan any further until Ross intercepted. A quick video call as proof and just like Marc had said, Sammie couldn't resist saying yes.

It was just after four p.m. and Sammie was coming for seven-thirty p.m. Megan had needed space, time to just breathe on her own. It was all too surreal. She had been employed by *the* Ross Huston and he was happy to invite her sister to dinner. It didn't matter how many times she said it over and over in her mind, it was just as crazy. She wondered what her Mum would think, whether Sammie would tell her. Perhaps having her sister back in her life would fill the void left when Christina died. She had never felt so lonely.

Christina's Mum had always tried to make her feel like she was part of their family. Christina was a couple of years younger than she was and still lived with them, so Megan spent a fair amount of time at their house. But even so, Megan didn't make it easy for them, she was quiet and reserved, finding their close-knit family unit uncomfortable. It didn't matter what Christina did, her Mum always embraced her and they always fixed it together. The bond between them was enviable; they looked the spit of each other and even shared the same left lazy eye. Everything Christina wanted to do, her mother supported her, including helping to fund their ghost hunting equipment to start their business. Their small home on the same council estate that Megan lived on with Scott, was brimming with love and Megan could never shake the sadness that it filled her with. It was just another thing she hated herself for. She hated that her own Mum turned her back on her, despite what she'd done. Christina would never have been discarded like that. *But then she never did anything that bad did she?*

As the tears stung her eyes, Megan pushed the negative thoughts away, grounding herself by focusing on her surroundings. The street really was picturesque. Her life was heading in a more hopeful direction and being here in this Cotswolds town, was the start of it. Megan approached the cafe she was in earlier. The waitress that served them was clearing some dishes from the table outside the front. Looking up, the waitress smiled and quickly beckoned her over.

'It was lovely to meet you earlier, I'm Emma.' The waitress placed a dish back down and wiped her hands down her apron before extending one of them for a handshake. 'It's always lovely when the Huston's are in town, are you a friend of the family?'

'Yes, sort of,' Megan replied.

'Well, any sort of friend of the Huston's is a friend of ours,' Emma giggled. 'Wait here just a sec.' She hurried inside the cafe.

moments later, Emma reappeared, handing over a mouth-watering cup cake. It was topped with swirling pink icing, garnished with slices of fresh strawberries.

'Here, only for our special guests,' Emma grinned.

Megan took the cake, 'Wow, it looks amazing, thank you.'

'The Huston's always create business for us. They're a bit of a tourist attraction around here.'

'They are the loveliest couple,' Megan agreed. *They really are*, she thought. Thanks to them, she may get her sister back and maybe even the rest of her family.

'They're so down to earth, always happy to chat to the staff and other customers. Ross is an excellent tipper too,' Emma laughed, her whole face lighting up.

'Deborah said this is one of her most favourite cafes.

Anyway I should get going.' Megan didn't think she could keep up the small talk with her mind whirring away.

She thanked Emma again for the cake and she hurried off, taking a bite into the deep frosting. Sugar can only be a good thing right now, she thought, trying to catch the crumbs, it might help her to stop feeling faint. She smiled to herself. No one had ever referred to her as a special customer before- a special anything for that matter. How nice for just a brief moment to feel important. Her smile quickly faded though as she recognised the policeman approaching her- PC Turner.

'Ah, you were up at the Huston's last night?' Turner stopped her.

'Yes, that was me. Any luck finding Kerry?'

'No, that's why we are in the area. Just popping into local businesses and houses making enquiries.' Turner held up the photo of Kerry.

Megan took a closer look at it. The woman in the picture was definitely the woman in her dream. Clear as anything, clutching her bleeding throat- it was Kerry.

'You might want to...' Turner said pointing to Megan's lips.

Megan quickly wiped her mouth suddenly aware it must be smeared with frosting. Wiping herself down, she bundled the remaining cake into the bin. Suddenly she didn't feel hungry anymore.

'So you've never met this woman,' the policeman continued.

'No. Wish I could be more help,' Megan said, and meant it.

'Are you still staying with the Huston's?'

'Yes, just for tonight though.'

'We may need to speak with them some more,' he advised.

'They did say they'd be happy to help in any way.'

PC Turner nodded briefly before his radio signalled for him

to leave. Megan watched him stride away. She couldn't get involved in any of it, there's nothing she could do. It was out of her hands. Her problem, however, was the Huston's ghosts. She had ghosts to banish and she couldn't let her sister's visit distract from that. She needed to plan the night's operation. And just like the beacon she needed, she found herself stood in front of a library. Internet access sprang to her mind. She'd see if she could research some of *Blind House's* history. Try and find out for sure, what she was working with. She was relieved to see that the Library didn't close until six- she had some time, so through the doors she went.

CHAPTER NINETEEN

TEN MINUTES LATER AFTER SIGNING UP TO THE LIBRARY, MEGAN nestled into one of the study booths and logged into the PC. She had to use her address to join the Library, but it was no longer her address and it stung. She pushed the pain aside; it'll do for now she told herself. She'll create a whole new little palace for herself soon enough and she'll have an address she'll be able to proudly use.

In the search bar, Megan typed in how to research the history of a house. Scrolling through the results, she realised that there probably wasn't going to be a way to do thorough research without registering and paying a subscription fee. She stared blankly at the screen for a moment, feeling frustrated not knowing where to start next. She started to type lunatic asylums but then got interrupted.

'Everything okay?' the lady said, peering over Megan's shoulder.

She smiled at the Librarian, with her white hair in a tight

bun and her crinkled eyes framed by spectacles. She looked like a librarian Megan thought- kind and well, librarianish.

'Yes, I think,' Megan answered, feeling a rush of hope that this lady could shed some light. Librarians know everything, right? 'I'm actually trying to research the history of a house... who lived there and stuff over a hundred years ago. I'm at a loss where to start.'

'Well in that case dear, you are in luck. It happens to be an area of expertise of mine. I've even published books on the process myself.'

Megan's eyes lit up. She needed a stroke of luck.

'Any house in particular?' asked the Librarian.

'Yes, actually, one local to here...Blind House, just on the brink of town, set back down the-'

'Ah, say no more dear, I know the house. I know it very well indeed. I know all about its history and I can show you all that I know. You just wait right here my dear, I'll be back in a jiffy.'

The stroke of luck was suddenly becoming more of a master stroke. Megan's stomach flipped at the thought of learning more about the house. Perhaps she could find things out that Ross and Deborah hadn't? Perhaps there's more to its sinister past- something that she could work with to help those poor souls to find peace. Morbid curiosity, fear, empathy for the victims- it all gave her a rush; a need to know more. Who exactly was haunting Blind House? And how many ghosts were there?

'This, my dear is all of my research on Blind House.' The lady placed a file on the desk in front of them. 'You see, my great-great-grandfather used to live there.' She pulled out a grainy newspaper clipping of a proud looking man with a thick moustache. 'Here he is, Aubury Holdstock. Dr Aubury Holdstock, that is. Tell me, what is your interest in the house?'

Megan couldn't take her eyes off the photo. *Dr Holdstock.* He looked like an affluent and gentle kind of fellow. What was he a doctor in? Could he have inflicted brutal punishment on his patients? She resisted blurting out too many questions. The last thing that she wanted to do was cause any offence- especially not to a family member.

'I happen to be doing a bit of work for the occupants... some housekeeping. The lady of the house said it's got quite a history. That it may have been used as a hospital for the insane? I guess I'm just curious, it's a beautiful house.'

The Librarian drummed her fingers on the file. 'Is that so? I'm presuming therefore that you are on about the Huston's. And I suppose that *Deborah* told you that these so called insane people were tortured and perhaps even butchered to death?'

'Oh, well no... not exactly-'

'Look,' the Librarian swiped up the newspaper cutting and read from the article which was dated 1878. She read how Dr Holdstock was one of the leading pioneer's in the care and treatment of the mentally unwell. How he won prestigious awards for his research and for the care of his patients. She then placed it on the table, other news reports one by one. Stabbing at them with her finger, one by one. 'Here, here and here,' she sounded exasperated as she pointed to the smiling families of the patients and the patients themselves.'

'Forgive me, I don't understand,' Megan said gently, 'The Huston's said that little was known about the house. That it was private so there was no public records about the place.'

'Well as you can see dear, there was nothing private and nothing to hide. I have spoken with Deborah and she has seen my research into my family's history. But she is still set on discrediting my great-great-grandfather. Making him out to be some sort of monster. You're not the first person she has told this to. It always gets back to me. It saddens me that the house never stayed in our family. We would have cherished its true history, not like these jumped up celebrities, with more money than sense. And its people like that, that people will believe anything they say just because they're famous.'

So this must be the historian that Deborah and Ian spoke with, Megan assumed. She noted the time. 'I think I really must be going. I can't thank you enough for your time. I didn't mean to cause any upset. It was lovely to learn the truth. The Huston's don't actually know I'm here doing this.'

'Any time dear,' the Librarian shuffled the papers back together. 'My name's Nancy by the way, should I be able to help you further.'

'Thank you Nancy.' Megan couldn't leave quick enough; she had to collect her thoughts.

Back out in the fresh air, she tried to make sense of what she'd learned. Why would Deborah make all of that stuff up about tortured patients? If she knew of Dr Holdstock, why did she lie about there not being any documented history? If the ghosts weren't that of tormented dead patients then who were they? This revelation didn't help her at all. If she couldn't make a connection with the spirits to help them move on then she was at risk of not getting paid. Would they refuse to pay her? She stopped and closed her eyes, praying that there would be no more supernatural action tonight. Then there wouldn't be a problem: they'd assume that she had already successfully moved the spirits on, pay her, then she could leave. Then she remembered her sister and prayed that would go well too. Too much was riding on tonight. Time stood still for a fleeting moment as she opened her eyes. Because there it was across the street from her. The black dog. Sitting there, watching her.

CHAPTER
TWENTY

'You look like you've seen a ghost?' Marc met Megan at the door with a genuine look of concern.

'Just nervous about seeing my sister. Is it okay if I take a shower?' Megan didn't really wait for a reply; she brushed past Marc and made for the stairs.

'Sure, I'll bring you up a coffee shortly,' he called after her.

Megan hurriedly closed her en-suite door behind her and ripped away her leggings, t-shirt and underwear. She felt hot and sticky despite the cooling September weather. She welcomed the powerful drenching from the shower. What the hell went on in this house? Are the Huston's hiding something? What happened to Kerry? And what the hell is that dog that's stalking her? The shower spray suddenly stopped then spurted out again, continuing to erratically turn on and off.

'Damn it.' Megan turned the faucet to the off position. The water spluttered out a few more times before staying off. Stepping out of the shower, she wrapped the large bath towel around her body, enjoying its comforting embrace. As she went to open the door she halted as it sounded like something heavy had fallen against it from the other side.

'Hello?' Megan jumped back. It was silent. She slowly pushed the door ajar, realising that there was nothing in its way, so pushed it open wide. Relief was temporary as sudden rapping to her bedroom door startled her again. Without waiting for a reply, Marc entered. holding out a mug of coffee.

'Sorry, I won't look,' he said, looking away in an over-exaggerated fashion.

'Thank you,' Megan stepped forwards and took the coffee. 'It's okay. I think there is something wrong with the shower?'

'I'll take a look later-'

'Ah Megan, good, you've started getting ready,' Deborah blustered into the room.

Megan looked at her hair which was still dripping down her shoulders and tried not to blush. This was all getting too cosy for her liking.

'I thought it would be fun to give you a little make over.' Deborah beamed, busying herself picking up items of Megan's clothing from her rucksack. 'As I thought, well you weren't prepared for all of this were you. Come on, I have many dresses you can try on. I could do with some girls time.'

'You really don't have to, I...' Megan tried to protest but Deborah's look said it all so she simply shrugged, 'Okay, yes then, thank you.'

'I'll leave you ladies to it then, before you put me in a dress too,' Marc grinned and backed out of the room.

Deborah took Megan's hand and pulled her from the room across the landing to her own bedroom. From the far right corner of the room, they accessed a separate dressing room. It was huge. She gasped at the rows and rows of outfits and shoes. Nothing looked out of place. Megan perhaps owned maybe three or four pairs of trousers/leggings and a handful of t-shirts, definitely only one pair of trainers and certainly no dresses, yet they never managed to stay neatly hung away. In fact today's attire was still screwed up on the floor in the shower room.

Deborah pulled a chair up for her at the beautiful antique style dressing table and proceeded to blast her hair dry. Once the noise of the hair dryer ceased, Deborah set to work adding some loose curls to Megan's hair using her straightening irons.

'So what have you got lined up ready for the ghosts tonight after dinner?' Deborah asked.

'I need to try and communicate with them again. Perform another vigil in each room and use the Ouija board. I'm hoping you will join in on the Ouija board, it really does work better with more people.'

'Best put my big girl pants on tonight then. If you get answers then what?'

Megan didn't have a clue, 'If I can find out why the spirits are restless, then I can encourage them to move on. If not then you may have to consider getting a priest in. There is only so much that I can do.'

'It's those poor patients that perished here. I know it is. I'd be restless too, poor souls. Yet I want to be able to sleep well at night in my own home again.' Deborah shuddered as she curled a length of hair around the irons.

Megan wondered whether she should mention her findings at the library earlier. She didn't want to risk getting in trouble for breaking any confidentiality thing. Although she was sure that she was careful about what she'd said to Nancy. It might even bring peace to Deborah if she could persuade her that there was no grisly past goings on in her home. So Megan took the chance.

'Actually, I popped into the library earlier and I got talking to the librarian, Nancy, she had a wealth of info on the house and it turns out she was a relative of the doctor that lived here.' Megan proceeded to fill in the rest of her findings.

'Yes that's the same story that Nancy spieled to me,' Deborah's tone had changed.

'You don't believe her?'

'The woman is just bitter and won't acknowledge the truth of her great-great-bloody-grandfather. Those newspaper articles were a mere smoke screen. At some point this house should have rightfully been hers but the family fell on hard times and sold up. She's holding onto an influential family heritage but it's all bollocks. Dr Holdstock was nothing but a monster.'

'Do you have proof of this?'

'I have proof enough in the ghosts here that are keeping me awake at night. There is no other explanation. None. My parents upped and left, leaving me with a haunted house. They are probably still laughing at me from Australia.' Deborah switched the straightening irons off at the wall with more force than needed.

'But Nancy seemed quite convinced of the truth,' Megan pushed.

'You witnessed what the spirits are capable of here. It's them. They've probably had enough of that wretched woman defending their killer.'

'Well I'm still hopeful that the spirits have already moved on. I acknowledged their suffering and told them to be at peace. All went quiet after that. So if that worked, then you were right all along about them.'

'I know I'm right.' Deborah pulled out a sky blue laced pair of knickers and matching bra. 'Here try these. They've never been worn. I have a good judgement for sizing. Now let's find you a dress.' She started leafing through the clothes rail.

Megan decided not to push the conversation further. Deborah was right, this house was definitely haunted. Too much had happened that she couldn't explain; nothing that she'd seen the likes of before. If only she could find out the real truth on who the spirits were, but she guessed that she'd never really know.

'Perfect,' Deborah waved a sky blue dress in front of Megan. 'Matches the undies, try it all on.'

Megan took the dress and Deborah left the room. She dropped the towel to the floor and slipped on the underwear. The bra gaped a little and the knickers were a tad tight, but Megan wasn't going to speak up about it. She just wanted to get the whole night ahead over with. What did she care about matching clothes? No one was going to see her underwear anyway. She stepped into the dress and with a bit of effort, managed to zip it up at the back herself. The full length mirror revealed that it fit perfectly. It was a simple style, skimmed her knees and had an elegant neckline. Her hair shone with her new curls and she felt like a different woman. That's the problem though isn't it, Megan thought. It's not her. Her sister won't be meeting the real her.

Thump. The sound broke Megan's thoughts as something thudded inside the wardrobe at the far side of the room. Her heart missed a beat or two. She took a deep breath; she should be getting used to these thumps and bangs now. She stepped over to the wardrobe and grasped the handle.

'Wait,' Deborah called as she entered back into the room. She hurried over to join her and placed a hand on the wardrobe door, blocking her actions. 'Some things are private,' she smiled sweetly at Megan. 'Right a splash of makeup and then we are done, just in time for your sister to arrive. Now sit back down.'

CHAPTER
TWENTY-ONE

S<small>EVEN THIRTY P.M. EXACTLY AND THE BUZZER RANG OUT</small>. M<small>ARC</small> winked at Megan before answering it.

'It's Ian. Will you relax; you look like you're going to be sick.' Marc offers to top Megan's glass of wine up but she stops him. 'You do look nice by the way.'

Marc was right, Megan did feel like she was going to be sick. She couldn't believe all of this was happening.

'Too right she looks nice,' Deborah shouted over from the other side of the kitchen, where she was preparing dinner with Ross. 'I'm nothing short of a perfectionist. How long did you say you hadn't seen your sister for?'

'About eleven years.'

'Oh this is so exciting,' Deborah clapped her hands together. 'What's better than a family reunion?'

'Chopping veg, that's what,' Ross mocked, whipping a tea towel at his wife, 'less chatting more chopping.'

Megan chuckled at them both. They were starting to feel like a normal everyday couple. They really were so generous with everything that they were doing. She took a gulp of her wine, determined not to have any more. Ian entered the kitchen and Deborah rushed over to give him a hug.

'Scotch, large, coming up,' Deborah informed him. 'We are going to have a wonderful evening and forget all of this sorry nonsense.'

Megan couldn't agree that a missing woman was nonsense. It was hard to imagine how awful Ian must be feeling though. There's a good chance he is still somehow under suspicion too. Her brief encounter with PC Turner earlier niggled at her. She wouldn't say anything though. It wasn't her place and she wouldn't spoil the evening. Then the buzzer went again.

'It's Sammie,' Marc grinned.

Megan held her glass up to Marc for a top up. Perhaps one more wouldn't hurt. Deborah gave Megan a reassuring wink and proceeded to fill Ian in on who Sammie was, whilst Marc went to greet her at the door.

Moments later Sammie appeared in the doorway. It shouldn't be possible for wine to lodge in the throat but Megan had difficulty swallowing her mouthful down. Sammie was stunning. She hadn't pulled out any stops with her skimpy glittery silver dress. The last thing Megan thought she'd notice first about her sister after all of this time would be her cleavage. But there it was.

'Sammie,' Megan stepped towards her, 'I'm really happy you made it.' Although Sammie gave her a big smile, there was awkwardness, so a hug and kiss didn't feel appropriate.

'I drove past the house a couple of times but got here in the end,' Sammie laughed.

Megan thought that her laugh was more of a hysterical nervous one. Ross strode towards her and introduced himself, then planted a kiss on both of her cheeks. Yes, she had definitely gone red. Marc offered to get her a drink. She asked for a small spritzer as she had to drive home later. After the introductions, Deborah finished off prepping the dinner whilst everyone sat around the table. Ross wanted to get the formalities out of the way. He explained to Sammie that Megan was working within the household and that she had to sign a waiver not to disclose any private goings on within the house. He explained that Sammie would need to do the same and to not go to the press with the nature of Megan's work. He would however be happy to have a few photographs of them together, which she can post on social media as she pleased. Sammie eagerly agreed and signed away. And then she asked,

'So what is it Megan does?'

Sammie listened, wide eyed, as she was filled in on everything. She chatted on about paranormal experiences of her own, how once she thought she'd seen a person late one night in her living room, went to say something to them but the image had vanished. Megan was relieved that Sammie didn't look completely freaked out and the conversations flowed effortlessly. Deborah announced that dinner was nearly ready, so Ross gently pulled Sammie up and said 'Right, let's take some selfies.'

Megan watched on, smiling from ear to ear as Ross posed with Sammie. They both took a number of selfies, raising their glasses, pulling faces and one with Ross planting a kiss on her cheek. Marc had done a cheeky photo bomb too. Megan was pleased that the attention was off her for a bit. No doubt she would get a proper chat with her sister later, but it was good that she was made to feel welcome first. It took the pressure off.

'You and your sister are quite different aren't you?' Marc

said quietly, shuffling closer to Megan. 'I'm sensing she has stacks more confidence than you.'

'Well things went very differently for us from our teens.'

'She's hot too.'

Megan rolled her eyes at him. Deborah announced dinner was ready to be served and asked Ross to help dish up. Steak, roasted vegetables and herby garlic new potatoes were plated up for everyone. Delicious, Megan savoured the sight of her dinner and the smell. She hadn't eaten so well in such a long time. Fresh, home cooked food was all but non-existent. Tinned food and cheap microwave meals were the normal for her and Scott. Now her stomach growled as she tucked in, promising herself once more that she would never return to her old lifestyle.

The conversation turned to Ross and he was happy to answer Sammie's questions, filling her in on some of his behind the scenes antics, name dropping his celebrity friends and future work he had lined up including becoming the new Inspector Dark.

'So it's true then, you are going to be him,' Sammie gleamed, 'I really hoped it would be you.'

'As good as but it hasn't been officially announced, so keep it under your hat for a few more days.' Ross put his finger to his lips, hushing her.

Sammie pursed her lips and made the scout's honour gesture.

Megan felt a little out of the conversations and was aware that she hadn't spoken much with Sammie yet properly. There was so much that she wanted to find out about her- her life, how she had spent the last eleven years.

'So what's your line of work Sammie?' Megan blurted into

the conversation, a little awkwardly- social cues had never been her strong point.

'I'm a beauty therapist,' Sammie replied, flashing Deborah a knowing grin.

Deborah looked delighted, 'Well then, a girl after my own heart. Ever fancied breaking into show business?'

'Oh my goodness yes, but I wouldn't know where to start,' her voice had become excitably high pitched.

'Well then, perhaps I can forward your details on to some of my contacts.' Deborah said.

Sammie looked like she might burst as she said that she would be ever so grateful. Megan was ever so grateful too. All this would definitely be putting her relationship back on track with her sister and hopefully make amends for everything that had happened in the past with all that she put her family through.

'Of course you both must have so much to catch up on,' Ross said. 'Why don't you both have a good catch up in the lounge whilst we clear everything away.'

'Can I show her the gardens?' Megan asked.

Sammie nodded enthusiastically as Ross said that it was perfectly fine.

'Hold on,' Marc said jogging from the room. He returned with a jacket and a thick hoody. He handed Megan the jacket and draped the hoody around Sammie's shoulders. 'It's cold out there.'

'Perfect gentleman,' Sammie blushed.

'Watch out for him,' Deborah mocked. 'He doesn't understand the meaning of the word gentleman.'

They all laughed as Marc put his hands up in protest. Megan believed that Marc must definitely have a way with the ladies.

He just oozed that kind of confidence. Anyway it stands to reason doesn't it, a good looking guy, best friends to a movie star. He probably wasn't as much in Ross's shadow as Megan had started to believe. Besides, from what Deborah had disclosed earlier, it was Ross that her sister had to watch out for. Even if that were the case, would Sammie mind Ross's advances, knowing he was married? Would she resist him? Megan couldn't even guess. She knew nothing about her sister's thoughts, her morals, anything. But she was about to find out.

CHAPTER
TWENTY-TWO

'So you've done alright for yourself,' Sammie said, as they stepped out into the garden which was glittering away with its solar lights.

Megan didn't really know how to answer that. She hadn't done alright for herself at all. She had been doing far from alright. She felt like she had literally fallen into this house and into this world and even though she had wanted out a few times already, she was sucked back in. Terrifying spirits and things that go bump in the night was anything but alright. Being in the company of a famous actor did not define her as doing alright for herself. Should she just nod and agree or admit that actually she had no home, no money and no friends? Deciding she didn't want to sound like she was after sympathy, she just nodded and tried to change the subject.

'Tell me everything. Are you married? Kids?' Megan asked.

'Yes and yes. I have a son. He's five now.'

'Oh wow, that's lovely, I'm pleased you-'

'Why did you do it?' Sammie cut her off abruptly.

Megan knew this was bound to come up. She had prepared herself for it. She'd prepared for years in fact, hoping that one day her family would give her the time of day to listen. That day never seemed to arrive though.

'I can't pretend to be able to justify what I did. All I remember feeling at the time was envy that Chloe, Sadie and Beth had boyfriends. Remember them from my year? They bullied me saying I was frigid and boring. I was so shy and quiet at school. Remember? I don't know, then Mum and Carl started getting more serious and yes he was younger than her and good looking. He took the time to get to know me. I never thought for a second it was anything other than in a step-dad kinda way. But I enjoyed the attention and I wanted those girls to know that I was getting attention, that it wasn't just them and that I wasn't boring. How ridiculous it all seems now but that's how I felt.'

'Mum and Carl are still together, you know,' Sammie sounded a little angry now. 'He's still teaching. You didn't fuck up his career completely with your sick lies.'

'There's not much more I can say Sammie. I've been punished over and over since getting thrown out of the house. I came clean immediately as soon as it sunk in how serious I messed up. I never thought of the implications. I just didn't mean... you know I even tried to take my-'

'Your own life? Yes I know. Mum was there at the hospital. She didn't want to talk to you but she looked through the window whilst you were sleeping. You broke her heart.'

Megan's eyes filled with tears. She had no idea that her Mum had been there. She knew that she had caused her Mum and Carl a lot of pain but there were times that she wondered whether she deserved everyone completely turning their backs on her. Her own mother cutting her off. Not caring if she actually was dead. But she had cared a little, she must have. She was there.

'A couple of days ago,' Megan continued, 'I went to Mortehoe. I sat on the dragon's back. Do you remember that place? I'd do anything to go back to then when we were kids. I wish I could change it all.'

'Yes,' Sammie half smiled. 'We would fly off and do battle. You always did have a big imagination. Always one for telling stories.'

There was an uncomfortable silence as Megan felt the sting of her sister's dig.

'I'm sorry. I'm just sorry for everything.' Megan's tears now fell freely. 'I've missed you so much.'

Sammie's own eyes started to shine, 'Perhaps you have been punished enough, perhaps it is time to stop all this anger between us.' She stepped in and welcomed Megan into her embrace. Laughing through the tears she said, 'Inviting me round to meet Ross Huston was a good move.'

They both laughed and hugged a little longer, until Marc burst through the doors interrupting the moment.

'Sorry ladies, but that's enough mushy stuff. Come in and join us, we have dessert.'

Megan wiped her eyes and they headed back inside after both agreeing that they would spend the day together very soon to have a proper catch up on everything that had been happening over the years. There was plenty of time for Sammie to find out that Megan was not doing so well for herself but for now all that mattered was that the first step had been taken.

As Sammie stepped back into the kitchen, Ross swooped over, grabbed her and waltzed her around the room. She didn't object and threw her head back laughing as he spun her round.

'Put her down,' Marc said, 'Let her try some of this gateaux, it's to die for.'

The others were already seated and tucking into layers of soft sponge, cream and salted caramel sauce. Ross pulled Sammie's chair out for her, picked up her fork and loaded it with some of the desert. He slowly and playfully spoon-fed her. Sammie giggled and wiped a little cream from her lips.

'Excuse me a moment,' Marc pushed his chair back and marched out of the room. Deborah and Ian were deep in conversation about something. Oblivious really to Ross's flirting. Megan thought she should feel more awkward but having her sister here and seeing her happy pushed any other thoughts aside. Sammie took her last mouthful of desert and explained that she really must be going home as she hadn't realised how late it was getting.

'Oh you must stay the night,' Deborah piped up. 'It's late. Stay, have a drink. Drive back tomorrow.'

Megan could tell Sammie looked tempted. She wouldn't blame her if she caved and said yes. It's not every day you get invited to a sleep over at Ross Huston's house.

After groaning Sammie said, 'Thank you so much for the offer but I can't. My husband is expecting me back, he's up early for work tomorrow and my son won't expect me to not be there. He copes better with advanced warning about things.'

'Have you got far to go?' Ian asked.

'It took me just over an hour to get here from Studley.'

Megan still couldn't believe that Sammie was living in the next town to her all this time and they hadn't so much as bumped into one and other. She wondered how many times they may have crossed paths without realising.

'Ian usually drives my guests around,' Ross said, 'but I've let him have the night off, I expect he's had a skinful now.'

Ian proudly announced that he was very much drunk as a skunk.

'Truly it's fine,' Sammie protested, 'It's a straightforward and pleasant drive and I'm not tired yet either. I'll be fine.'

Marc reappeared looking flustered, 'Megan, you have to see this.' He held up his phone to her. 'Think I've got another ghost on film.'

Everyone huddled round the phone to see a black shadow move across the doorway to the guest bedroom- the guest bedroom that Megan was staying in. Marc explained that he had heard a thump against the door like something falling into it as he passed. He couldn't see anything when he checked. Out of interest, he checked the footage on his app and saw the black shadow.

Megan didn't feel drunk but she still felt like she had suddenly sobered up. They all went a bit quiet at the reminder that sinister things seemed to be going on. They had temporarily forgotten their fear of the house.

'Definitely a good time for me to leave,' Sammie said.

Everyone took turns planting kisses on Sammie's cheeks as she prepared to go. She thanked the Huston's for their enormous generosity. Megan hugged her one last time and Sammie told her to make sure she phoned her tomorrow to fill her in on everything. She also thanked her for getting her an invite; it was a night that she'd never ever forget. With that she got into her car and pulled away from the drive.

'Right, I'll get my Ouija board out then.' Megan said with all seriousness. 'Back to work.'

CHAPTER 23
BLIND HOUSE 1878

THIS WAS THE SURPRISE. PATIENT NUMBER ONE'S HEART THUMPED AS she dragged herself over to the woman sprawled out on the floor screaming an ear piercing scream. Number One tried to reach out to her but the woman clapped her wide eyes on her and screamed some more.

'It's okay, shh,' Number One soothed but she realised that there was no soothing this.

The woman tried to stand, her mass of black curly hair falling in front of her face. She screamed out as her legs buckled beneath her.

'I think my legs are broken,' the woman panted through her sobs.

'Mine are too,' Number One gently edged closer to her.

'Look at you,' the woman gasped, 'what's happening? why-'

Number One realised that she must look terrifying. This was terrifying. 'What's your name-'

The door swung open, banging against the wall. The Doctor hurried through, fussing, putting the white coat on.

'Why have you done this to me? What's going on?' The woman cried out.

The Doctor strode over and struck her around the face. 'The Rules, don't talk unless spoken to, don't look me in the eye, know your place. You are here for treatment.'

The woman looked to Number One, looked at her wounds, the blood, the dirt, the chains. Realisation flooding her senses. Number One looked back at her defeated, sorrowful.

'From now on, your name is Patient Number Two,' the Doctor explained, pulling over a length of chain. One utterance of your real name, either of you, and it'll be electric shock treatment, you'll never leave and I'll target your families. Understand?'

Number Two nodded then screamed out as cuffs were clamped around her ankles. The Doctor wrapped a gag around her mouth to muffle her screams, 'You need to grow a fucking back bone, get some resilience. But that is why you are here; these are things we can work on.'

Number One reached out to Number Two again and this time the woman let her put an arm around her as the Doctor went off to the check the equipment. The whites of Number Two's eyes were turning pink as she hyperventilated through the gag. Number One told her to try and stay calm, that it would be easier. She saw the Doctor holding up a sack and she knew what was coming, she knew it wasn't going to be pleasant but she knew it wasn't the worst. She squeezed Number Two's trembling shoulder. 'It's hard but stay calm,' she whispered. Number Two nodded and tried to regulate her breathing but as the Doctor approached it became impossible.

'Back off Number One,' the Doctor ordered, roughly placing the sack over Number Two's head.

Number One felt powerless but knew it was best to follow orders. She wasn't going to make it worse for this woman. This unsuspecting woman, confused, frightened, just as she was. This was her a week ago. She could do nothing but watch. The Doctor poured water over Number Two's face, holding her down, telling her that the sensation of drowning would cleanse her. Madness, the Doctor is mad and the truth will out. She can't call the Doctor by name in this small world of hell but if she gets out... when she's out, the whole world will know it, she'd make sure of it.

The Doctor ripped away the sack from Number Two and laughed down at the woman gasping and spluttering on the floor. 'You need to change into the appropriate attire now.'

'You okay?' Number One mouthed to the other woman.

She didn't answer, she curled up shivering and crying into the filth-ridden floor, whilst the Doctor went to fetch her white cotton night gown. Number One couldn't find the words, didn't know what else she could say, how she could comfort her. Her own body- every inch of it screamed with pain. She was anything but comfort to this woman, she was an image of things to come.

'You know, Number One,' the Doctor exclaimed before forcing Number Two to dress, 'treating two patients could become exhausting and rather time consuming. You've improved this past couple of days. Perhaps you can be released later tonight. Would you like that? To go home?'

Number One had been tricked before and felt the pain for giving the wrong answer. Everything was a test, a mind game. She simply nodded, keeping her head down not to look directly at the Doctor.

'So be it then, in a couple of hours I shall return to finalise the arrangements for your release.' The Doctor continued to struggle with getting the gown onto Number Two.

Number One kept her head low. One false move or sound could change the Doctor's decision. Could it be possible she would get to go home, that she would just be set free? Then what? Number One knew where she was, she knew who the Doctor was, she knew everything. So the Doctor would just let her go? Number One had tried to imagine that she would get out of here many times, that she would be snuggled at home with her parents again. But she now knew for sure. She knew that she would die here. She would die tonight.

CHAPTER
TWENTY-FOUR

Megan requested a few minutes to set up and prepare. What she really meant was that she was dying to get out of the skimpy knickers that she was wearing and put her old faithful's back on. She kicked off the delicate blue undies then rummaged in her bag for her own pair. Pulling them up, the relief was instant. She scurried into her en-suite and gathered up the pile of clothes that she had left there earlier. The door closed behind her abruptly. Panic set in. The door wouldn't open.

'Hello?' Megan hammered on the door and rattled on the handle. Why won't it open? There is no lock on the door. *Thump.* There was that sound again as if something or someone had fallen into the door. Megan backed away. No, she panicked and lunged back at the door. It still wouldn't budge. 'Let me out, help. Hello?'

The door swung open and Megan was startled to see Marc standing on the other side.

'Problem?' he said.

'The door wouldn't open.'

'Odd. There's no lock on it.' Marc said checking both sides of the door.

Megan wanted to scream that she knew the blasted door didn't have a lock on it. She swiped up the blue knickers that were still lying on the floor and bundled everything into her bag. There was literally no privacy around here.

'The ghosts feel angry.' Megan said. 'You know, I've met Nancy from the library. She said the private hospital here was peaceful and the patients well cared for. If Deborah is right then perhaps the spirits are feeling ignored. That they are seeking justice and no one is listening.'

'Ah Nancy and Deborah have had this ongoing feud for months,' Marc explained. 'Even before the hauntings started- before any strange things started going on in the house. Deborah was convinced this house was dodgy before we even realised that it was. Nancy couldn't convince her otherwise.'

Megan didn't know what to make of that. How Deborah could be so certain without real proof. She wasn't sure that spirits could be classed as proof. Not even with everything that she and they had already witnessed.

'Anyway, I'm ready,' Megan said. 'Can you call the others? We need to do a seance in this room.'

Marc nodded in agreement and did as she asked whilst she set up the Ouija board table. Once more, she placed the cat balls and the K2 EMF meters around the room. She decided against using the spirit voice box again, it just irritated her. If the other equipment didn't offer anything then she might consider using it later. It would offer some entertainment value if nothing else. She wondered if she had time to quickly put her leggings and t-shirt back on, now her sister had gone, she just wanted to feel like herself again, but then again she didn't want to offend Deborah after she had made an effort for her. She'd keep the dress on.

Everything was set up. Megan was relieved that Sammie had gone home. She was self-conscious as it was doing all of this in front of the Huston's let alone her estranged sister too. Her neck was stiff and she realised she probably hadn't relaxed a muscle all evening. She reached down to touch her toes, held herself there for a few moments then stretched up rubbing her neck. The sound of water falling halted her effort to relax. It was the shower. She popped her head around the en-suite door and the shower was blasting out water at full pelt. *Strange.* She turned the faucet off, completely confused. Stepping back into the bedroom she continued to stare in amazement as the cat balls and K2 EMF meters were all flashing away in the dimly lit room and then they stopped.

The sound of the others approaching filled her with relief. It must have just been the vibrations of their footsteps setting everything off. It didn't explain the shower though. Her hopes of no more paranormal activity were diminishing nauseatingly fast.

'I'm not sure I can do this,' Deborah whined as she entered the room first, not able to take her eyes off the board in the centre of the room.

Ian, Ross and Marc followed in behind her, spreading themselves out around the table.

'Ouija boards are actually very safe,' Megan attempted to reassure Deborah. That is what she had been told on past ghost hunting events. Event organisers would tell you that though wouldn't they? Who could actually know for sure? 'The important thing to remember is to close the board properly afterwards to prevent any spirits becoming trapped in here with us.'

Deborah didn't look like she found that reassuring.

'We didn't have any luck with this last night,' Megan explained. 'But with two more of us, we may have more luck.' She placed a compact torch on the corner of the table so it illuminated the board. She then instructed Ian to turn the bedroom lights off as he was nearest the switch.

Everyone rubbed their hands together to build the energy. Once they were all in position with their fingers lightly touching the glass, Megan called out the instructions to the spirits- advising them how to use the board to communicate with them. She thought it best to start with what she already knew about this room. She had been trapped in the en-suite and had twice heard something fall against the door. Marc had also heard something similar and then discovered a shadow by the door on camera.

'Is there a spirit with us here tonight? Please answer yes or no,' Megan called.

Everyone remained silent for a few moments. Megan had said that sometimes it can take a beat or two for spirits to reply. And then it happened. The glass moved. It edged its way to the word 'yes.' Deborah made a kind of strangled mouse sound as the glass came to a stop.

'Good, thank you,' Megan said. 'I feel that you were trapped in your previous life. Were you trapped?'

The glass slid slowly away from the word yes and then straight back to it with some force.

'Okay. I think you were trapped behind a locked door. A door you kept banging on for help but no one came. Am I right?'

Once more the glass shifted from the word yes then straight back to it.

'Were you a patient here in this house?'

The glass shot over to the word 'no' with more force than before.

'Okay, who is actually moving this glass?' Deborah squeaked.

Everyone looked at each other and in unison declared that it wasn't them and that their fingertips were only lightly touching the glass. Then there were echoes of gasps around the table as all of the equipment around the room lit up. Three dull knocks sounded on the bedroom door. Knock, knock, knock.

'Holy shit,' Ross whispered. 'You all heard that right?'

'No one take your fingers off the glass, we can't lose the connection now,' Megan swiftly said. She had noticed that they all looked like they wanted to bolt from the room- as did she.

'So who were you then?' Megan called out again calmly. 'Can you spell out your name for us?'

It went so quiet Megan was convinced that they had all stopped breathing. The glass moved. It slid over to the arch of letters, moving back and forth over them as if undecided. Back and forth and then it stopped over the letter 'P.'

'Good, keep going, we are listening,' Megan said, feeling exhilarated. Her fear seemed to have turned quickly to excitement; feeling the buzz as if she were back on a ghost hunt with Christina. Experiencing the wonder about how all of this was happening- attempting to get to the bottom of the unexplained. Helping this spirit was all that mattered now. She needed answers. Something very wrong had happened under this roof and she needed to find out what. She didn't blame Deborah now for thinking the worst about her home.

After a beat, the glass moved to the letter 'A' followed by the letter 'T' and then 'I' and so on until it had spelt out the word 'PATIENT.'

'But it said that they weren't a patient?' Ian piped up.

The glass hadn't finished though. It slid up to the arc of numbers above and rested over the number one and there it stopped.

'Patient number one?' Megan asked.

The room turned cold. Everyone felt the chill raise their gooseflesh. The torch flickered off by itself, the equipment stopped flashing and the glass shot from the table, clattering to the floor and then Deborah screamed.

CHAPTER
TWENTY-FIVE

Marc remained in the room with Megan after the others had fled downstairs.

'That was heavy,' he said.

'That was definitely something else, I'm shaking.' Megan picked up the glass from the floor. 'I need to close the Ouija board down properly but I reckon it's too late. The glass falling from the board is not a good sign.'

'Are we screwed then?' Marc asked.

'No more screwed than before I guess. The spirit is already behaving negatively. Chances are it could now get worse though if it's gained more energy.'

Megan placed her finger back on the glass and thanked the spirit and called out goodbye in hope that closing down the session properly would help stop things from becoming worse.

'So were they a patient here or not?' Marc said still none the wiser.

'I don't know, this whole thing is such a mystery. We need to take a break and re-group. We can't give up now.'

'You know I nearly doubted you, Miss Ghost detective. It appears you do have the gift.' Marc smiled at her and helped fold her table away.

Megan laughed, 'So you don't think I'm a loon for dragging you around the gardens last night looking for a demon dog?'

That had been playing on Megan's mind. She had felt utterly stupid despite being certain that there was a dog stalking her. But every so often a wave of embarrassment washed through her at the thought of dragging Marc around the gardens in the middle of the night- a complete stranger.

'Oh I do think you're a nut... but a gifted one,' Marc laughed 'Best fun I've had in ages.'

Megan actually believed him. She wondered if he did actually manage to go out socialising much or whether he was always at Ross's beck and call. Did he have many other friends? He obviously struggled to keep a girlfriend. Megan hoped she wasn't blushing at her thoughts. What did it matter to her about his love life? Social life? Anything? For the first time in a long time though, she felt awake. She was doing something exciting; she was growing curious about this celebrity lifestyle and she was fascinated about the history of this house. She had also reconnected with her sister. Who would have thought that working with the dead could make her feel so alive? She didn't want to shy away from everything anymore; she was keen to embrace it.

'Who the hell's that?' Marc said as the front gate buzzer sounded out, 'It's not far off midnight.'

Megan shrugged and wondered if perhaps Sammie had come back. They both headed downstairs to be met with Ross.

'It's the police again,' he said rubbing his face.

'For Christ's sake,' Deborah muttered as she joined them by the front door with Ian.

Ian looked pale and Deborah rubbed his arm and reassured him not to worry. Marc opened the door to Detective Page and PC Turner.

'Forgive the late hour,' Page said, 'may we come inside.'

Marc stepped aside and allowed them into the reception area.

'Is everything okay?' the Detective continued, observing everyone looking a little strained.

Megan wanted to scream out that no it wasn't all okay, the house is haunted and them turning up at this very moment was not the best timing. Deborah, Ian and Ross had just bolted downstairs terrified to then be confronted with the buzzer going. It was clear that everyone was on edge. But she couldn't scream that, she remained quiet, hoping that this was actually going to be good news and that they'd found Kerry.

'It's late officers,' Ross said gently, 'we were just starting to settle for the night.'

Deborah then put on that huge over-the-top enthusiasm that she does so well, 'How can we help you? Any news?'

'Sadly, still no news on Kerry,' Page explained. 'Obviously, we are growing increasingly concerned and door-to-door enquiries have led us nowhere. Kerry's husband and wider family are becoming desperate and are frantic with worry.'

'I feel so terrible about this,' Ian spoke up rubbing his forehead, 'I don't know how I'm going to forgive myself for not taking her to her front door,' his voice unsteady.

'No Uncle,' Deborah soothed, 'you're not just to blame. She didn't want her husband catching her being dropped off by you. He didn't know where she was and that was down to all of us.'

'Best not to dwell on blame at this stage,' PC Turner smiled awkwardly at Deborah.

Page appeared to scowl at Turner, 'The reason we are here, is to advise you... and I'm glad that you, Ian, are here to hear this, that we shall be filming a reconstruction early tomorrow morning before sun rise and that Kerry's husband and parents will be making a public appeal.'

'So how is this going to work then? Is my name going to be all over the news tomorrow?' Ross said. 'You know this could really harm my career if my name-'

'At this present time, all we need to show is that Kerry was leaving this area after an evening with friends, by car, the route she travelled, and the point that she was dropped off. Actors will be used and the same make and model of Ian's vehicle. We have already begun talks with your legal team in how to manage this so you'll be kept in the loop.'

'Thank you, God I hope she's found and soon,' Ross said.

'Enquiries will be ongoing, so we may need more from you in the coming days,' Turner warned.

'So I hope you're planning on staying local, all of you?' Page asked.

'Yes, we'll do what we can to help,' Ross said with Deborah confirming and Ian quietly nodding his head.

'We'll leave you to it then, and sorry again for the late disturbance,' Page said.

As the two officers headed out, Turner looked back and awkwardly nodded and waved. Page was seen gently shaking his head. Marc closed the door.

'Not much of a page turner are they, those two,' he said, his attempt at humour lost as Deborah scowled at him. 'Right, so where were we then? Ghosts?'

CHAPTER
TWENTY-SIX

'I. AM. NOT. STAYING. HERE. ANY LONGER,' DEBORAH ERUPTED, dismissing the sudden interruption from the police. 'Something bloody well touched the back of my neck when that glass dropped,' Deborah continued to wail. 'Ian get me away from this house. Now.'

Ross made several attempts to reach out and comfort Deborah but she kept brushing him away pacing back and forth.

'Debs, Love, you can't go now and Ian can't take you anywhere,' Ross insisted. 'Ian's pissed and you're drunk, we've all been drinking.'

Deborah all but screamed back at Ross, 'Drunk or not, I'm not staying in this fucking house.'

'Look, let's just get a taxi back to mine then,' Ian offered, already punching the number into his phone, 'it's late and there's nowhere else to go that's close by.'

Ross rubbed his face, 'Fine, we'll just get some stuff together then.'

'We'll?' Deborah scoffed, 'Oh no big man. No way are you coming. You're staying right here to help sort this shit out.'

An argument ensued between the married couple with Ross being accused of never stepping up and always having other people running around after him. Deborah was then accused of being no better.

'Whoa,' Marc intervened, 'Deborah, c'mon. We are talking about ghosts here. Can't blame Ross, he doesn't know what to do. None of us do. Look, he's just as scared as you are.'

'Jesus Christ,' Ross despaired, 'I'm not scared, there still has to be some rational explanation for all of this. I just want to be with my wife that is all.'

Deborah let out a high pitched laugh, 'Well you know what Ross, I am scared but no, I don't need you. My uncle will take care of me. You just help Megan with whatever she needs. I've said all along that patients died in this house. They never got justice and they're taking it out on us. It's about time that Nancy learned the truth about her sodding great-great-whatever-grandfather.'

'But it's not proof though is it,' Ross looked exasperated.

Deborah shot him that look which warned him not to say another word. She announced that she'd just go and grab her overnight bag and hurried from the room. Seconds later she was back poking her head around the door, 'Well don't leave me to go upstairs on my own, Ross,' she snapped.

Ross shook his head and followed her out.

'Poor sod,' Ian laughed. 'He's better off here with them ghosts, he'll get more peace.'

'Well I'm staying,' Marc said looking seriously at Megan.

Her stomach did a little flip. He could look sincere when he wanted to, and she finally admitted to herself that it was okay to find him attractive because he was. She couldn't remember the last time that she had looked at a guy and felt remotely anything. She was still certain that no one would ever see anything in her but she was more awake now to others around her. Christina would have definitely approved. Just how long had she felt dead inside for?

A scream cried out from upstairs making everyone jump then rush from the lounge. Deborah came running down the stairs, barging past everyone. Ross followed close behind carrying her bag.

'What on earth?' Ian asked.

The blood had drained from Deborah's face and she was visibly shaking, she couldn't speak.

'We heard a woman crying,' Ross said, also looking like he'd lost his glow. 'In our room, clear as anything, a woman crying. Then we heard a whispered voice saying, "Get out." Then Debs felt something touch her neck again.'

The gates buzzer rang out.

'Thank God,' Deborah's voice shook, 'It's the taxi.' She took Megan's arm and looked her in the eye. 'Please help them, those poor women. If you need a priest, anything, just whatever you have to do. I'm scared yes but the ghosts are the victims here. I just want them at rest. I wish I was brave like you.'

Deborah then ran from the house without kissing her husband goodbye. Ian followed, stumbling down the doorstep. Megan thought that it was probably a blessing for Ian that he was so drunk. It wasn't exactly the relaxing night to forget his worries that he'd hoped for. He'd gone from feeling guilty about not dropping Kerry on her doorstep to being in the middle of a supernatural fight for justice.

I wish I was brave like you. Megan repeated those words to herself. Well she wasn't that brave for a start but to have someone like Deborah wishing she was anything like her, was a huge compliment- a woman who had just about everything going for her wished to be a little bit like her. It may seem like a silly thing to pinch yourself over but Megan did just that.

'To be honest, I'm surprised she lasted this long,' Marc said.

'She wouldn't have even been here if she hadn't had to come back to see the police.' Ross replied, looking weary. 'The sooner we leave for Ireland the better.'

'What? It's like only a couple of days now tops that you'll get the go ahead?' Marc's eyes lit up, remembering that they would be out of this place soon anyway provided this police matter didn't drag on.

'Yeah, it shouldn't go tits up now but if it did then we're going straight back to the States anyway. I'm not hanging around here a moment longer.'

There was silence as they all felt the need not to be there any longer than necessary, looking around the hallway, then at each other- feeling the chill.

'Right then,' Megan rubbed her hands together, 'we potentially have a spirit known as Patient Number One who may or may not have actually been a patient. He/she said that they were trapped here. We are assuming a female as you have heard women crying and Deborah is convinced that patients were tortured and killed here. Deborah may well be sensitive to the spirit world so we can't rule out her gut instincts. It's all pointing to that she could be right. I now need to try and ask them what they want.'

'Fine,' Ross said, 'let's go back upstairs then, but can we leave the lights on?'

CHAPTER
TWENTY-SEVEN

Megan nodded to Marc that she was ready so he flicked off the lights. Ross's defeated expression vanished into the blackness for a moment until Megan switched on her torch to a dimmed setting. Marc took the torch and shone it over to the tapestry.

'Look how scary the figures look in the torch light, with the shadows and stuff. Almost looks like they're moving.' He mocked an evil laugh whilst moving the torch to under his chin, lighting up his face.

Ross snatched the torch away and put it back on the table. 'How can you even joke right now?'

Megan had to agree that it wasn't funny. The last thing that she needed was the thought of the black dog in the picture with the red eyes moving, she shuddered.

'You know the drill,' Megan said and they all began by rubbing their hands together. Fingers back on the glass, Megan called out, 'Hello Patient Number One, are you still here with us?' Nothing. 'I know you're angry but we want to help you. Does the name Dr Holdstock mean anything to you?'

The glass moved a tiny amount but no more. They patiently waited but still nothing.

'Is it just you Patient Number One or are there more of you?'

The glass moved. It slid over to the arc of numbers and rested on the number two.

'Two of you? Thank you. How can we help you? What do you want?' Megan willed the glass to move, to spell it out clearly. At this point, she hadn't felt so desperate for anything. Help the spirits to move on, get paid and start a new life. Really, what was so hard about that? *Please*, she begged. But nothing.

The glass didn't move, they waited but it didn't move. A few more questions later and it still didn't move.

'Perhaps we need to move to a different room and try?' Marc suggested.

The glass swept off the table with such force it cracked.

'Whoa okay now it moved,' Megan gasped.

Ross snapped the lights back on, 'I can't cope with this shit. Why aren't they saying what they want? Why don't they want help? Victims? My arse. They are fucking with us and I want out. We should all get out.'

'You know Deborah will kick your ass if you turn up at Ian's,' Marc reminded him.

'Shhh,' Ross hushed him.

Megan couldn't believe her ears. A woman crying, she could hear it.

'See there it is.' Ross stormed around the room, looked in the en-suite, under the bedding, in the cupboards. Then charged from the room, 'Where the hell is that sound coming from?'

But it stopped and no one could make out where it had

been coming from. There was no explanation. Megan felt light-headed, it was a heart wrenching cry. They followed Ross down the stairs to the kitchen. Everything looked in place as it should. Ross checked the knives were where they should be and the contents in the cupboards were in one piece.

'I don't believe they can hurt us,' Megan tried to soothe Ross's anxieties. 'Just tell yourself its only sounds. They can't hurt us. I'll do a lone vigil in one of the rooms. Perhaps if I talk to them one to one, woman to woman, it'll make a difference?'

'Makes sense,' Marc agreed.

'I do think that if I can't get rid of the problem, you will need to vacate the house and get a priest in or a team more experienced.' Megan didn't want to be defeated but she could see how scared Deborah and Ross were so she had to be honest if she couldn't do it. She already knew deep down that was the case. This was something she could never have anticipated.

'This just can't be happening,' Ross was serious. 'This cannot get out to the press- none of this can be made public. The more people involved the more chance of that happening is. I'll be a laughing-stock.'

'That's all you ever think about is your ego,' Marc sniped.

'Back off Thorne,' Ross glared at him.

'Fear can make us act irrationally,' Megan quickly stepped in. 'Please just leave me to it, go get a drink, sit, relax.' It seemed a difficult thing to ask them to do, relax, but she was all out of more inspiring advice.

No one spoke for a Moment then all at once, they noticed a slight movement from the hanging saucepans. Heavy based saucepans hanging in size order beneath the cupboard, swaying with a gentle clanking sound. It briefly held the three of them in a trance.

'Is there a breeze in here?' Marc spoke up first. He was

closest so reached to steady one of the saucepans. The clanking heightened as the saucepans swayed in more of a frenzy, clattering against each other and against the wall. Four pans swaying, clanging and banging. Marc froze in front of them, mesmerized- baffled.

'What the hell?' Ross sounded short tempered. 'What the hell do you want?' he roared.

Marc stepped back and the saucepans settled until they were gently tinkling then stopped. 'Well that shut them up?' he laughed but soon pursed his lips because Ross's expression told him it was no laughing matter.

Ross threw a towel at Marc and stormed out the kitchen, stating he would be in the lounge.

'I suppose I better follow him; he won't want to be in there on his own. He just won't admit it,' Marc said. 'Are you sure you'll be okay on your own?'

'You shouldn't wind him up,' Megan scolded. 'Of course this is scary stuff, are you not scared at all?'

'Yes, no, I don't know. It's a bit unreal isn't it?' He ran his fingers through his hair.

Megan couldn't work him out. It bothered her that he seemed to get enjoyment out of Ross's fear- Ross who was his so called best mate and not to mention his employer. It was Megan's dream to work with her best mate, Christina, to escape the drudgery of their jobs at ST Style. They spoke about it often, how to get out, to start their own business, throwing ideas around until they settled on ghost hunting. Now she wondered whether their friendship would have held up as business partners. Would they have fought? Would Christina have got tired of doing most of the work and Megan being the useless one? Megan didn't know and she couldn't compare her life to that of Marc and Ross's so she pushed the thoughts aside. Besides, she'd do anything to have Christina back and to find out how well they'd be working together now, at this moment.

'I'll be fine. It's what I'm being paid to do. I'll scream if I need you,' Megan was only half joking.

Marc and Megan left the kitchen and met with Ross who was standing at the far end of the hallway with his back to them. He was standing perfectly still. Had he been made of stone he would have been the perfect statue.

'You alright bud?' Marc asked.

He didn't move. Marc approached him and he didn't so much as flinch.

'Ross?' Marc peered round to see his face. It was blank and unmoving.

Megan joined them and squeezed Ross's arm. 'He's in a trance,' she said softly.

Ross remained rigid. Unnerving.

'He looks like he's seen a g-' Marc soon shut up.

'For Christ's sake,' Ross snapped, suddenly moving. For a second it looked like Ross might swing for Marc. He grabbed the collar of his shirt. 'I'm not in a trance. But yes I could have seen a ghost. I heard a noise from in there,' he gestured to the second sitting room, 'a dull thud, then a dragging sound- as if something heavy was being dragged across the floor. I open the door and I think I see something move from the window. I take a closer look and there is a figure of a woman, an old lady I think in the distance by the trees. She stood staring and then disappeared. I look down at the floor on my way back out and look...'

He showed them to just inside of the doorway to the sitting room. He pointed down to the wood flooring. Five deep scratches swept across one of the panels.

'Fingernail marks,' Ross said, 'Like someone was being dragged across the floor.'

Megan knelt to closer inspect the markings. 'It's not possible,' she said. 'Anything could have made these marks, are you sure they weren't here before, have you been moving furniture?'

'No they weren't there yesterday and they weren't there this morning. Look at them, you can't miss them.' Ross's voice shook. 'And there was definitely someone outside.'

Marc looked at Megan, 'Do you want me to get the gun?'

Megan gave a loud sigh, 'No, no more guns,' she cringed at the thought. 'Why don't you both go check the CCTV. Leave me in here. Seems like the best place for me to start.'

Ross didn't need telling twice, he turned on his heels and headed to the main lounge. Marc nodded to Megan and followed after him.

Megan looked out of the window and couldn't see more than shadows and moonlight. This was possibly a really bad idea but she had no choice. No matter what, she was going from here- from this house, come daylight. Her enthusiasm and change of heart to embrace everything was vanishing as quickly as it came. They can get someone else in to ward off these spirits. Someone else can feel terrified- anyone but her. She took a last look around the cosy sitting room whilst the lights were still on so she could keep her bearings. The door was closed, she flicked off the lights and was plunged into darkness.

CHAPTER 28
BLIND HOUSE 1878

Patient Number Two sobbed uncontrollably in Number One's arms. The Doctor had left them alone for now but would be back soon.

'What time is it about?' Number One soothed. Time had stopped meaning anything to her. Number Two had just arrived; she must know the time. It would be nice to know, to feel a sense of something normal.

'It was close to eleven p.m. I think when that fucki-' She couldn't finish her sentence she screamed out again in pain, her legs felt like they were burning. She wiped away the snot on the sleeve of her gown. 'I can't stay here, my son needs me, I need to get out...'

'Shhh... just be careful what we say, they are watching.' Number One feared what was to come and knew better than to make it any worse.

'How long have you been here?' Number Two asked shuffling slightly back to get a better view of Number One's battered appearance.

'Since last Saturday.'

'A week? No... no... I can't, I have to-'

'Listen, no one knows I'm missing. My family think I'm on holiday. They wouldn't think to look for me. You have a son, a husband. They'll be out looking for you straight away. My family will soon notice that I haven't returned. We have to believe help is coming.'

'My husband thinks I'm staying the night with a friend. He didn't know where I really was.' Number Two broke down again.

That was Number One's last speck of hope diminished as quickly as it came. No one knew where this woman was either. No one was looking. It must be between midnight and one a.m. now, and the Doctor would be back within a couple of hours. So before dawn broke, before the rest of their small world awoke to realise that something was wrong. Before their families would come looking.

Number One brushed away a clump of damp dark curly hair away from Number Two's face. 'Let's stay strong. Tell me about your son.' Both women huddled together, both of them trembling.

'Louis is nine. He's ten next week. He's funny, always up to mischief, playing practical jokes. I can see him on stage- a comedian. He just has one of those expressions. He makes you smile. Soon he will be in double figures though. Ten. Where does the time go? I have to see him reach that milestone... I have to get out- he needs me...'

'I don't have kids. I can only imagine. I'm close to my folks though. They have a gorgeous spaniel who I dote on. People say they love their dogs like children. I'm missing his soft hugs and waggy tail.' Number One's voice trailed off. Perhaps this wasn't the way to stay strong. Her gut told her that she wouldn't survive the night. The Doctor wasn't letting her go and she was finished with her. She hadn't thought seriously about having children yet but now she wouldn't get to. There's nothing like being robbed of chances to make you realise that you want more, to experience more, to live more.

Number Two screeched out in pain again, 'My legs are too painful, I can't do this. We need to fight back. We need a plan.'

No answer came. Number One had tried a few times earlier in the week but the punishment got worse. There is only so much fight you have in you when your legs are broken and your whole body is screaming in pain. Number Two still had a chance. If she was kept here a few more days, then help will come. She just had to get through a few days and she'd be better off towing the line and making it easier on herself. Number One was out of time; she was convinced of it but Number Two had a chance.

'One way or another, the Doctor is getting rid of me tonight. You must listen,' Number One pleaded. 'Just always stay calm and follow instructions. Just survive this okay. Hang on for as long as possible. Your husband will find you.'

Number Two suddenly looked up, eyes wide with realisation, 'I told my best friend where I was. The one I told my husband I was staying with. I didn't tell her the address but she knows who I was meeting. That's it. They will find me... us.'

But not before the nights out. Number One squeezed her new friend's hand, 'Yes, just hang on in there okay?'

Number Two nodded. The sound of the heavy bolts sliding across the door cut the conversation dead. Number One's heart hammered against her ribs. It was time.

CHAPTER
TWENTY-NINE

MEGAN'S EYES STILL HADN'T ADJUSTED TO THE DARK. OPPRESSIVE INKY blackness smothered her, stroking her with shadowy fingers. She brushed away the tickle from her cheeks, fearing she was being touched. Her throat thickened, suppressing her rapid breathing. Now would be a good time to turn upside down, she thought. It was only natural to have a panic attack in these situations, right? She hung over the arm of the sofa and breathed in for five and out for three. She scrunched her eyes shut and willed her brain not to think about the spirits, she delayed calling out to them. Why reach out to something you don't want to receive? *Don't look for what you don't want to find.*

Feeling a little more at peace, Megan sat herself down crossed-legged in the centre of the room as if to meditate. She was kicking herself for not having her torch with her though. She spent some time thinking about her sister and about how excited she was to meet up with her again, how her loneliness would now be left behind, how it may help build bridges with her mother too. She thought about Devon and her new start and how she might delay going there if things worked out with her sister. No matter what, she would never go back to Scott. The thoughts kept her distracted for a time, still reluctant to make contact with the spirits. She had resolved she'd be out of her depth so didn't see the point in trying. Another professional could come in and take over. They were welcome to it.

That was until she heard a scrape. 'Hello?' she whispered. It was no good; she turned her attention back to the scratches on the floorboards- imagined someone being dragged along against their will. She replayed the crying she heard, felt the grip around her throat from last night, someone had suffered. *'Damn it.'* she cursed softly.

'Patient Number One? Are you here? It's just me now...I think you tried to show me how you suffered. Show me again. I want to understand what you went through. I can help you get justice.'

Silence. Then there was a tap at the window. Megan stood with a start. She was afraid to get a closer look. She didn't want to see an old lady standing out there in the dark, lurking, watching her from the shadows. Tap, tap again. Perhaps it was just a branch swaying. The wind had been picking up. She felt her way gingerly closer to the window, but soon jumped back. What she saw was the unmistakable outline of a large hound. She scrambled back panting, made for the light switch but her stomach squeezed with intense pain- a burning, crushing pain. The pain brought her to her knees as she doubled over, not having the strength to cry out.

The pain subsided, it only lasted a minute or so but felt much longer. It had knocked the wind out of her so Megan stayed where she was, drawing her knees up to her chest and hugging herself tightly. 'Please go away. Please go away,' she pleaded. What did that dog want with her? As if she didn't have enough to deal with. The dog is not why she was here- it's not what brought her here. Why was it always around? *Think,* she thought back to the first time she saw it, out of the window at the Needleworks and Mill. Nobody else saw it, even though she was pleading with the group to look.

She'd had a bad row with Scott, she'd met up with Christina ahead of their ghost hunt that night who did her best to persuade her that now was the time to leave him, that she was worth much more. Megan had insisted that she couldn't think about that right then, she wanted to forget him for at least the night, she didn't want their night out ruined. They arrived at the location and after the initial meet and greet, the group went straight into a séance. The leader asked everyone to talk to the spirits through their thoughts, to introduce themselves- to tell the spirits a bit about themselves to show that they meant no harm. All Megan could think to them, whoever was listening, was, *'Hi, I'm Megan, no one loves me and I'm truly alone. Perhaps you feel the same?'* A few minutes was given for this, then the circle was broken and that's when Megan saw the dog through the window.

The hound had sat at the roadside watching as Christina lost her life later that night- the same dog and it'd been appearing to her since. She was still convinced it was waiting to take her life too- to escort her to the other side. It was just biding its time. Megan wondered if that time was now close. She'd asked to feel Patient Number One's suffering and that was directed at her stomach. Megan rubbed her middle and sniffed away the tears. She wondered if the spirit now wished her dead too. The window tapped again.

Megan couldn't bear it; she scrambled up and hit the light switch on, she stepped back and felt something brush against the back of her neck. She turned to see a figure, tall and all in white. They were face to face and then it vanished as quickly as it came. Megan screamed. It was a scream which summoned Marc and Ross running into the room. They found her curled up cowering on the floor. Marc put his arm around her rigid shoulders and helped her to her feet.

'What happened?' Ross said, flustered.

Megan looked to the tall lampshade that Ross was standing next too. It had a white shade laced with tassels. Was that what she saw? Was the sudden bright light playing tricks on her frightened mind? Megan couldn't speak. She was disorientated and confused. 'I thought I saw...'

'Let's get you out of here,' Marc said, still holding on to her.

CHAPTER
THIRTY

'What did you see?' Ross demanded, pacing the main lounge.

'I thought I saw a woman- a ghostly woman, right in front of me. But she vanished. I think that it must have been the lampshade. I feel like an idiot,' Megan said sounding washed out.

'Anything else happen?' Ross pressed on.

'Not much,' Megan decided not to mention the hound. 'I heard a few taps on the window, couldn't see anything though. I had a pain in my stomach, I asked the spirit to show me her pain and moments later my stomach felt like it was being sliced open.'

'Shit, didn't that happen last night too? Except you were strangled weren't you?' Marc said.

Megan rubbed her throat at the memory. It was too much of a coincidence for it to happen twice- to ask to feel their suffering twice and then to experience pain twice. That was no panic attack, neither times were. She was all too familiar with panic attacks and yes they could present with pain but nothing like that, nothing like your stomach feeling like it was being sliced open with a hot poker or your throat being squeezed to the point you can't breathe, that it could actually kill you. She decided that she would not be trying that tactic again. It was more than enough for her to get the message that these spirits had greatly suffered in some way.

'But we are no closer to getting rid of these... these ghosts.' Ross was beginning to sound irritated.

Megan had to be honest, 'I can't do it. You'll need a priest, I think. Someone to cleanse the house properly.'

Ross continued to pace, getting more agitated. 'How do they do it? Cleanse with what?'

Megan wasn't sure. She was back to feeling unprofessional, not knowing enough about the business she was in. Quick, think on the hoof she thought, she pictured a priest walking through a house, something from a movie she may have seen- a priest waving a pot of something which was smoking. But what was it, Incense? A type of herb? Say something, anything, 'They burn sage and sprinkle holy water.' Yes, that sounded about right she thought. Faith is something she needed more of- confidence and faith in herself. Knowledge was there, she just needed to trust herself. She was sure that she wasn't too far off the mark.

'Can't you do that? Why a priest? Seriously what difference does it make?' Ross crouched down before Megan as if he were ready to supplicate.

Taken aback, Megan looked to Marc who merely shrugged. 'I don't know. I can't bless water and make it holy, I guess. If I had the water and herbs, I could try?'

Ross's eyes widened and he lifted a finger, suggesting that he had an idea. He hurried from the room. Marc sat himself down next to Megan.

'Honestly, are you okay?' he asked with sincerity. 'You must be exhausted, if only we could rewind to when we were eating and drinking and laughing hey.'

Megan rubbed her eyes. Yes, she was exhausted. It'd be easy to forget herself, to just allow herself to cry, to storm from the house saying she wanted no more part of it, but this was her job. If nothing else, she had a strong work ethic. 'I could murder a coffee to be fair,' she half laughed.

'I think a coffee is the least we can get for you,' Marc said. 'Anything else, anything at all, just ask.'

Megan appreciated his kindness. Sammie was right, he was a gentleman. Her stomach did another flip. This was ridiculous she thought, she couldn't find Marc that attractive, he was good looking yes, but he was a cocky idiot and totally out of her league. But when he looked at her with sincerity in his dark eyes and showed kindness it weakened her. It's not what she was used to- it confused all her feelings and unnerved her. She hoped she'd successfully talked herself out of having a crush on him and was relieved that Ross burst back into the room. He was waving around a jar of herbs.

'Sage, see, I have some. Here you go. This'll do, right?' he said handing her the jar of supermarket branded dried herbs. 'Thank God for spice racks.'

'Well I guess... I could-'

'Please just try,' Ross pleaded, 'burn it, spread it, burn the fucking whole house down, I don't care, just get rid of the ghosts.'

'He wouldn't normally swear just ignore him, he's tired and stressed-' Marc said in jest.

'Please, will you try?' Ross asked again, with an exaggerated grin for Marc to see.

'I'll do anything for a coffee,' Megan agreed. 'Find me something, a dish or something to burn it in and I'll give it a go.'

Ross looked relieved. Getting anyone else in the house really was the last thing that he wanted. He instructed Marc to make the coffee and to find a suitable dish because he wouldn't be staying. Ross had made it clear that he was leaving them to it and that he didn't care if Deborah would throttle him for abandoning the house. He was going.

'If I don't get some kinda sleep, I'm going to suffer later. I've got interviews lined up later today, it's gone four a.m.,' Ross furthered his excuses.

Marc looked like he was holding back some sarcastic response to Ross leaving, to say something like that he was a coward, a deserter or something. But no he just said, 'Don't blame you mate. We'll manage.'

Ross took no time in grabbing his jacket and headed out of the front door. No sooner had he said he was leaving, he was gone- just like that.

'Unbelievable,' Marc scoffed. 'Anyway… coffee. Just you and me then ghost detective.'

Megan felt weak, but she clung to the fact that it was just gone four a.m.. Just a few more hours until sunrise, until daylight, until she hands her notice in. Strong work ethic or not, she wasn't staying here another night. They would be forced to get someone else in, she was done.

'Oh I forgot to ask,' Megan suddenly remembered, 'did you check any CCTV footage? Did you see anything else? Did you get the figure that Ross thought he saw in the garden?'

'We looked, but nothing. We don't think the cameras out the back quite reached that part at the side, seems to be a bit of a blind spot. Let's check the images from when you were in the second sitting room. If you want to that is?' Marc pulled up the correct camera image on his phone app and handed it to Megan whilst he prepared the coffee.

Reluctantly, Megan looked through some of the footage. She was scared of what she'd see. The images weren't the best in the dark. Marc had said that the cameras were only fairly cheap ones, which were quick and simple to throw up when needed. But Megan could see the glow of herself sitting then standing then walking to the window, then falling to the floor. It was then that she noticed specks of light dancing around her. Orbs or specks of dust, either way there they were flitting around her frame and nowhere else. She then watched herself run for the light switch and as she did there was a sudden bright flash of white light. As quick as a flash of lightning, it was gone and the room was illuminated with its usual light and everything was as it should be; although the lampshade that Megan thought was a ghost was very gently swaying.

'Anything?' Marc asked, handing her a steaming hot mug.

'Nothing conclusive,' she said. She was reluctant to show Marc what she thought she saw. She'd had enough of looking like a crazy person. She shuddered though and as much as she had longed for the coffee, she now found it hard to swallow. She had felt terrible pain in that room and she feared that whatever spirit it was meant her great harm.

'Let's drop a match in this sage then and get it smoking, sooner this is done the better,' Megan jumped from her stool. 'Let's start in the second sitting room, if any room needs cleansing then that one does.'

CHAPTER
THIRTY-ONE

Megan gently blew on the smouldering heap of sage. 'It stinks,' she said. 'Let's be quick, I think it's all going to just burn out and we won't get round the whole house.'

'Can't believe that we are trying to bodge a house cleanse; Ross should just get a priest in the stubborn idiot,' Marc said. 'C'mon then.'

'Winging it is becoming a mantra of mine,' Megan laughed. She could just about see the humour in this or she had gone past the point of being terrified and had finally lost her sanity.

As they were in the kitchen, Megan called out there first as the smoke wafted around, 'I bless this room, Spirits please leave, move on and find peace. It's time for you to leave.'

They hurried next to the second sitting room, Megan avoided looking over to the window, she did not wish to see anything move from outside. She repeated the words she had spoken in the kitchen as she swiftly paced the room allowing the smoke to spread. They repeated this process out in the hallway, up the staircase, along the landing and in each of the bedrooms. They had even gone into Ross and Deborah's bedroom, even though Ross had previously mentioned he didn't want her investigating in there. But Megan had figured that Deborah had already allowed her in there and there was an urgent need to be thorough.

'So that's everywhere then?' Megan double checked.

'That's everywhere,' Marc confirmed, 'I guess we might not find out if it's worked until tonight? We don't have much spooky goings on during the day.'

But she wouldn't be here tonight, Megan had already made a promise to herself that this was it, no more, she was finishing her part in this crazy situation. She could finish now even, call it a day, it was nearly five a.m. Surely her work here was done. She could be at her sisters in an hour, maybe she'd be awake? She has a young child after all. Perhaps she'd offer her breakfast. Surely she'd be dying to know the rest of the gossip from after she'd left.

'Perhaps not,' Megan said, 'but I really have done all that I can do here. Ross is going to have to get someone more experienced in if things haven't settled down. It's time for me to head home, well somewhere... well I need to get myself sorted, so I must get going.' Megan felt her cheeks begin to redden as she tripped over her words, aware that she must sound pathetic.

'But you'll get some sleep first won't you? You know you're very welcome to and Ross will be back in a few hours, he'll want a full report. I don't want our adventures to end yet, it's been fun.'

'I wouldn't say fun exactly.' Megan scrunched her face up. Then she realised that Marc did have a good point. She did need to wait for Ross to come back. She needed paying. 'Okay, I'll stay and get some sleep until Ross gets back.'

Marc showed her back to her room, 'Are you going to be

okay? You know if you don't want to be on your own, I could kip on the floor for a bit?'

Megan couldn't tell if he was joking. No she didn't want to be on her own, not for a second. Space on her own was something that she was always perfectly content with, but not in a haunted house, not when she was weak with fear. But she couldn't say yes to him.

'No, really I'll be fine, you don't need to do that.'

'Perhaps I do need to. I was thinking more that I didn't want to be on my own.' He playfully bit his fingertips and mocked an expression of fear.

He was joking. 'Well just scream if you need me, I'll come save you.' Megan smiled.

'Seriously, I am worried if you're okay. You've been swept up in a lot here haven't you? You must think we're all nuts. For someone who claims to be anxious, you've got more courage than anyone I've ever met.'

Now she wasn't sure if he was being patronising. 'Ghosts and missing women? I'd say that was a lot. But I'll be fine, honestly go and get some sleep.'

'I guess that reconstruction will be underway around now then, if they wanted to do it before daylight.'

Megan didn't know what to say. She felt uneasy that Ross still insisted on keeping his name out of it. Surely it would come out soon enough. Goodness knows how Ian must be feeling. He must be under suspicion still, he must be. She shuddered and then yawned. Marc was right, all of this was draining.

'I'll leave you to it then,' Marc said yawning in return, 'but honestly, if anything happens, or you need anything, anything at all, you know where I am. Don't feel on your own.'

He wasn't joking. It was that look again, like he genuinely cared, that sent waves of tingles around her fatigued body. She insisted that she was fine and after him asking her a number of times if she was sure, he finally left her alone, to Megan's relief. She didn't want the fuss, as kind as it was of him it was just something she wasn't used to and found it all a bit too much. It panicked her as much as being left alone in a haunted house.

She used the en-suite but this time she propped the door open with her trainers. There was no way that she was going to set herself up to be trapped in the room again. She decided not to shower too as it had been playing up before- anything not to add to the drama. She sprawled across the bed, sinking into the deep mattress. She really would miss this bed. Sleep didn't come straight away, she found herself listening for bumps and knocks and replaying events in her mind. It all started to not feel real. What explanations could there have been? How could she debunk all that had happened? She couldn't. She tossed and turned a number of times but did eventually give into fatigue and drifted off to sleep.

Once more Megan found herself in a pitch black room- musty and dank, suffocating. Faint distant sobs grew nearer, closer until she felt the breath of the sobs in her ear and the brush of hair against her cheek. Megan had lost her voice, she couldn't speak. Her throat tight, her breath restricted. A figure in white with roughly chopped blonde hair lit a candle, illuminating herself, showing her white night dress stained and grubby. Another woman stepped into view, dressed the same but she had long dark thick curly hair. Megan had seen her before. 'Can you help us?' the woman said. The blonde woman pressed her finger to her lips, 'Shhhh,' she whispered. She had the look of terror, of a woman about to die. And so she did, she fell to her knees before Megan as blood pumped from her stomach flooding her night dress crimson. The woman with curly hair looked on with an expression of lost hope for a moment before blood drained from her throat. She dropped down next to the other, both now collapsed at Megan's lap. She still couldn't gasp a breath or scream out. She stroked each of their heads with trembling hands but their hard skulls turned to mush and collapsed under her touch.

Megan shot awake, layered with sweat and as her eyes adjusted to the darkened bedroom she set eyes on the tapestry as two red pinpricks of light came from the hound's eyes. Megan screamed.

CHAPTER
THIRTY-TWO

Megan shot from the bed and ran to throw the curtains open to see the efforts of the sun emerging. Marc burst through the door.

'Are you okay? What-' he gasped looking to Megan as she slid down to the foot of the window shaking.

'Something terrible has happened in this house,' Megan's eyes were now full with tears. 'Something terrible has happened to Kerry. I know it has.'

'What? Wait, Kerry? As in Kerry, Ross's missing friend? How do you mean?'

'She came to me in my dream and it's not the first time. Each time she bled out from her throat asking for help. She was wearing a white gown.'

'And what are you thinking? That she was harmed in this house?' Marc joined her sitting on the floor, looking more than confused.

'I don't know but it was so vivid, as vivid as we are talking now. She was there and she was with someone else, another woman, also suffering. Why am I dreaming of Kerry?'

'Look, honestly, it's just a jumble of things isn't it? Your mind making sense of everything. None of us know where Kerry went but she left here happy and in one piece. We all saw that she did. It's normal to have nightmares after all of this isn't it?'

Megan knew that he was probably right. But it was so real and Kerry had appeared to her twice now, it was all too strange. Tears were now in full flow and Megan stood and made her way to the tapestry.

'This hound, its eyes were glowing red, it was staring at me,' she pointed, scared to physically touch it.

Marc rubbed his face, 'Look, I don't know what this obsession with black mutts are but-'

'I know what I saw,' Megan snapped. 'I can't do this anymore, we didn't use holy water, we should find some. Is there a church, there must be a church, we could get some ask for some-'

'Megan stop,' Marc joined her and tried to rub her arm but she brushed him away. 'Let's just take our time and think, I really don't think-'

'No there isn't time, women were harmed here, butchered even, Deborah was right about this house. I've been choked, I felt my stomach slice open...' She suddenly pictured the blonde in her dream and her stomach wound. 'Oh God... we need to get help. I'll go to a priest, I don't care what Ross says, I'll go, these women need peace. All the things that have moved, all the noises, we have to do something.' Megan didn't care anymore that she was sounding hysterical, she wiped her eyes. 'I wish I was brave. I wish I could carry on but this is too much, we have to do more.' Her tears continued and she ran from the room.

Marc chased after her to the top the stairs. 'Wait,' he called, 'don't be hasty, you're tired-'

'Enough, I'm terrified, I have to go, I have to do something.' She ran to the bottom of the stairs and Marc was hot on her heels.

'Please stop,' Marc pleaded. 'Look it's gone too far... I've gone too far. Please you need to listen.'

Megan spun round to face him, her eyes red and tear-stained.

'It was all me okay,' he said softly with a look of remorse.

'What?' Megan looked completely thrown.

'It was me; I did all this to wind Ross up. It was just a big joke on Ross to scare him. Look.' He rolled his sleeve up to reveal a kind of armband. 'It's magnetic. I can move saucepans and knives with a wave of my arm. I have small Bluetooth speakers set up around the house. One tap of my phone and a knocking noise can sound out or a dragging noise or a creepy voice asking for help and yes the crying women too. I made those scratches on the sitting room floor. I had smashed those glasses in the cupboard. I played the noise afterwards. We opened the cupboards and it looked like it had just happened. The images on camera- I created them.

Marc gave Megan some time to process what he'd explained so far. She looked dazed, confused and then anger took hold. There is always a breaking point isn't there? When it doesn't matter how dignified and professional you try to be, there is always a point where none of that matters anymore. Megan had always tried to be her best self since everything she had put her family through as a teenager. She had towed the line, been polite and worked hard. But that point had now arrived for Megan- fatigue and disbelief had consumed her and she swiftly punched Marc in the face.

He recoiled back, clutching his cheek, 'Whoa okay, I probably deserved that, but you know none of this was personal against you. I was careful to make sure you were okay. I assumed you wouldn't get too scared as this was your job and what you're used to.'

'Of course I was bloody terrified, you've taken me for a complete idiot... oh my god, you've been laughing at me all this time-'

'No I-'

'You've driven Ross from his home and Deborah, was it your plan to terrify her too?' Megan's tears were now hot, her mind was whirring, so many questions. Why? Why the hell would you-'

'Everyone else is collateral damage I guess. It was Deborah banging on about this house's history that gave me the idea. She believed it was haunted before it was. I just wanted to make Ross suffer, just a little. I knew behind his bravado he was a coward. He thinks he's up there as some bloody hero because of his movies... far from it in reality. He's pissed me off one too many times, stealing my girlfriends from me. Sarah was the last straw. I may not have known her long but I was taken with her and then Ross swoops in like he always bloody does and now she's cut me off.'

'So you did all this?'

'Okay yes it was getting out of hand, I was putting a stop to it today anyway. It was just meant as my way of revenge without risking my job. I'm asking you nicely not to tell him. We'll say the cleansing worked and it'll all go back to normal.'

'No, I'm not part of your game, I'm not a plaything for your fucking enjoyment. You scared the shit out of me. You've made a fool of me. But what about the pains I was feeling? You didn't do that...'

'Panic attacks. It must be. Just all coincidences. Please just trust me you have nothing to fear-'

'And the Ouija board? Patient Number One?'

'That one wasn't me, but someone else must have moved it, there's a trick to these things isn't there?' Marc continued to rub his cheek, 'I'm sorry okay?'

Megan's tears fell once more, 'No not okay, I can't believe you did this to me, to Ross and to poor Deborah. It's beyond a joke whatever Ross has done to you. You should have just tried talking to him.' Megan didn't wait for a response, she bolted up the stairs to gather her things.

Marc waited at the foot of the stairs until she returned, 'Please consider staying and play this thing out. I can pay you for your time?'

Megan had mentally had enough; the shock was making her feel ill. There was no strength left in her to carry on in this house, under this roof with these people, with Marc the psychopath. That's how she now saw him. Any trust was gone. And she'd almost begun to care for him. She thought of how nice he'd been to her, how caring. How he never seemed that scared, how he put up with her crazy talk of black dogs, how he was happy to walk the grounds with a gun. It all makes sense now. She knew in her heart though that the black dog was a separate issue, one that appeared before she arrived at the house. That one was for her alone to deal with another time.

'I'm leaving, tell Ross I cleansed the house and then left, tell him what the hell you like.' Megan left through the front door and this time Marc didn't try to stop her.

She slipped into her car and started the engine. The petrol gauge showed that there wasn't much hope of reaching Devon.

She thought about going to her sisters but then what? How could she just turn up with nothing- as nothing. She'd think that she only wanted to get back into touch for money or something. Megan was not wishing to be a burden on her family not ever again. There was no way that she was going home to Scott either. She was sick of being treated like an idiot everywhere. There was only one place left that she could think to go to for now. To the one person who loved her for who she was. The gates opened and she sped away from the property.

CHAPTER
THIRTY-THREE

A GENTLE PATTER OF RAIN STARTED TO FALL OVER REDDITCH Crematorium, Megan hardly noticed it. Her petrol gauge had just hit the red as she pulled into the car park. She had nowhere else to be. Nine-eighteen a.m. and the grounds were peaceful. Megan gently jogged over to the memorial gardens where Christina's ashes were scattered. Despite the dampening grass, Megan dropped to her knees in front of Christina's memorial plaque. 'Oh Chrissy, I miss you. We would have been so much better at all of this together. I'm so hopeless without you. Everything is a mess. I don't know what to do...' Megan's voice trailed off as she was overcome with tears.

The rain started to fall a little heavier but Megan remained on the grass feeling numb. She hadn't wanted to entertain dark thoughts but they now dominated her. What if she had successfully killed herself back when she was fifteen? Had the last decade or so meant anything to her? Would she have been sorry she'd missed it if she wasn't around? The future wasn't promising either. It was Scott that had found her unconscious following her overdose. He too had been a troubled teen and shared the same block of sheltered accommodation. That's how they met. She often wondered why he bothered calling for help when he would just end up treating her so cruelly. She was just his plaything, that's all she ever was to everyone it seemed.

Her tears were uncontrollable as she wished out loud that Christina was still here with her. Megan missed her and Christina's family missed her, she had meant something to at least someone. Perhaps Megan's sister would now miss her if she were to die right here and right now? Isn't it worth living so no one else feels this pain? 'I want to live Chrissy, but I don't know what to do,' she sobbed taking a handful of grass and picking through the blades. She became aware of a dark shadow from the corner of her eye so looked in its direction. She scrambled backwards on her bottom as her eyes met with the large black dog.

Paralysed with fear, Megan cried, 'What do you fucking want with me?' Everywhere she turned this hound was there. She stared at it, braced herself, it had come for her. It sat and stared back. It didn't move and its eyes were deep red. She closed her eyes and scrunched up her face, her trembling body ready to be taken. But nothing. She opened her eyes and the hound had gone.

'Are you okay? Can I help you in any way?' Where the hound had sat, a lady had appeared. She was holding up an umbrella and looked concerned.

Megan couldn't stop crying and shook her head.

'Have you lost a loved one?' the woman asked.

'My friend,' Megan said hoarsely.

'I lost my husband a few weeks ago,' the lady added. 'I have a flask of tea and cups and a waterproof covering for the bench. Will you join me?'

Megan didn't know if she had the strength to stand and she was now shaking with the cold and wet. But this lady looked warm and kind and it was enough to get her to her feet. The lady handed Megan her umbrella whilst she got them settled on the bench with a hot drink.

'I'm Sue,' she said, 'there isn't anything more painful than this is there?'

Megan took a sip of tea and savoured the mouthful. 'I'm lost without her,' she said meekly, without the energy to speak up.

'It sure is a cruel world as they say,' Sue smiled sympathetically.

'It's cruel and people are cruel to each other, I've been cruel, I don't know why I thought I may deserve better than this.' Megan poured her heart out, not meaning to.

She was still furious at Marc. How can people who have everything still be so hateful to each other? Why all the childish games? Ross treating women that he sees as beneath him as his playthings, holding Deborah back from pursuing an acting career, holding Marc back from having happiness of his own. And then there was Marc and his actions, terrifying her and his friends as some act of revenge. *What is wrong with people?* Megan thought, but she had been no better in the past, how could she judge?

'I'm a firm believer,' Sue said 'in being kind to yourself. There are enough people out there who will give you a hard time, so whatever you've done, cut yourself some slack. You can build your own happiness; you don't need anyone else. And your friend, I'm sure will watch you every step of the way.'

Megan managed to give Sue a smile. She knew that she was

right; she had already come to the conclusion that she didn't need anybody but she had nothing to be going on with. No money, no roof over her head. She didn't know where to turn next and she was exhausted. Lack of sleep was wearing her down even more. She considered going to her sisters again, but thought better of it. She wasn't going to turn up on her doorstep like this. Perhaps there was a homeless shelter or refuge she could go to. Yes, Megan decided that she would just head to the local council offices and see if they could help her, point her in the right direction. She had to start somewhere.

'Thank you,' Megan said, 'I feel silly for being so-'

'You are not silly for grieving. Don't apologise for yourself. Goodness knows I've learned that these past weeks.'

Megan handed Sue back her cup and thanked her again. A kind face and a few kind words was just what she needed. It at least gave her the lift she needed to take her next step. She said goodbye to her and headed back to the car. Before she reached it, her phone rang and her stomach sank. It was Ross. Had Marc come clean? Was he going to be mad with her for leaving? She didn't think she could cope with the drama, not even for someone like Ross Huston, but she cautiously answered the phone anyway.

'Ah Megan, hi,' Ross sounded relieved that she had picked up. 'Sorry you'd left before I got home. The local press have got wind of our ghost problem and now it's all online, it'll be all over the national press any time now-'

'But I never-' Megan jumped in defensively.

'No, it's okay, I know you didn't. The wind that blew that piece of gossip to the press was my delightful wife, Deborah. She made a few phone calls to her contacts with the press during the night. She figured the only way to get the spirits to move on was to get some proper justice for the victims, it'll get historians investigating properly into this Dr Holdstock bloke.'

'And she didn't check this plan with you first?'

'Wish she bloody had, I've already had my agent on the phone to pass on contact details for paranormal investigators and mediums willing to help. I've got reporters wanting access inside the house for interviews and pictures. I've refused. Not happening. They're getting no more than what they've already got.'

'Perhaps getting a medium in would-'

'No, absolutely no. This is exactly the attention I didn't want. Look, Deborah and me both want you back tonight. Marc has said you have cleansed the house and he believed it's worked. But just to be sure, we'd like you back. Then I can tell the press to fu... go away. Perhaps my wife will let this whole thing go finally.'

Megan already knew it had worked because there were no ghosts in the first place. Ross and Deborah deserved to know the truth but she didn't feel comfortable with dropping Marc in it, despite how cross she was with him. He obviously hadn't come clean yet. It's really up to him to explain himself.

'I can't,' Megan said without needing to think. She was going to uphold the promise to herself not to be taken for a ride anymore.

'Please, look, I haven't paid you yet have I? Text me your bank details and I'll deposit cash for work done so far right away. And I'll double it tonight if you please agree to come back. And why don't you invite your sister over again for moral support? Please?'

Damn it, Megan found herself agreeing again, but only if she received money owing so far. How could she refuse another night for her sister to spend at her favourite actor's house?

She'd do it for her. Besides Megan now knew that there were no ghosts. Nothing to be scared of now, so why the hell not. They ended the conversation with Megan agreeing to just turn up sometime before the evening and not to speak to any press in the meantime.

CHAPTER
THIRTY-FOUR

Megan squealed at the figure displayed on the screen of her mobile banking app. Two thousand pounds, she drummed her feet on the floor of her car and clapped her hands. Like Ross had promised, he had instantly transferred over the money. But two thousand pounds though and he said he'd double it later. Another realisation hit, remembering that Deborah had offered to match whatever Ross paid her and Marc had offered her cash too. She could be more than quids in if they kept their word. This was just the silver lining she had desperately needed. Before driving away from the cemetery, she gave herself time to reflect. Yes, everyone in the Huston household was crazy and on a different planet to her but she decided to push her morals aside. She needed this job to survive so it was okay to be a bit selfish and to just go with it. First things first she needed to go into town and purchase a couple of nice outfits for potential interviews. Settling down in Devon was starting to feel possible again. She also needed petrol, phone credit and food. She squealed again at being able to get everything she needed. Yes, she'd get herself sorted and then phone her sister. She blew a kiss towards the direction of the memorial garden and drove away.

No sooner had Megan pulled up into the car park to the shopping precinct then Sammie phoned her.

'Have you seen the news?' Sammie asked excitedly, 'They have a feature on Ross Huston's house being haunted.'

'Yes I know, I haven't seen it yet but Ross has told me.'

'Oh my god I still can't believe you're friends with Ross Huston, tell me everything.'

'Actually, I was going to call you shortly. Fancy another night at Ross's? He has invited both of us. It will involve some ghost hun-'

'Yes, yes and yes,' Sammie screamed down the phone.

Megan had to hold her mobile away from her ear, 'Perfect. I'm in town right now, can you meet me, I'll buy you lunch. I can fill you in on everything before tonight?'

'Yes I'll be straight up, I'm not working and Liam's at school so I'm all yours.'

They ended the call. Megan smiled widely. She was going to buy her sister lunch. She was having lunch with her sister and she could afford it. Both things had felt impossible just an hour ago.

∼

Within half an hour, Megan had purchased a new outfit, changed in the public toilets and met with Sammie at one of the restaurants in the hub of the town centre. The food arrived and Megan all but dived into her all day breakfast.

'Wow, hungry?' Sammie laughed.

'I think my body is desperate for the fuel. I've been up all night. Probably had an hour's sleep if that.'

'No way that you get to sleep at Ross Huston's house. Fill me in then.' Sammie said tucking into her lasagne.

Megan methodically worked through the events of last night. The Ouija board and how it had spelt out 'Patient One,' the saucepans moving on their own, how she thought she'd seen the figure of a woman in the second sitting room, how Deborah and Ian bolted from the house and later followed by Ross. What she didn't include was the fact that Marc was responsible for it all. But as Megan was talking, she realised that there were too many unanswered questions that Marc couldn't have been responsible for, that Megan still couldn't debunk. She had to be careful not to reveal what Marc had admitted too, not that she didn't trust her sister but now that it was all over the press, she thought it best to just keep quiet for Marc's sake. However, she wondered why she was having conflicting thoughts about why she should care about "Marc's sake."

'Have you told Mum that you've met with me yet?' The thought suddenly occurred to Megan. Well it hadn't suddenly occurred to her- she'd been plucking up the courage to broach the subject since they'd arranged to meet. It was more that she'd suddenly blurted it out.

Sammie looked a little sheepish, 'Not yet. I thought... I just thought, I'd get to know you a little better first so I can make my own mind up about you.'

'Does Mum talk about me then?'

'Not really, not anymore.' Sammie must have clocked Megan's face fall. 'Oh don't look so injured. Remember what you did? I don't mean to sound nasty but you really hurt her. Mum struggled for a long time after dad died. She confided in me after everything, just how hard it was when we were both so young. No money and no support. Depression hit her hard.'

'I don't have much memory of our childhood. I remember our holidays and her laughing and the games we'd play.'

'But that was once things started to improve- when she'd found decent work with a decent salary and the grief was subsiding. Meeting Carl made everything perfect. She was at her happiest. You ripped them apart with your lies. She believed you straight away over him. He was suspended from work immediately and the police were involved and social services. You nearly ruined him.'

Megan felt the anguish of what she'd done wash over her again, 'I was completely stupid, naive, I just didn't understand what I was doing. I was just trying to fit in. It doesn't make any sense to me now what was going through my mind. But I never expected Mum to cut me off completely. Just chuck me out like that. I'm her daughter.' Her eyes started to burn again thinking about Christina's relationship with her Mum.

'Carl said it was you or him. How could he carry on living with us... with you. Mum chose her happiness and security.'

Megan's tears fell. This is not how she wanted this meet up to go but it all had to be said. She had to hear it. Sammie took her hands.

'I'm here now okay? Mum drummed it into me that there was a darkness in you. I've been thinking about you a lot and was toying with the idea of getting in touch. We're older now and time's moved on.'

'I've changed, I'm not who she thinks I am...' Megan wiped her tears away roughly.

'It'll be okay, let's just take this one step at a time. We have stacks of time to get to know each other again. And you need to know that I couldn't be happier to have my sister back.'

Sammie walked around the table and threw her arms around her. 'Let's forget all this now, c'mon what about tonight, what's the plan? We need some fun.'

Megan nodded. She understood what her sister was saying- just take it step by step, day by day. It was more than she could have hoped for just a few days ago. 'So tonight then. Do you want to drive up with me?'

'I'll make my own way up I think,' Sammie looked thoughtful, 'yes because then I'll have my car and I can leave whenever. I best discuss it with Simon first, not that he has a choice,' she laughed.

'He sounds like a good catch,' Megan chuckled.

'Oh he is... and he knows I'm in touch with you. He throws his hands up and says he's staying out of girls stuff. He's well jel that I've met Ross though.'

'You didn't tell him-'

'No, I said you're his housekeeper. I signed a contract and I kept my word. I figured it was a small lie.'

Megan was relieved; at least Simon was one more person that wasn't trying to talk Sammie into staying away from her. She settled the bill, which may have been a small thing to most, but it made her feel amazing. After hugging and kissing Sammie goodbye, Megan set off to do a bit more shopping; get a few more outfits, goodness knows she needed them.

As she wandered around the department stores, Megan felt uneasy once more about the events from last night. She had convinced herself that it was safe now- now that the ghosts were all of Marc's doing but as Sammie was coming, she suddenly felt uneasy again like she didn't want her in danger. But Marc had promised to stop it all now hadn't he? Then she thought about her own experiences that didn't make sense. She needed some extra insight. Like the general public would be now, she was more curious than ever to find out more about Dr Holdstock. Ghosts or no ghosts, Deborah was still convinced that patients were wrongly treated in her house. She wondered if she could pluck up the courage to go and see Nancy at the Library again. She wondered what Nancy would make of today's news reports. Perhaps she shouldn't interfere? But then again if Nancy could still persuade her that Dr Holdstock was a kind doctor, then maybe she would feel more relaxed about tonight. She was very much aware that she was trying to justify visiting the Library to herself; the fact was she just couldn't resist.

CHAPTER
THIRTY-FIVE

A LITTLE AFTER TWO-THIRTY P.M., MEGAN ARRIVED BACK IN Charlington, loitering outside of the Library, hesitating whether to go inside or not. Once more her anxiety was getting the better of her, holding her back from being the decisive, assertive woman she longed to be. Nancy might be cross with her, she might think that she had something to do with the news reports. Then again Nancy might not care, she might think nothing of it. She might not even be working today. But what if she was angry? What if she demands to know everything that goes on inside of the house and Megan is sworn to secrecy. She signed a waiver; she'll be taken to court and fined thousands of pounds that she couldn't afford. She'll be worse off than she is now. Megan rubbed her forehead, why did she have to overthink everything? Overthinking was crippling. It often left her debilitated, unable to actually move forwards or plan anything.

Call it divine intervention but the heavens opened and a sudden downpour forced Megan through the doors. She wiped the rain splatter from her face and submitted to now being inside. It's okay she thought. She looked around and decided to just find an empty booth and use the internet. She'd wait for the rain to cease then she'd leave. Perhaps it would be best not to interfere, she wouldn't seek out Nancy, she wouldn't snoop further. It was out of her hands though.

'Megan, how lovely of you to pop back dear,' Nancy had clocked her and didn't waste time making a beeline for her. 'I suppose you're after more of my research?'

'No, well really I was just wondering how you felt about the-'

'About Blind House being haunted? About that witches public noxious slander against my great-great-grandfather? She may not have named him in her accusations but it doesn't take long for nosey busy bodies and crazy mediums and the like to start digging and assuming. I've already had one reporter from a magazine on the phone. They don't hang about do they?'

Megan thought that calling Deborah a witch was a bit extreme, after all she was only trying to get to the bottom of the so called hauntings; truly believing that people had come to harm. It may sound crazy but she was only trying to help, wasn't she?

'Are you going to show the press your research? You have plenty to show that Dr Holdstock was an honourable practitioner,' Megan pressed on.

'You bet I am. A reporter from that magazine who phoned is on their way over tomorrow for an interview. I'll soon tell them it's all stuff and nonsense. A haunted house indeed, how ridiculous,' Nancy spat. 'You've been in the house, haven't you? Have you seen any ghost stuff?'

'Not exactly, but I can't really talk about what goes on

inside of the house. As an employee, I'm under strict confidentiality.'

Nancy huffed out loud and raised her voice, 'Huh, I'll tell you what I think about Ross Huston's confidentiality rules... Julie, over here.' She called over to a lady who was placing a pile of books back onto the shelves opposite to where they were standing. 'This is my daughter Julie,' Nancy introduced them both.

'Hi,' Julie said shaking Megan's hand.

'Megan here is employed by Ross Huston and has been working up at the house. Had to sign her life away so as not to talk about them to anyone. Go on tell her about your friend Kerry,' Nancy urged her daughter.

Megan's stomach lurched; surely she doesn't mean the Kerry who has gone missing?

Julie looked about her cautiously as if careful who was listening. 'My best friend Kerry worked for one of Ross's charities that he heads. He treated her to a dinner party up at Blind House for all of her hard work. He insisted that she sign some waiver agreeing to complete secrecy. She couldn't even tell her husband where she was going. So she didn't. Now she's missing, no one has seen her since Saturday night.'

'But she told you where she was going then?' Megan asked trying to look like she didn't already know.

'Yes, she couldn't help herself. We've been best friends since forever. She knew I'd never tell,' Julie's expression fell to one of regret. 'I kick myself every day that I didn't speak up much sooner when Kerry first didn't show up. I thought I was being truly loyal to her, but by Monday, when she didn't return home or to work, I was convinced that it was no longer the case that she was spending time at the Huston's. I'm an idiot and I let her down. I wasn't the great friend that I thought I was being.' Her eyes welled up.

'No love, we've been through this, don't you dare cry again,' Nancy scolded her. 'It's all the Huston's fault, if it wasn't for that bloody waiver.'

'I did see the police out on the high street yesterday asking if anyone had seen her,' admitted Megan.

Julie sniffed and nodded, 'I did go to the police eventually and told them her last movements. Her husband knows now too, he was so upset that Kerry didn't tell him.'

'But no one else bloody well knows do they,' Nancy tutted. 'The police are up the Huston's backsides too. More bloody confidentiality malarkey. We're not to tip off the press, said they're handling it all. But the bloody Huston's can go to the press stirring up goodness knows what.' Nancy flapped her arms getting more agitated.

Julie suddenly looked alarmed at Megan, 'You won't tell-'

'No, honestly no. I've signed one of them waivers anyway,' Megan saw the irony and half smiled.

'Anyway,' Julie continued, 'Perhaps the Huston's didn't have anything to do with Kerry's disappearance. There's that other woman I saw missing on the news this morning from Broadway. Missing a week apparently before anyone noticed. Hope they aren't connected. It's so rare to hear of this kind of thing happening here in the Cotswolds.'

'Poor wretch,' Nancy muttered. 'Anyway, I will not be keeping quiet about the facts that I possess about Blind House and its history. I've not signed any bloody waiver. That Deborah wants to thrash it out in the press then so be it. She'll look like the crazy witch that she is by the time I've had my say.'

'I don't think you can compete with the Huston's popularity, Mum,' Julie said, 'If they say ghosts are real, their followers will believe it.'

'Poppycock,' Nancy scoffed.

Megan was keen now to get online and read up on what Deborah had already reported. Before heading to a booth, she reassured both ladies that she really didn't have anything to do with any ghostly goings on in the house. It was a lie but she did want Nancy's trust as she could see both sides. She also wished that Kerry would be found safe and well. However, her stomach knotted around the bad feeling that somehow she knew that Kerry was far from safe and well.

CHAPTER
THIRTY-SIX

Megan typed 'Ross Huston haunted house' into the search engine and there it all was. Popular gossip magazines, local and national press all buzzing over a haunted house scoop. Deborah was quoted as describing the ghostly goings on inside the house and how terrified she'd been. She then continues to discuss her theories of the historical torture of patients. Nancy was right, she doesn't actually name Dr Holdstock but she gives dates that the house was used as a private residence for the insane, so it wouldn't take a lot of digging to investigate the owner of the property. Some historian or medium could take the credit for seeking justice for the victims. Deborah was just pointing them in the right direction.

Megan is also mentioned although not by name. Deborah admits to getting a paranormal investigator in who confirms that the spirits present are that of deceased patients. She even discloses the use of the Ouija board and the fact it spelt out *Patient Number One*. Megan didn't know how to feel. It felt like she was reading about somebody else. She was only grateful that her name was kept out of it. The thought of any attention sent flutters through her stomach. Ross was stated as declining to comment, with some articles claiming it was a publicity stunt ahead of the imminent announcement of his role of Inspector Dark.

Marc must be feeling guilty of some sort, Megan wondered. His tricks had gotten out of hand and caused all of this public speculation. He must realise that he'd gone too far. She wondered what he had to say for himself, what was he thinking? A flush of embarrassment hit her hard as she recalled punching him in the face. How could she look at him again? Did she overreact? No, she told herself. He had terrified her and had taken her for an idiot. He won't be able to have it out with her at the house, not in front of Ross, not if he wants to keep his secret. Still, Megan wasn't sure she could face him.

She sat staring at the screen a while longer, re-reading some of the articles then she thought back to Kerry. All of this stuff written about the ghosts, Megan knew was a hoax but something still niggled at her about Kerry. Call it a premonition or whatever but Megan felt that Kerry was trying to tell her or show her something. It sounded ludicrous to herself especially as she had never really believed in any of that stuff. She didn't believe that spirits could communicate with her in any way shape or form let alone visit her in her dreams. She used to have vivid nightmares as an adolescent she seemed to recall but grew out of them. In fact she rarely remembered her dreams now at all. She wasn't even sure she had any.

But now there was news of another missing woman. Megan typed 'woman missing from Broadway,' into the search engine. A picture of an attractive blonde popped up. *Sarah Lees Missing for just over a week. Sarah left her home last Saturday 25th August for a week- long break in the Cotswolds. She never arrived to check in at the hotel and has not been seen since. Her family became concerned after Sarah didn't return home as expected on Saturday 1ˢᵗ September. She was finally reported as missing on Monday when she didn't turn up for work. We are now appealing to the public to see if anyone knows of her whereabouts.* There was a video link to an appeal by Sarah's mother to help find her. There was also reference to Missing Kerry Beck and that they are not being treated as connected at this stage.

And then it dawned on Megan. The last nightmare she had with the vision of Kerry, there was another woman. She was blonde, but her face wasn't clear now in her head. Could she have been Sarah? Megan pushed the thought away. She was beginning to sound even more crazy. She wasn't having visions about missing women. She had no gift, her mind was simply overwhelmed with everything that had happened, of course she was going to have nightmares. Who wouldn't have nightmares faced with ghosts and witnessing all that she had. Another thing she had Marc to thank for- giving her nightmares. She cursed under her breath.

'Worrying isn't it?' Julie said appearing from behind, looking at Sarah's image. 'Two women vanishing so close together.'

'Yes,' Megan agreed, hitting the shutdown button. She didn't know either women and wasn't in any way connected to them. She felt for them and wished them to be found safe of course, but for now she needed to distance herself from thinking about them before she really did send herself crazy.

'Her last known movements are unknown,' Julie continued, 'she left for a holiday in this area and then nothing. Just like Kerry. Wonder if she ended up in secrecy at the Huston's too. Can't help feeling sceptical about them now.'

'It's probably best not to speculate,' Megan said sympathetically. 'I know it's worrying for you, but the Huston's do seem like honest and kind people. They have really helped me out. The police will find them, I'm sure.'

Julie nodded but her look said that she wasn't convinced.

'I'm heading off now anyway, it was nice to meet you.' Megan smiled but found herself momentarily blocked by Julie's frame.

'If you hear anything, if Ross gets in touch with Kerry, you will tell me, won't you?' Julie said, her voice desperate.

Megan pursed her lips and nodded in agreement. Julie side stepped and allowed Megan to leave. Back outside and the rain had stopped. Megan wondered whether to head straight to Blind House or to kill some more time. And then it hit her. Sarah. Marc's girlfriend's name was Sarah, wasn't it? He said that he hadn't heard from her, didn't know where she was. *Surely not*? That would mean that she really was last seen at Blind House. Marc said he hadn't heard from her since she spent the night there and Ross had made a pass at her, or something. She looked back at the Library doors and shuddered. No, she wouldn't go back and tell Nancy and Julie. She wasn't certain of her facts. She wasn't going to stir up any further trouble.

It had to be a coincidence; it must be a different Sarah. Megan couldn't comprehend two women going missing from the Huston's. It didn't look good. No, they were respectable public figures, famous, popular. Back to Blind House, it is then, Megan took a deep breath. If Sarah was the woman that Marc was seeing, she would find out soon enough. Marc would know about it by now.

CHAPTER
THIRTY-SEVEN

Driving away from the car park, Megan resisted the urge to stop and phone her sister to cancel her plans to come over tonight. The thought of two women going missing after a night at the house didn't sit well, she'd rather Sammie didn't get involved. Why were the family so keen to invite complete strangers round when they claimed to enjoy their privacy? Why were they so insistent for Megan to keep going back when she made it clear that she couldn't do anymore? Something didn't feel right. Deborah had gone public now, they could easily afford to get any top paranormal investigator in.

Overthinking again, Megan breathed in for five and out for three. But doesn't over thinking protect you from ending up in danger? Isn't it best to consider everything? No, overthinking stops you from forming a relationship with your sister; stops you moving forwards with your life. In for five and out for three. Megan approached the gates to Blind House, alarmed to see a number of vehicles blocking the entrance. She waited, signalling to turn in. A man with a camera jogged over to her and she wound down her window.

'You visiting the house? Are you a friend of the family?' The man was brash, poising his camera ready.

'Can you move your cars please?' Megan gulped down the nerves. She considered putting her foot down and just abandoning ship.

Another man jogged over, raising his camera over the first man's shoulder, taking a few snaps of Megan.

'I'm from the national press love, have you seen any ghosts in the house,' he shouted, continuing to take pictures.

They were then quickly joined by a frenzy of reporters.

'Do you believe the house is haunted?'

'How do you know the Huston's?'

'How scared is Ross Huston?'

The questions were flying at her and the cameras were flashing. Megan held her hand up to shield her face. Breathing in for five and out for three was now impossible. She couldn't even drive off as she was surrounded. She wound her window back up and sat her ground feeling she might vomit if they didn't leave her alone soon. How do celebrities put up with this? She longed to be inside of the house with the ghosts than out here with these vultures. In fact she wanted to scream out of the window that there were no ghosts. It's all a bloody hoax. Megan wanted to cry and she almost did but as quickly as the reporters surrounded her, they had backed away, getting into their cars and parted a way for her.

Relief washed over her, she could still put her foot down and get far away from the house, from everything, but she didn't, she crawled the car up to the gates and reached out for the intercom. She knew she had said this to herself last night but this time it really would be one more night and this time would be different. There were no ghosts. She had said it the first day she had knocked on the door to Blind House. *Ghosts aren't real.* Christina would have made contact with her by now. Knowing that without a doubt and Marc's confession together, Megan knew there was nothing to be scared of. As for missing women, the thought of Ross Huston having something to do with it was ridiculous. He was idolised by millions of fans. Besides, Megan reminded herself that Sarah may not even be the same Sarah that Marc was dating.

The gates opened and Megan pulled up on the gravelled driveway. The gates closed, shutting out the reporters and Megan observed them in her rear view mirror quickly swarming back around the gates with their cameras flashing. She looked towards the house again to see Marc jogging over to her. Her stomach knotted remembering that she punched him in the face. He opened her car door and smiled anxiously at her.

'C'mon let's get you inside. That lot hounding you?' Marc said nodding over to the reporters.

The same questions were being shouted through the gates as the reporters desperately tried to get Marc's attention. He kept his back to them and ushered Megan inside of the house.

'Ah Megan, sweetheart, bless you for coming back,' Deborah beamed a huge smile and rushed to hug her.

Megan was a bit taken aback by her welcome and awkwardly returned the hug. No one was ever this pleased to see her. It's not that she disliked hugs but when strangers did it, it set her teeth a bit on edge like nails on a chalkboard scenario.

'Strong coffee, two sugars right?' Deborah released her embrace and guided Megan through to the kitchen to be greeted by Ross and Ian. 'Now my backup is here, she will agree that justice for our spirits is the way to move them on for good. Right, Megan?'

Megan nodded too afraid to disagree with the lady of the house. 'Nothing is for certain but yes it's a positive way forward,' she said, her voice almost trailing off. 'I needed internet access so I popped into the library again,' she began to proceed more cautiously when Deborah raised her eyebrows, 'Nancy collared me and told me that she is meeting with reporters tomorrow to fill them in on her great-great-grandfather... don't worry I didn't tell her anything, she tried to ask... I just said I knew nothing. She thinks I'm your cleaner.'

Deborah laughed, 'I bet she's loving the opportunity to gush about her bloody family history. She won't be laughing when reporters and historians do their digging and find out the truth. People will start coming forwards, you just watch.'

'It'll be fascinating to see what's unearthed,' Megan admitted.

'So tonight, you communicate with the spirits, those poor souls and tell them that they haven't been forgotten and we're doing everything we can so they can finally rest in peace.' Deborah clapped her hands together, looking pleased with herself.

Megan noted that Ian just sat there quietly and Marc stood defensively in the corner still appearing anxious. He definitely lacked his usual charisma. He couldn't look at her and was messing with the sleeves on his hoodie. She wasn't sure if she felt pleased that he appeared to be feeling awkward, that he knows he screwed up.

Ross busied himself tidying away some crockery, opening and closing drawers with more force than needed, obviously ignoring what Deborah was saying, 'Did the press bother you?' He directed his question to Megan.

'Ah take no notice of the press,' Deborah threw her hands up, 'you weren't bothered were you Megan? She's a natural.'

Megan wanted to say that well actually she wanted to vomit in her car, she was that nervous. But once more, she found herself agreeing that she was fine. Deborah handed her a mug of coffee. Megan clocked Ross raising his eyebrows and nodding his head towards Marc.

'Would you mind leaving us for a short while Megan, we have a few private matters to discuss.' Ross smiled, firmly knotting a tea-towel around his fingers.

'Stroll round the garden Megan?' Marc offered gesturing to the patio doors.

Deborah clapped her hands together again, 'Yes go make the most of the last of the afternoon sun, can you believe it was even raining so much earlier?' She shot another of her dazzling smiles.

Megan couldn't help but think that Deborah's over the top cheerfulness was a bit forced. She expected that she and Ross had been fighting over the whole press thing, he was certainly coming across as tense, biting his tongue, not wanting to cause a scene. Making her way over to Marc, she hugged her coffee to her chest. Thank goodness for caffeine backup, the last thing that she wanted right then was to be alone with Marc. She was hoping to avoid it but no chance of that now. She knew his secret, now what was he going to do?

CHAPTER
THIRTY-EIGHT

'I WANT TO THANK YOU FOR NOT SAYING ANYTHING,' MARC SAID, not quite able to meet Megan's eyes.

'It's not my place, although I think you should own up, look how out of hand it's got.' Megan tried not to sound angry. Being in close proximity with him again brought back how hurt she felt. He had terrified her with his pranks. She had started to accept the fact that she had found him attractive and was enjoying his company despite feeling completely out of his league but that had changed. Now her skin prickled to be near him.

'I didn't see this coming. Never expected Deb to go to the press. The thing is I can't admit to anything now, mate or not, Ross will fire me... I am sorry you got caught up in this.'

Megan walked off towards the statue of the Roman lady, stopping to study her fixed expression. Her stone face was still sorrowful and always will be. If the statue could see and hear everything, what stories could she tell? She couldn't though, not without a voice, with her stone lips pressed together unable to speak up.

Megan had a voice though, 'I heard on the news that another woman went missing from nearby. Her name is Sarah something, I wondered if...'

Marc rubbed his neck and paced around her, 'Yes it's my Sar- the Sarah I was seeing,' he swiftly moved in closer to Megan. 'As far as Ross is aware, no one but me, him, Deb and Ian knows that she was here the night she disappeared. A week before Kerry disappeared.'

'But you have to tell...'

'No not yet, that's what they are discussing in there now. No one knows she was here. This on top of Kerry vanishing will cause a shit storm for Ross. This could damage his career. His agent and production team are announcing him as the next Inspector Dark at any time. As far as we know Sarah left here perfectly fine. Ross said that she walked out of the gates and that was that. I've checked CCTV and it does show her leaving.'

Megan's head was swimming. How could they not tell the police? She thought about how guilty Julie was feeling for not speaking up earlier about Kerry's last movements. Time was of the essence. 'But if it's all innocent, the police-'

'C'mon you know that's not how the media work, it'll ruin him. Listen...' Marc's eyes darkened, 'another reason, I'm not risking getting fired yet, is that it doesn't matter how innocent you say it is, Ross let her walk out of here late at night alone. What did he do to make her want to leave? She never came to me, called me, what? She didn't even call a taxi?'

'But the police-'

'We're all sworn to bloody secrecy aren't we. We have to do whatever Ross and Deborah say. He'd have my ass in court and yours. He doesn't know that you know about Sarah. I'm gonna find out why she left the way she did.'

'So what do you actually think Ross did to her to make her want to leave without saying anything? To just sneak out?' Megan pushed.

'I think that he came on to her and she refused his advances, but how heavy he came on to her I don't know. It must've been strong enough for her to bolt like that.'

'Have you considered that perhaps she didn't refuse him, so that's why she left because she couldn't face you?' Megan hoped that was more the case and not that Ross forced himself onto her.

'Perhaps,' Marc replied quietly, 'God he can piss me off sometimes,' he erupted kicking away a stone.

'Deborah told me that they have an open relationship.'

'He could have anyone. Anyone. But he has to get his kicks out of trying to get one over on me and take the women I care about. Can you see why I wanted to get at him? You think I'm an arse? What kind of a mate does that?'

Megan gave up trying to argue. She did still think he was an arse but she was getting a clearer picture now of how hurt he was feeling. She'd never understand why, as mates, they couldn't just talk about this rather than this one-upmanship thing they had going on between them. Defeated, she knew that now she had two of Marc's secrets to keep. She drained the last bit of cooled coffee and looked again to the statue. *I guess now I don't have that voice.* She walked off further up the path, the sky now darkening. Marc followed and they walked in silence. On the second lap, they stopped at the top of garden so Megan could admire the archway some more.

'Your sister's coming tonight isn't she?' Marc broke the silence.

Megan's stomach flipped; she had almost forgotten. She had figured that surely Ross wouldn't want Sammie round tonight now. She wasn't even sure why he was still happy for her to be here. *It doesn't make any sense. It just wouldn't normally happen would it?*

'I ought to check with Ross if it's still okay for her to come. It must be bad timing for him.' Megan had lost Marc's attention. He was looking over to the far left of the lawn which backed onto the woods. He raised his hand to hush her for a moment.

'There's someone standing over there in the trees, can you see?' Marc picked up the pace towards where he was pointing.

Megan squinted and followed him and sure enough she spotted the head of a figure peeking out from the trees. 'Yes, there's someone there,' she said.

Marc broke out into a jog and shouted, 'Hey,' to whoever it was.

By the time they had reached the spot, there was no one to be seen. The figure had vanished. They quickly scouted amongst the trees but nothing.

'Goddamn reporters. Bet they got in.' Marc kicked at the earth. He'd have to check all the fencing and up the security but it was getting too dark now.

'It looked like an old woman to me, from the distance,' Megan said.

'Reporters come in all blasted shapes and sizes,' Marc seethed. He admitted that they never stop trying his patience.

Megan had a flashback to Ross saying that he saw an old lady watching the house from the woods last night. *Stop it.* Megan scolded herself. It won't help now to start getting creeped out. It was just a reporter like Marc said. It made perfect sense. There were no ghosts and everything felt on edge enough with everything going on. They made their way back inside. Megan placed her mug by the sink and looked around the empty kitchen. She shook her head remembering how she felt seeing the saucepans moving and when all the cupboard doors and drawers were open and the glasses smashed. *Unbelievable,* she thought once more. But then she thought about the feeling of being strangled and rushing to the sink because she had sworn her arm was gushing blood. That had been real. That hadn't been one of Marc's jokes.

Marc suggested that she could go to her room for some space and to freshen up before the night if she wanted. She agreed. She couldn't think of anything she wanted more right now than to just be on her own for a bit, but first she wanted to find Ross and check that it was still alright for Sammie to come over. If not then she could catch her sister before she left home and not have a wasted journey. Deep down Megan hoped that Ross would now say it wasn't convenient for her to come because once more Megan didn't feel the slightest bit comfortable. Her new relationship with Sammie was in its fragile early stages and she didn't want to risk breaking that. Things were too on edge here, too unsettled and more to the point she was starting to wonder what Ross Huston was actually capable of.

CHAPTER
THIRTY-NINE

Raised voices came from within the main lounge, so Marc and Megan held back from entering the room.

'For the last time you're making a mistake,' they heard Deborah shriek.

'My decision is final,' Ross yelled back before bursting through the door.

Megan and Marc jumped back allowing Ross to storm past them to the stairs. Deborah plastered on her big grin once more and encouraged Megan in to join her.

'You'd think he'd be in a better mood,' laughed Deborah. 'He's due a video call with his agent. His announcement as Inspector Dark is imminent. They are jumping on this haunted house publicity, striking at the opportunity. He should be more grateful, he really should.' Her mouth was now set to a thin line.

'Thinking of which,' Megan braved, 'It's not too late for me to cancel Sammie coming over. You have enough going-'

'Absolutely not, she is more than welcome still. I insist that she does. It's the least we can do for you after all you are helping us with. Ross will be leaving for Ireland any day now then, looks like I'm staying here so I want nothing more than to feel safe in my own home. Oh and Ian's just popped home, I can call him see if he'll drive her.'

Megan felt a sudden twinge of guilt. She wasn't helping. She knew now that there was nothing to help with. She felt like she was taking their money for nothing. Scamming them even. *I am scamming them, I'm nothing but a con artist.* This didn't sit well with her, it's far from something that she felt proud of doing. When she first arrived here, she wasn't sure of what she was doing but she was at least going to use the little ghost hunting skills she had to make an effort. But now this was different. The game had changed. She knew for definite there were no ghosts and that she was merely covering up for a twisted, childish prank. Deborah would be furious with her if she knew the truth. She glanced at Marc who had that nervous look again. Looking at her as if he could hear her every thought, pleading with her not to say anything.

'If you're sure, then thank you.' Megan forced a smile, 'She's happy to drive herself though.'

'Marc, can we talk?' Deborah shot him a firm look.

'I'll take my stuff up and freshen up,' Megan said, relieved to be leaving them to it. They clearly have much to sort out between them. Megan just hoped they decide to go to the police about Sarah. By the sounds of it, that was not an option that Ross was willing to go for. All Megan could do was stay out of it. It wasn't her place.

She scooted along the hallway, grabbed her bags and hurried up the staircase, stopping as Ross popped his head around his bedroom door.

'Ah, I thought you were Deb coming up,' he said. His eyes were pink and puffy. *Had he been crying?*

'Are you okay?' she asked gently.

'It's just all of this media attention. You'd think I'd be used to it. Truth is it's a pain in the ass,' he half smirked.

'I can only imagine.'

'You're a breath of fresh air, you know that Megan?'

'I am?' She didn't feel like a breath of anything. She looked at him confused as to what he meant.

'Come, sit with me for a few minutes,' he widened the door to allow her through.

She didn't actually want to; she was craving her own space but she didn't want to be rude. He pulled a desk chair out for her and he perched on the edge of the bed opposite.

'You know why I call this place home over my house in Beverly Hills? Because it's less in your face. Less surrounded by pretentious, fake arseholes. It's natural here, I can be myself.'

Megan thought about the house she was sitting in right now, by her standards it was very much in her face, positioned in an affluent area and not to mention it was enormous. How nice to be in a position whereby this type of house is less in your face than a more extravagant property you own. What would he make of the pokey flat that she'd just left behind?

'What I'm trying to say,' he continued, 'is that this is my normality here. I just get that bit more freedom. Hard to explain. Am I making sense? All this going on... it's...'

'Unsettling?' Megan offered.

He smiled back at her, 'Yes unsettling.'

To be fair, Megan thought, anyone would feel unsettled with all of this going on, famous or not, wealthy or not. He was still human. It was an eye opener to see *the* Ross Huston sat before her now, looking vulnerable. He looked drained. The bulk of his shoulders slumped forwards. She wondered how many people actually saw this side of him. Kerry may have done. And what side of him did Sarah see? She quickly stood.

'I really need to freshen up for this evening.'

Ross stood and closed in on her, placing his hands on her shoulders, 'Thanks again for all you're doing. Do you really think the ghosts have moved on?'

Megan felt her whole body stiffen at his close proximity; she nodded giving fleeting eye contact, 'I'm as sure as I can be.' She willed him to step away from her. It took a few beats too long, but he looked her in the eyes, nodded and released her.

'I reckon dinner will be around eightish, just shout if you need anything.'

She thanked him and made a beeline for her room. She couldn't imagine what all this pressure must be like for him and to be in the public eye too. You really did have to watch your every move. The bed welcomed her back as she flung herself onto it, nestling into its cushioned embrace. She buried her head into the pillow and quietly screamed into it. For a split second back then, Megan was all but certain that Ross was going to kiss her. Christina would be having a field day if she was up there watching her. She did feel some sympathy for Ross but she refused to be swept up into any more games- Marc's or his. It was just a matter of hours now before she could prove the so-called ghosts were gone and she could move on. Ross wanted normality and she wanted hers. It was the only thing she could really relate to him over.

So there are no ghosts, no need to be scared of this room anymore. She sat up and looked around. The tapestry was just a tapestry, it was nothing sinister. The nightmares were just that- nightmares. The shower was just a faulty shower. The door was just a sticky door- no demon had held it shut. Everything was just a normal thing and everything was peaceful. She was in the exquisite home of a famous movie star and that's all there was to it. Time to relax and enjoy the moment. She'd tell herself that until she believed it. And she had new clothes. She squealed again at the thought, jumped off the bed and unpacked some stuff, hanging it in the closet. It was time to take a bit more care of herself and her things. She sent texts to her sister arranging her arrival then she set her alarm to get an hour's sleep. She didn't know how she was going to function for the rest of the night if she didn't at least try to get a power nap in. Things are going to be okay, she told herself to relax and drifted quickly off to sleep.

CHAPTER 40
BLIND HOUSE 1878

'Emotions can hinder us,' the Doctor said, setting out a range of sharp implements on the table. 'All of this crying and snivelling coming from the both of you... how is it productive to your sanity? Patient Number One, come here, take a seat.'

Number One looked to Number Two whose eyes were wide with panic. She knew better than to disobey. Sitting in the chair was going to happen whether she dragged herself there or was taken there in pieces. So she left her trembling friend and shuffled over to the table and chair then hauled herself up.

'Good,' The Doctor praised Number One and made a note in the book. 'I've seen a change in you these past days Number One... hence it's time for another assessment. See if we can't get you out of here, back to your loved ones.' The Doctor flicked back through past notes muttering 'yes, yes,' a few times. 'Your mind is becoming more robust, more capable. Let's see if that is the case. Are you ready to be released back into society? Can you know your place and where you fit in amongst the pecking order without issue or rearing your head?'

Number One bit her tongue, *don't speak, know your place.* She nodded gently with her eyes down, she wouldn't look up and she couldn't dare to look at Number Two anymore. The Doctor ran a finger across the selection of scalpels that had been placed in a row in size order. But the Doctor decided against any of them and swiped up the knife instead.

'Let's see if we can master those emotions which hold you back so terribly. No more outbursts, no more shrieking, no more being ill-tempered. Are you following Number One?'

Number One nodded, fighting every nerve not to shake. If the Doctor meant it then she could be home, back to her family, back to when time mattered. She was cracking, slowly cracking and close to breaking. With all her strength she shut out her surroundings and pictured a calm garden, her garden and the smell of home baking from the kitchen and the beautiful face of her mother calling her to tell her dinner was ready and her dog nuzzling her with his soft fur and kind eyes. She wasn't here with this monster pointing a knife at her.

'Remember, one sound and you will remain here indefinitely.' The Doctor slowly circled the knife around Number One's left eye, barely touching the clammy skin. The knife then moved to her throat, down to her breastbone where the tip rested for a minute, pressing more firmly through her night dress into the flesh and then it withdrew leaving only a scratch.

The Doctor made a quick note in the book then waved the knife once more in front of Number One's face, smiling a wicked smile- the kind of smirk which turned Number One's blood cold. She couldn't stop the gooseflesh but she steadied her shaking, *I'm in my garden, I will not speak, I know my place.*

The Doctor stood tall, stepping back, turned and strode to Patient Number Two. The Doctor stroked the Patient's curly hair then clutching a handful firmly, the Doctor circled round the back of her, pulled her head back by her hair exposing the fullness of her throat. Without hesitation and with one swift motion, the knife sliced across her flesh, deep and final. The blood spilled down her white cotton night dress and the doctor looked into the whites of her startled eyes. Patient Number One screamed. She buckled to the floor and howled.

'You lose,' the Doctor laughed.

CHAPTER
FORTY-ONE

THE SHOWER MAY HAVE BEEN FAULTY BEFORE, BUT IT WAS WORKING fine now. It rained down over Megan as she massaged shampoo through her hair. She felt invigorated after her power nap. It was just what she needed. She wondered if Deborah was going to drag her away for another makeover. Perhaps not tonight, she had too much else on her mind. At least Megan had something half decent of her own to wear now. She would do her best to make an effort on her own as she had already decided it was time to look after herself better.

She turned off the soothing spray and wrapped a huge fluffy towel around her. She did feel truly spoilt. She'd never owned such a towel. Only knew faded threadbare towels which were only just big enough to cover the essentials. Luxury towels were not an essential item when you could only afford tinned food. She allowed herself to feel angry again for Scott dragging them both down into so much debt, using her, spending all of her money on drugs and goodness knows what else. Anything but the bills. Her hard earned cash from the job she worked hard at despite it making her miserable. She was struggling to be that responsible adult, that better person. She didn't want to be that teenager that everyone hated and turned their backs on. It was a stupid mistake. But despite her best efforts, Scott kept dragging her back down.

No, she told herself off for going over old ground. She'd done something about it now and was moving on. She pulled on a smart pair of fitted black jeans and a red gypsy style top which revealed her shoulders. Not over the top but it felt almost pretty and was as designer as she was used to getting. She bent over to touch her toes, allowing the rush of blood to her head to clear her thoughts.

'I'm here.'

Megan straightened up with a start, as the robotic voice sounded out.

'I'm here.'

What the hell? It took Megan a few moments too long to realise what the sound was. Her heart thudded before relaxing to its usual rhythm. She opened up her bag and pulled out her spirit voice box- the gadget meant to sound out the voices of the dead.

'Blasted thing,' she cursed. Of all her ghost hunting equipment, she thought this one was the biggest nonsense. If spirits were able to communicate words through white noise which the spirit box picks up then surely they would have much more to say other than odd random words. Not once on a ghost hunt has one of these boxes communicated anything other than incoherent nonsense. All it must do is pick up the odd words from radio stations or perhaps it records and plays back the odd word. Being technically minded was certainly not her strong point but she was sure that whatever words were coming out from that gadget was not a ghost.

It was the same with the torch she used during a vigil. She'd place a torch down and invite a spirit to turn it on. Megan had witnessed the torch turning on a few times on different ghost hunts but *really?* She thought. If a ghost could turn a torch on why doesn't it turn the whole room lights on or touch something more obvious? Which led her back to considering poltergeist activity- chair stacking, opening cupboard doors, throwing things across the room. Why would spirits bother with this? Unless they were angry? Why are all ghosts angry? Surely there are kind ones too? If a ghost could move things why don't they open a door for you or put the kettle on and make you a cuppa or help with the housework? Why is it always stacking and throwing things? Marc had staged poltergeist activity in the kitchen and Megan knew it didn't feel right, but she had believed it was real. But it was a hoax, of course it was. *See, it just wouldn't happen.*

The Ouija board offered something a bit more plausible, with spirits guiding the glass to spell out names and sentences which made sense- revealing messages that were of some importance and had meaning. However you couldn't rule out human interference. Who, stood around the table, was actually pushing the glass? It can be done so subtly; it was usually impossible to tell. No, nothing was an exact science and these gadgets proved nothing. Megan was satisfied that she was thinking logically again. However she did have complete respect for those that believed in ghosts, after all her best friend had. Christina had her own experiences and Megan respected that. She would never think her a liar or a crazy person. One night during a ghost hunt Christina had sworn that something had been holding her hand when there was no one else around. There was something about that which had given Megan the creeps the most. But she was satisfied with her own beliefs, it's hard to believe in something that you haven't witnessed for yourself. No, there are no ghosts- not here and not at all.

Never-the-less, Megan would get all of her gadgets out tonight safe in the knowledge it would all be okay. Tonight she would simply be confirming that the spirits had vanished or moved on (not that they were ever there). It would also be entertainment for her sister. Yes, it would all be great, they would have a laugh. It'd be more relaxed and tomorrow she could move on, start her new beginning, her new life. Megan checked herself out in the full length mirror and she liked what she saw. She felt fresh and new. Her hair was still damp and wondered if she could go and ask Deborah if she could borrow her hair dryer and perhaps some lip gloss too? No more feeling awkward, Deborah was more than generous and she was never made to feel uncomfortable. Not wanting to be any trouble was just her anxiety talking, yes, she would go and find Deborah now and ask her.

Before leaving her room, she examined the tapestry. *There, you are not the image of the hound that's stalking me*, Megan traced her finger lightly around the snarling black dog. She wondered how much this tapestry was worth or if it was even an original? It looked old but the colours weren't faded enough to be really old. She leaned into the battle scene and delicately pressed her cheek against the coarse material. In a weird way, her thinking was that if she gave it a hug, she would be less afraid of it, she would bond with it. Satisfied that she had made peace with the tapestry, she stood back from it. Anything untoward she saw in the images was once more just her overactive and anxious imagination talking. No, there are no ghosts, now she just needed to convince herself that there was no hound of death stalking her either. Perhaps she needed some psychiatric help with that or some sort of counselling? She was seeing things and it wasn't normal. She had decided to look after herself better and she intended on sticking to that promise.

CHAPTER
FORTY-TWO

Downstairs was quiet. Megan pushed through into the living room to find it empty. She peered into the second sitting room and felt a sudden chill run up her spine. The last time that she spent time in this room had completely unnerved her. The tall lampshade stood where it had been before, where it always stood because it doesn't move. It didn't move then either. It wasn't some ghostly figure like she had convinced herself she'd seen. Megan closed the door and rubbed her arms. She didn't like that room. She quickened her steps to the kitchen but that was empty too. Where were they all?

Back in the living room, Megan perched on the pristine white sofa. This sofa unnerved her too but for different reasons. Never had she been more terrified of creasing a sofa ever, so she stood back up and took the opportunity to get a closer look at the pictures on the wall and the awards in the glass display unit. A BAFTA: Megan caught her breath as she suddenly recognised the BAFTA award gleaming at her from its central position in the cabinet. She had seen the awards given out on television and the emotional speeches from some of the recipients. It felt unreal to see one up close.

There were a number of photos with Ross and his co-stars and other famous friends. Megan hadn't been much of a fan before but she found herself eager to catch up on Ross's films. It'd be surreal to watch them now she had met him and spent time in his house. Her stomach flipped, *I'm in Ross Huston's house.* She was still going through waves of feeling indifferent to working for a famous actor, to not believing she actually was. The next unit along housed a few various bottles of brandy and crystal glassware. Megan hadn't been much of a drinker in recent years but the sudden urge just to have a mouthful was overwhelming.

Drinking cheap neat vodka was a phase she went through in her early twenties to try and drown out reality. The reality was though that it just fuelled the fights between her and Scott. It took a while but she realised if she didn't rise to his temper then things never turned out as ugly. Did that make her weak, she wasn't sure, but she had more self-control when sober. Her submerged hurt, sadness, anger would spill out after a few vodkas and she hated the lack of control. The vicious cycle had to break if she was going to improve her life. Sadly Scott never shared the same aspirations. It was down to him and only him which drove her away.

She was now here in this house; fate truly was unpredictable. Megan decided to pour herself a small drop of the brandy and inhaled the aroma deeply. She wondered if she could actually get used to this lifestyle after all and to drink for the enjoyment and the flavour of it rather than for stupid self-harm purposes. She clasped the chunky crystal glass and took a closer look at the pictures over the fireplace. Wedding photos. Deborah was breath taking in her figure-hugging, vintage style wedding dress. The detail in the gown was glorious, all framed in an exquisite pure silver frame. The guest list would have been incredible, she thought. Pushing thirty and feeling completely hopeless, Megan had come to the conclusion she'd not so much as get a whiff of a wedding dress. Perhaps she didn't want to, not anymore.

She strolled over to the large window. The curtains were closed so she gently moved one aside to peer out onto the driveway. There they were. Deborah was at the gate talking with the reporters. Marc was close by her side. The image that Megan had of Marc being a handsome strong bodyguard had all but vanished now. He was close to being that fantasy, the kind of man a woman might go for. But no. His behaviour had let him down and Megan was still mad at him, *unbelievable*, she sighed to herself once more. She carried on watching them. Deborah looked like she was laughing, throwing her head back, gesturing with her arms- animated. She did have a presence about her. The reporters didn't take their eyes off her. Not for a moment. Megan took a swig of the brandy and instantly coughed from its strength.

'Not used to brandy?'

Megan jumped; she hadn't heard Ross approach her from behind. She blushed but she blamed it on the heat from the liquid.

'No not at all, that obvious,' Megan laughed and cleared her throat. 'I'm sorry, I hope it was okay? I couldn't resist trying a little-'

'You're more than welcome,' Ross grinned, taking the glass from her. He strode to the drinks cabinet and poured her another measure before helping himself to one. 'Here,' he handed back her glass.

Despite initially craving the taste of the brandy, Megan

didn't feel that drinking any more was a good idea but she was too polite to say so and accepted the drink.

'Deborah is giving the reporters some of her time. It's a ploy to get rid of them... give them something, they'll leave faster,' Ross smirked. 'You must find all of this overwhelming. Please drink... you won't taste a finer Cognac.'

Megan put the glass to her lips and let the smooth warmth from the liquid slide down her throat. She instantly felt herself flush again. It was strong but that one mouthful soothed her nerves.

'It's divine,' Megan said, not knowing the best words to use to describe fine alcohol.

'Two and a half thousand pounds worth of divine,' Ross winked.

Megan didn't hide her shock. She gasped, 'It never is? You shouldn't waste this on me,' she suddenly felt like she was handling something delicate and she was just a clumsy child.

'It's no waste,' Ross looked at her sincerely. 'We are celebrating, and you're here and part of it now. In a couple of hours I'll be doing a live video call on tonight's Lewis Lee Show to announce myself as the new Inspector Dark. It's all been rushed but sometimes that's how it goes.'

'That's incredible,' Megan raised her glass as if to say cheers, 'I hope I'm not going to get in your way though, I don't wish to-'

'Megan, why do you always feel like you're in the way?'

She felt her cheeks burning, all she could manage was to take another drink, anything to distract from sounding pitiful anymore.

Ross gently brushed past her to look out of the window. 'We need these reporters gone. I don't want them here at the time I go live. Lewis Lee has exclusivity and those blasted reporters can wait their turn.'

'My sister will have to fight her way through them, she'll be on her way,' Megan said peering over Ross's shoulder to share the view.

'Ah yes. We are going to have a memorable night,' Ross smiled warmly at her.

His close proximity sent a shiver shooting up Megan's spine. His crystal blue eyes were intense this close up. She stepped away; he was once again getting too close for comfort.

'Looks like they're coming back inside,' Ross relaxed the curtain. 'Now let's hope the paparazzi piss off. I could still strangle Deborah for all of this.'

Megan hoped that he was joking because his tone suggested otherwise. She took another mouthful of the two and a half thousand pound liquid and willed any tension to vanish before Sammie arrived.

CHAPTER
FORTY-THREE

'Timed that well, it's starting to rain,' Deborah said breezing back into the house. Marc shut the front door behind them and leant back against it looking relieved that bit was over with. 'Did you see they were starting to leave? Happy now my Love,' Deborah shook off her jacket and affectionately rubbed Ross's shoulder.

'Yes because guess what?' Ross's eyes twinkled.

Deborah paused for a moment but it sank in quickly, 'You are being announced tonight? You're going live?'

'You got it. At nine on the Lewis Lee show, all very last min obviously but my agent has pulled it off.'

Deborah shrieked and threw her arms around her husband, 'Your fans are going to go nuts, I can't wait for the public's reactions.'

'You must be done in after all that press stuff,' Ross said releasing his wife. 'Why don't we order in some food?'

'No, you know I couldn't stomach another person arriving at the house, not even a delivery driver. No, I'm going to cook us up a feast. Oh and Marc, we need champagne we must have champagne. The finest. What have we got in the cellar?'

Cellar? Megan didn't know there was a cellar. Why hadn't they mentioned it before? Megan should have thought before that a house this size and old was likely to have a cellar. Nothing more creepy than the thought of doing a vigil in a dark cellar. Megan shuddered, thinking perhaps she didn't actually want to do that and was relieved that over the last couple of nights, she hadn't had to go down there in search of ghosts. It would have just added to the nightmares she'd already faced. Marc would have had a field day terrorising her in a dark cellar. No, she pushed the rising anger down again. What's done is done and at least Marc had come clean now. She was curious to see the cellar now she knew there was one though.

'Can I come with you?' Megan piped up after Marc confirmed that he was sure that there were a good few decent bottles of champagne down there.

'Sure but it's not very exciting,' he said looking bemused.

'Oh and Deborah,' Megan said coyly, 'It might not be too late to cancel Sammie coming over if you don't want anyone else-'

'Don't even say it,' Ross laughed. 'For the last time we want her here, it's no trouble.'

'I'll get supper prepped,' Deborah winked at Megan and she flounced to the kitchen.

'I best have a shave,' Ross said rubbing his chin and made his way up the stairs.

'Cellar then?' Marc looked sheepishly at Megan.

'Lead the way.'

Marc led Megan through the kitchen, into the pantry. Megan looked puzzled. She had been inside the pantry before and hadn't noticed a doorway to any cellar. The door turned out to be cleverly disguised as part of the wall. Wire racks were fitted to the door, holding an assortment of vegetables and the handle was a decorative brass hook, like others fixed around the pantry. In fact, now that she could see that it was a door, she couldn't unsee it. Marc pulled the brass hook, swinging the door open.

'Secret door. I like it. Clever,' Megan said impressed.

'Enjoy the surprise while it lasts,' Marc snorted, 'Once you know it's a door, you can see it's a door and then the fun has gone.'

Megan smiled; she had already figured that one. The doorway led to a narrow stone staircase which curved down to a compact cellar. The dimly lit room was framed with wine racks, not all of them full. There was not much else apart from a few cobwebs.

'So why didn't you show me the cellar before,' Megan asked Marc as he slid a champagne bottle from its holder.

'Unless you're blind, you'll see it's not worth mentioning,' Marc looked around the confined space and grinned sarcastically.

Megan rubbed her arms. He was right, it probably wasn't worth including in the tour of the house. It really was a small space for such a large house and it was far from welcoming.

'Why is it so small?' Megan blurted out at the thought.

'Bit personal,' Marc grinned wickedly, 'ah, you mean the room.'

Megan dismissed his humour, 'It's such a big house.' She ran her hand across the stone wall and pushed firmly. The stone felt cold to touch. She leant into the wall, turning her ear close to the stone.

'There are no more secret doors; if that's what you're thinking,' Marc said.

'I thought I could hear something.'

Megan remained listening at the wall, her breath touching the coolness of the stone and the palm of her hand pressed against it. What Megan was not aware of was what was on the other side of the wall. A transparent hand matched Megan's, pressing against the wall from the other side. The rest of the figure leaned into the wall listening. After just a few moments, the ghostly figure in a long stained white gown and matted dark curly hair, sank down to the floor. There she stayed perfectly still, except for the trickle of tears from her eyes.

Megan shot back from the wall as she felt a shock of biting cold sting her hand.

'There are no ghosts; you know that now, right?' Marc said awkwardly. 'In fact,' he grinned, 'if anyone should be jumpy in a dark confined space, it's me. I am after all in here with someone who has a pretty mean right hook,' he mocked, rubbing his cheek.

Megan wanted to find a witty comeback but the words got lodged in her throat. She had nothing and she wasn't about to say sorry for hitting him, in fact she'd quite happily do it again.

Marc pulled out another bottle of champagne, 'She's going to want two bottles, c'mon let's go back up.' As he turned, Marc managed to walk into the corner of the adjacent wine rack, catching his side as the whole thing rattled.

Megan stifled a giggle as he yelped clutching the two bottles. He really was clumsy, she thought. Goosebumps prickled her arms and she shuddered again, relieved to be heading back up the stairs. No, she definitely didn't want to do a vigil in here. Christina would have been all over the whole dark cellar thing, Megan was sure of that but she confirmed to herself that she didn't need to. Like Marc said there are no ghosts. One more night to prove to the Huston's that the so-called spirits had moved on then she could move on. She could move on and leave them to deal with missing women and their bizarre relationship dramas. Megan would just keep reminding herself of this, it eased her anxieties and in doing so helped her move forwards. *One more night, their problems are their own and I can start my new life.*

'How long were we down there for?' Marc laughed as they both entered back into the kitchen and surveyed the scene before them.

Ross was sat at the table already clean-shaven and he was joined by Deborah, Ian and Sammie. They were sat around laughing, with wine in hand and something bubbling away on the stove. Sammie leapt from her chair and rushed to Megan for a hug. It was like they had both walked into a parallel universe.

'We were only in the cellar ten minutes at the most,' Megan laughed, 'we didn't hear you arrive.'

'Ah, it's well sound-proofed down there,' Ross confirmed.

Marc placed the bottles of champagne down and lifted his shirt up at his hip to inspect the scraped skin inflicted by the wine rack. Megan clocked Sammie raising her eyebrows as she couldn't take her gaze off Marc's small, exposed area of flesh. If only Sammie knew what an arse Marc could be, Megan thought. Perhaps she would confide in her when all this was over and she'd ceased working for them. Tell Sammie that beneath their good looks and success, they were all crazy people. Sammie looked incredible again, Megan pictured her at home in front of her mirror applying her makeup and trying on numerous dresses to look perfect. She felt another glow of happiness that she could do this for her estranged sister.

'I'll put these on ice,' Ian said picking up the champagne.

BLIND HOUSE

'Are you staying for celebratory drinks tonight?' Marc asked Ian.

Deborah jumped off her chair clasping her hands together, 'Yes he is,' she beamed. 'We wanted him on standby to drive Sammie home so she could have a drink, but she's agreed to stay the night so Ian gets the night off.'

Megan looked at Sammie nodding excitedly and she went in for another hug. She couldn't believe that she had the company of her sister for the whole night and Sammie looked like she'd struck gold, her eyes sparkled along with the spray of golden sequins across the neckline of her dress.

'You'll be wanting a top up then,' Marc said opening a bottle of red.

Megan tried to refuse but Marc wouldn't take no for an answer and filled her glass. Deborah said she'd have one shortly and set about preparing the dessert for later. Ross was set to go live in twenty minutes in the sitting room and she wanted to be ready to sit and watch him on the TV from the second lounge.

'Do you get nervous?' Megan asked Ross.

'Nah, not really, not anymore...' Ross didn't expand any further, his phone vibrated so he picked it up. He covered the mouthpiece and whispered, 'It's my agent, gotta set up, see you in a bit.'

Deborah blew Ross a kiss as he left for the sitting room. 'Why don't you all take your drinks to the lounge and get comfy. I'll join you in a sec,' she said as she attacked the bowl of cream with a hand whisk.

'Lead the way sis,' Sammie grinned, excitedly linking Megan's arm.

Both Ian and Marc grabbed a bottle of wine each and they headed to the lounge. Megan pushed through the door to the lounge first and promptly dropped her glass on floor. She froze. But in the blink of an eye it had gone. The black dog. It was sat there at the far end of the room facing her. It was there then it was gone. Red wine flooded around the shattered glass.

'Shit, I'm sorry, I-' Megan stumbled over her words.

'It's okay,' Marc said darting back to the kitchen for something to clean it up.

'You okay?' Sammie asked her sister.

'Yes just stupid butter fingers, typical of me.' Megan steadied her breathing.

Ian guided her to sit down and reassured her that the glass wasn't expensive and Marc would have it sorted in no time. Megan sat down reluctantly. She didn't want to sit down; she wanted to run and keep running. That dog. She'd almost forgotten about that dog. It was still coming for her. There may be no ghosts but that death hound was waiting for her. She started to shake. Marc hurried back in immediately dropping to the floor to soak up the spillage and sweep up the glass.

'See all good,' he laughed, 'these wipes are amazing, I've spilt red wine many a time.'

Megan thanked him. At least it wasn't in the gleaming white sitting room, she had feared doing that the whole time she'd been in the house. Deborah entered the room and handed Megan a fresh drink. Ian turned the TV on and they all sat around excitedly chatting in expectation of the Lewis Lee Show. There was no running for Megan. The night was just beginning and she could only hope that the black dog did not return.

CHAPTER 44
BLIND HOUSE 1878

NUMBER ONE INSTINCTIVELY DRAGGED HERSELF OVER TO NUMBER Two's body, knowing nothing could be done. But she placed her hand over the gaping wound in her throat anyway to try and stem the bleeding. She was dead.

'How moving,' the Doctor sneered, 'but you've now failed your assessment. You will remain here indefinitely.'

'She had a son,' Number One stuttered through her sobs.

'A son who will grow up more capable now. A son who will thrive with a little tragedy in his life. Look at you, you disgusting thing, covered in someone else's blood. You need a bath.'

'Fuck you,' Number One took the Doctor off guard as she swiped away the Doctor's legs.

The Doctor crashed to the ground and Number One didn't waste time straddling the body and squeezing her hands around the Doctor's throat. The Doctor wrestled back, clawing at the infected sores on Number One's wrists. She tried to retain her grip despite the sheer pain but she could no longer hold her position sat over the Doctor. Her legs screamed at her. The Doctor felt her weakness and with one thrash, overthrew her.

The Doctor grabbed the bucket of drinking water by the trough and doused Number One with it, 'I said you need a fucking bath.'

Number One lost her fight and curled up as the icy water stung her sore flesh. She reached out and held Number Two's hand. She hadn't expected this. She expected Number Two to go on and get away from here, to be found, to be with her son and husband again. The Doctor cut her down like she was nothing. She thought back to a week ago, the evening she had met the Doctor, before she was captured. She couldn't have imagined anyone to be capable of this, especially not the Doctor. You put your trust in certain people don't you and then they surprise you, in the most cruel and sadistic way. Does the Doctor's family know? *Does he know?*

'Right, you need to eat. Let's see how long we can keep you going for,' the Doctor said offering a chunk of bread. 'You can watch the process of your friend here decaying. That'll be interesting won't it?'

Number One shook her head, refusing the bread. She started to hyperventilate.

'Take the bread, you need your strength,' the Doctor insisted, forcing it into Number One's hand.

Number One batted it away, sending it skimming across the floor. 'What was her name?' She stammered through choked sobs.

'Ah how precious. I'm impressed that you at least stuck to that rule. But then again you knew you were being watched. It doesn't matter what she was before. She was a stupid little do-gooder and I saw through her and her vile ulterior motives. Her name? Her name was... Patient Number Two.' The Doctor laughed a side-splitting laugh.

'You thought she was vile?' Number One felt the rage surge through her unable to hold back, 'You slit her throat, you're a sadistic fraud and you will burn for this. You will rot in hell, I will fucking make sure of it.'

The Doctor, still laughing, scooped up the chunk of bread from the floor. 'You will eat this.'

Number One clamped her lips shut as the Doctor tried to force-feed her the bread, pushing it hard against her clamped teeth.

'Eat it or I'll make you eat her,' The Doctor spat pointing to Number Two.

Number One parted her teeth allowing the bread to fill her mouth. As soon as the Doctor stepped away, she heaved and spat, spitting out every filth ridden crumb. The Doctor stormed over to the table and retrieved the knife. Number One scuttled back against the wall. She pressed herself hard against it as if she could just mould into the wall and pass right through it. The Doctor approached her slowly. Number One made one last-ditch effort to get to her feet, her will to survive kicking in. Trying to use the wall for support, she screamed out as pain seared through her legs.

'How pathetic, perhaps you would like a hand?' the Doctor mocked offering out a hand.

Number One swiped the hand away, lunging at the Doctor's middle, screaming as she did. She was met with the knife as it was plunged into her stomach. She dropped to her knees clutching the bleeding wound. 'We will fucking haunt you,' she managed to mouth before the Doctor plunged the knife in once more. Blood trickled from the corner of her mouth as she collapsed completely. She pictured the faces of her Mum and dad smiling and full of love. There they remained with her until she could think no more, until she could breathe no more.

CHAPTER
FORTY-FIVE

As soon as the live video call on the Lewis Lee Show ended, Deborah rushed out of the lounge and threw herself into the arms of her husband as he left the sitting room. He picked her up and swung her round before she pulled him into the lounge to join the others. As he entered the room, Marc and Ian applauded him so Megan and Sammi joined in.

'That went well mate,' Marc said fist pumping Ross.

Ian also got up and patted Ross on the back, 'Love how you handled that question about the house being haunted, that what's-his-face soap star bloke person didn't know what else to say to that did he, brilliant.'

'Yeah that was quick witted even for you Ross,' Marc laughed.

Deborah shot them all a look, 'Okay, now we don't want the ghosts to distract from Ross's achievement but don't think I'm letting it all lie and disappear. The spirits in this house need justice. The truth will out, I'll make sure of it.

'Jesus Debo-' Ross tried to say.

'No, let's not argue about this tonight my love, besides, we have guests.' Deborah snapped and her word on the matter was final.

'So is this house actually haunted,' Sammie chirped up, 'It's not just a publicity stunt?'

Ross confirmed that they all believed that the house was haunted, that too many strange things had happened that they couldn't account for, but that Megan had now cleansed the house so hopefully that was the end of it. 'I did not want it in the press though,' he barely said in a whisper in Sammie's ear, fully aware that Deborah was stood right there listening.

'Oh the dinner,' Deborah gasped.

She rushed to the kitchen and everyone followed. Deborah flung open the oven door to be met with a bellow of smoke.

'Didn't time that well, did I?' Deborah coughed as the smoke plumed past her.

Megan zoned out from the laughter and bustle around her as she watched fingers of smoke claw their way upwards- actual fingers. The fingers rolled and clawed up and up until they curled into fists, swirled and vanished.

'You alright?' Marc asked her. 'Told you, don't worry about spilt wine. Hey, it brings new meaning doesn't it to smoked salmon,' he laughed gesturing over to the blackened side of salmon now resting on the worktop.

Megan feigned a smile. Deborah had declared to hell with it and started taking pizzas out from the freezer.

'Guess Inspector Dark's body will have to be his temple from tomorrow,' Ross laughed patting his firm abs.

Sammie was straight in there helping Deborah unbox the pizzas and disposing of the packaging and asking what else she could do to help. Megan felt a twinge of envy. She admired how her sister was so naturally sociable and mingled and fitted in with ease. She could have been a friend of the family for years. For once, Megan wished she could be more like that without cringing to herself pretty much every time she spoke. Ian handed her a glass of champagne and she gratefully took it.

'To the new Inspector Dark,' Ian cheered raising his glass.

Everyone joined in the cheers and Megan felt the light bubbles dance on her tongue. She couldn't imagine how much this bottle had cost remembering the shock of the brandy. The next ten minutes was spent with Marc reading out reactions from Ross's twitter feed. Ross's phone had also started to go off from celebrity friends wishing him well. Sammie pulled Megan down to sit next to her at the table and squealed in her ear that she had to keep pinching herself and thanked her again for bringing her here.

Megan knew why she was feeling uneasy- it was seeing that dog again. Something wasn't feeling right and everything began to feel negative. It wasn't long ago that Sammie was on Facebook publicly saying that she didn't care when she thought Megan was a missing person. Now she was her best friend. They wouldn't be speaking now if she hadn't been invited to Ross Huston's house. But that was okay wasn't it? Megan tried to shift the negativity, Megan had done a terrible thing, it was okay that her sister hated her for it, wasn't it? Would Sammie want to stay in touch once Megan finished working for the Huston's or would she simply cut her off again?

'So where are you living now?' Sammie asked Megan, 'you'll have to give me your address so I can come and visit and stuff.'

It's as if Sammie had read her mind. She felt a small wash of relief at the thought that her sister would keep in touch. But she didn't have a home. She had nowhere to live yet.

'Just tell her the truth,' Marc piped up after overhearing the conversation.

The room went silent. It's doesn't matter how noisy a room full of chatter is, you can bet everyone will hear a word which might spark gossip. Like the word truth. Now all ears wanted to hear what this truth was. Megan started to feel hot and briefly thought about punching Marc in the face again.

'What?' Sammie asked.

'It's nothing,' Megan replied firmly.

'She's family,' Marc pushed, 'she might be able to help. You're in quite a bit of shit to be fair aren't you?'

Megan glared at Marc, shaking her head at him.

'Well?' Sammie asked.

Megan wasn't ready to discuss her private issues with her sister. She didn't want her sympathy or for Sammie to feel there was another motive for her getting in touch. People are too quick to think that an estranged family member would only be getting in touch for money, and that wasn't the case. There were good reasons why Sammie would not care for Megan's problems. It's all very well Marc sticking his nose in trying to help but he didn't know the full story, he didn't know what Megan did to her family all those years ago. She deserved her bad luck and that's all there was to it.

'Megan's homeless,' Marc said with some compassion after Megan hadn't answered.

'What? Why? What's happened?' Sammie clasped Megan's hand.

Megan pulled her hand away, it felt like her skin was on fire, she was getting so hot. Ross, Deborah and Ian closed in around her.

'It's nothing, I- I just- it's just that- I'm trying to- things have-' Megan stumbled over her words thinking how best to word it all.

'She escaped her abusive arse of a boyfriend and has been living in her car?' Marc clarified.

Now Megan really wanted to punch him and then she wanted the floor to swallow her up.

'It was just for one night, the night before Ross contacted me. I will find somewhere, I just haven't had the time yet, I've been here working,' Megan said meekly.

'Bloody hell sis,' Sammie put her arm round Megan, 'Did you not have money for a hotel?'

'Reading between the lines, I think that fella of hers bled her dry,' Marc scoffed.

'Jesus, what did he do to you?' Sammie asked.

Megan felt her eyes stinging and distracted herself by taking a big gulp of champagne.

'Can I just fill you in later? Now isn't the time, but honestly I'm okay and it's all fine.' Megan stood up and walked over to the oven, 'Shall I help take the pizzas out, they look done.'

Ross followed her and put an arm round her, 'We had no idea you were in a mess. I know what it's like to have nothing, I've been there, I've been vulnerable like you. Don't be too proud to ask for help. If I can help, I will.' He wiped an imaginary tear away from the corner of Megan's eye.

Deborah brushed past them and opened the oven door with force, ordering Ian to help ready the plates. Marc grabbed some bags of prepared salad out of the fridge and set the table. Once the pizzas were sliced and dished out, everyone got stuck in. Megan however found her mouthful of pepperoni hard to swallow. The atmosphere had changed and now she felt like everyone was looking at her differently, especially Ross who now couldn't take his eyes off of her.

CHAPTER
FORTY-SIX

'We need music,' Deborah sang, pirouetting over to the stereo. She cranked the music up.

'We've just got rid of the ghosts; don't think we need to wake the dead again do we?' Ross laughed covering his ears.

'We're celebrating aren't we?' Deborah grabbed her drink with one hand and pulled Sammie up from her chair with the other.

They both danced around each other whilst singing along to the tune. Megan could tell that Sammie was no stranger to the dance floor. Partying was just another thing that Megan had little experience of. Ross got up to grab another bottle of wine. Marc leaned into Megan, pointed over to Ross and whispered, 'watch him.' Before Megan could reply, Marc had walked away and headed out of the kitchen.

Ross waved the bottle at Megan and she shook her head.

'Honestly no more for me, I'm still on duty. I've work to do later, remember,' Megan covered her glass, denying access to it.

'Well why don't you take the night off, let's forget these blasted ghosts.'

Megan was a bit taken a back. He had been nothing but desperate to ensure that the ghosts were gone earlier. 'I'd rather we stuck to the plan. If we do a séance tonight and I sense that the spirits have really moved on then wouldn't that put your mind at rest quicker? You could get onto the press and tell them there are no more ghosts.'

'Like Deborah is going to ever let it lie, no matter what.' Ross looked over at his wife and let out a sigh, 'You're right though, the sooner I'm sure I won't have any more knives thrown at me the better.'

Megan could have easily told him then at that moment that she was sure that wouldn't happen again. Little did he know that it was really Marc, his best friend, throwing the knives. But she bit her tongue once more. 'Besides,' she said, 'I really need to leave tomorrow.'

'You can stay another night if it helps you out. Can't have you sleeping in your car.'

'No,' Megan answered a bit too abruptly, 'With what you've paid me, I can get a B&B. Honestly, I'm keen to get myself sorted. I'll be leaving first thing.'

'I meant what I said earlier, you're a breath of fresh air. Your boyfriend sounds like a complete dick. Who'd want to hurt you?'

All Megan could do was shrug. This conversation wasn't going to continue. She came here to work, not to get personal. The kindness the Huston's had shown her had blown her away, she looked over again to her sister and pinched herself, but she wasn't one of them and had no intention of exposing her life any further.

'C'mon, one more drink. At least enjoy yourself before

things get serious looking for ghosts.' Ross aimed the bottle at her glass once more.

Again, she refused him, blocking access to her glass. Ross placed the bottle down in defeat then took her hands, encouraging her to stand up and dance with him. Megan resisted but Ross was not going to give in so she relented, at least this way the conversation would end. He spun her round and she did so awkwardly, he then wrapped both of his arms around her and swayed with her in time to the beat. Megan felt uncomfortable at first but then she surprised herself by relaxing into his embrace. It had been a long time- too long to remember, since Megan felt the warmth of a real hug, one with genuine affection. She'd had mate hugs off Christina but being wrapped up right now in a man's strong arms felt good. Megan wished Christina could be here for this, she'd go nuts. Megan was dancing with *The Ross Huston*. For a moment and just for a moment, this is how she felt and then reality kicked her. She didn't want to dance around in strong arms, she didn't need it. She needed to be on her guard, so she pulled away from him and went back to her chair but not before feeling Deborah's icy glare on her back.

Megan puzzled once more over Ross and Deborah's relationship. Deborah said that they had an open relationship but why did it feel that she was now throwing daggers at her because Ross was showing her some attention. Surely it's not a big deal? Perhaps she was imagining it, she thought. She watched Ian joining in, dancing around the other three and Sammie showed no sign of letting up, shimmying and grinding her hips. Megan grabbed the bottle of wine from the table and poured herself a measure, just one more wouldn't hurt, she hoped it would just be enough to cloud her thoughts a little, but not too much.

Marc re-entered the room and joined her at the table, 'You okay?' he asked her.

Megan nodded and pushed the bottle of wine in his direction. He helped himself to a glass.

'I've said it before,' Marc said, 'but you and your sister are so different.'

'You shouldn't have told her my business. I wish you hadn't.'

'Thought I was helping.'

'She hates me, you know, she's hated me for years. I don't want her sympathy. I don't deserve it.' Megan was suddenly aware that she was slurring a little. Perhaps she had already had a little too much and she instantly regretted what she'd just said.

'So you're just gonna punish yourself forever? Leave the ghosts of the past behind. Join the living, live a little.'

Both Megan and Marc looked up with a start as the others erupted into a loud cheer as Ian presented a bottle of Sambuca and insisted on drinking games.

'Excellent,' Marc said.

'It looks like everyone's drunk enough,' Megan laughed.

'Excellent,' Marc said again, 'That's the plan.'

Megan looked at him puzzled.

'I need Ross so drunk that he blabs. He always does. He's a shit drunk. He's going to tell me what he really did with Sarah. Kerry too for that matter. They didn't just disappear; I just know they didn't.'

A shiver shot straight up Megan's spine. She looked at Ross now slamming shots and laughing. *He couldn't be capable of harming anyone, could he?* She wanted to tell Marc just to inform the police about Sarah's last known movements but bit her tongue. They had been through it already and Marc was determined to be sure of his facts first. If he was wrong then Ross's career would be ruined for nothing if it made the press and that also put Marc's own job on the line and not to mention Deborah's reputation too. Megan drained her remaining wine, unaware that there was a black dog lying at her feet under the table.

CHAPTER
FORTY-SEVEN

IT GOT TO ELEVEN-THIRTY P.M. AND MEGAN WAS ITCHING TO GET HER ghost hunting equipment out and to make a start. The sooner she could get it over with then the sooner she could go to bed and sleep. She longed to be asleep, to wake up, then to leave this place. But everyone was drunk- drunk and having fun. She feared that if they partied all night that they would just talk her into staying yet another night to try and make contact with the dead to ensure they'd gone. She said she'd be leaving in the morning and that was that. She decided to carry on without waiting to be instructed.

Everyone was so busy laughing at something that they didn't notice Megan slip out of the kitchen. She made her way up to her room and hesitantly opened the door. She didn't know why she should still be feeling a bit scared. Nothing was going to go bump in here- not anymore. First things first, she threw herself on the bed, hanging herself over the edge. Her head was feeling a little fuzzy from the alcohol but she wouldn't have described herself as being drunk. The fuzziness felt extra soothing as the blood rushed to her head. She breathed in for five and out for three.

'What are you doing,' Marc's voice boomed out from nowhere.

Megan jumped up with a start, 'I just needed five minutes.'

'Upside down?'

'Yes,' Megan said flatly. 'It's time we finished cleaning up your mess. I want to get the Ouija board out and prove there are no ghosts here. You do promise there will be no more tricks?'

'Yes. I haven't done anything else yet have I? Look, I wanted to scare Ross because he pinched Sarah off me. It was a stupid practical joke. But now Sarah is missing, so I have bigger fish to fry. This is more serious now don't you think?'

Megan nodded. She just hoped that she and Sammie wouldn't be getting caught up in this feud tonight. She wouldn't want her sister's night spoiled. She gathered her equipment up and asked Marc to help carry the Ouija board table down to the second lounge. Megan decided that's where they'd start. Once in the room, Megan set about laying out her equipment whilst Marc gathered the others.

Deborah, Ross, Sammie and Ian all but staggered into the second lounge.

'Well isn't Megan the life of the party,' Ian jeered.

Deborah laughed but then on a serious note said, 'No, Megan is quite right. We are paying her to do this, let's get on with it.'

'I've not done any of this before,' Sammie said looking wide-eyed at the pieces of equipment Megan had laid out.

'Stuff happened the other night when we did this...weird stuff, but nothing to worry about now.' Deborah clapped her hands together, 'I can already feel a difference.'

'That'll be the Sambuca,' Ian laughed.

Ross linked his arm with Sammie's and said, 'Yes, don't be scared. We are sure Megan has moved any ghosts on. This is just to make sure.'

'That's rich, you telling someone not to be scared,' Marc scoffed.

'Piss off Marc, you didn't have a knife thrown at you! Anyway,' Ross addressed Sammie, 'It was all full on when you arrived earlier, there's some paperwork I need you to sign, just some confidentiality stuff... as you're staying the night. Can we do that now before my drunken brain forgets? We won't be a mo guys,' he said as he led Sammie away.

The spirit voice box that Megan had just turned on crackled to life. It sounded like a radio station with zero signal.

'We'll start without them,' Megan said. She pointed out the various things that she'd laid out around the room. The small torches which turn on when a spirit's energy is present and the K2 Meters and flashing balls that will light up if there's a presence in the room. 'Let's form a circle.'

Ian flicked the lights off first before they circled round holding hands. The spirit voice box remained softly crackling in the background.

'Hello, it's me Megan. If you are here with us tonight spirits, please make yourselves known.'

Silence.

'There are some gadgets around the room that can light up. Can you make them light up for us please?'

Silence.

'Or you could talk to us. Use the white noise. Tell us if you are here.'

Ian burped. The belch caused the group to jump and then

erupt into laughter- except for Megan. She knew doing this with a bunch of pissed up adults was going to be difficult.

'*She's watching.*'

The laughter quickly stopped. The spirit box had spoken. It was distant, almost robotic.

'Did you say, "She's watching?" Who is? Could you repeat that please?' Megan spoke up hushing the others.

A few moments passed, '*The Woman.*' The voice came again.

'What woman?' Marc butted in, 'Where is she?'

'*You lose.*'

'Lose what?' Megan replied.

There was no answer. All four of them looked around the room. Marc went over to the window, picking up one of the torches. It was the first time Megan had known the spirit box to say something coherent and to answer a question with a response that almost made sense. But she wasn't buying it. The group seemed tense all of a sudden and were sobering up fast. Marc slowly pulled the curtain back. There was some lighting outside from the lamps surrounding the house. Ian joined Marc and pulled back the other half of the curtain further. Huddled together, the group looked out into the darkness. Nothing.

'There,' Deborah squealed, 'look over there by the trees, is someone there? A figure which looks like it's wearing something reflective?'

'Oh yeah,' they all said in quick unison.

But what they thought they saw had quickly vanished.

Deborah ran for the lights. 'Didn't Ross say he saw an old woman in that very spot just the other night?'

'Yeah,' Marc said, 'actually we saw someone there too earlier today, didn't we Megan? I ran but the person vanished by the time I got there. When all the reporters were outside. Thought one had got in.'

Deborah slapped Marc's shoulder, 'Security Marc, what the fuck do we pay you for.'

'Woah, I checked the boundaries and all was secure.'

'Would you say that person we just saw was a woman?' Ian asked.

'Hard to tell,' Deborah said and the others agreed.

The lights were switched back off and Megan called out to ask who this woman was. The spirit box crackled and buzzed, it then said the word *toast* and then *bicycle*.

'Ah it's just talking nonsense now,' Ian said.

'Yes, but someone is on our property,' Deborah snapped.

'I'm not convinced someone is really out there,' Marc rationalised, 'Look I'll grab Ross and Ian can come too and we'll go out there and search the grounds?'

'Where the fuck is Ross? How long does it take for Sammie to write her bloody signature?' Deborah sniped through gritted teeth.

She stormed for the light switch again but halted in her tracks. Each item that Megan had placed around the room lit up in unison. The torches shone, the balls flashed away and the K2 meters lights flashed. Megan looked to Marc who had his hands up in protest as if to say he didn't touch anything. Deborah smacked the lights back on and nearly had a heart attack as the door opened simultaneously. Ross and Sammie entered the room.

'What have we missed?' Ross said.

Megan clocked straightaway that Sammie looked different. She looked flushed and less relaxed, like she'd just been caught with her hand in the cookie jar. Megan guessed that she had more than the guilt of cookies on her mind. Deborah filled them both in but Megan was quick to rationalise it all. The group were moving around and the lights would set off with vibrations. The K2 meters would go off if there were mobile phones nearby. It wouldn't be too far-fetched to think that the odd member of the press was lurking around outside either. Megan needed to make sure that the Huston's believed the ghosts were gone without dropping Marc in it and none of what was happening so far was helping.

CHAPTER
FORTY-EIGHT

'Do you know what we all need?' Marc piped up, 'Another drink.'

Megan knew that Marc was on a mission to get Ross blind drunk but this really wasn't helping either. There was no way she was going to be talked into staying another night, she needed everyone to take this seriously tonight and let her finish her investigations.

'Okay take a break but then let's use the Ouija board, all of us,' Megan said almost pleadingly as the group departed for the kitchen. 'Sammie hold on. Stay and help me?'

Sammie looked reluctant but quickly seized the opportunity to be alone with her sister, 'Oh God, you never guess what happened,' Sammie clasped her hands around her mouth.

Megan raised her brows but had a feeling she already knew. Sammie looked like she might burst.

'So, I sat down with Ross and signed some document, promising to strictest confidentiality...' Sammie let out a squeal and took a couple of rapid deep breaths.

'Well, spill?'

'I signed it, then he threw it to one side... oh my god... then he stroked my face-' Sammie paused, biting into her thumb, 'he said, "Good, now I can do this," and kissed me, like really kissed me. He put his hands on my waist, he stroked my neck, his hand slipped inside the back of my dress-'

'Sammie, you didn't-'

'No, no, that was it, I pulled away because it was a bit intense...he took me by surprise and oh my god he's married, and I'm married.'

Megan didn't know how to think because she knew that Deborah was okay with Ross *being* with other women. Well at least that's what she said. Sammie did look a picture, she was biting her lip, then grinning madly, then scrunching her face up.

'*Ross Huston* kissed me,' she squealed again.

'I'm not surprised, look at you. You're beautiful. But be careful, okay? Everyone's had too much to drink-'

'I know, I know,' Sammie kept her hand firmly across her mouth.

Megan got Sammie to help put the gadgets away. She didn't want them lighting up anymore and getting everyone thinking that ghosts were doing it. She decided to stick with the Ouija board.

'Look at me,' Sammie laughed as she switched off the lights and flashed a torch in front of her face. She made a ghostly cackle.

Megan laughed, enjoying the light relief and grabbed another torch to join in. They knelt on the sofa to look into the mirror hanging above it, pulling faces and laughing at the spooky shadows cast around their features. Sammie felt her head spin from the booze and collapsed into the corner of the sofa giggling. Megan looked down at her and smiled, shaking her head at her drunk sister. She turned back to the mirror and held the torch under her chin, until her face in the reflection was no longer her own. It was no longer a shadowy likeness of herself, but a different face completely. It was a woman with blonde hair, and she was grey and black tears rolled down her cheeks and then another face appeared behind her with a head of black curly hair. They both suddenly screamed and were sucked backwards, they were smaller and smaller, distant, then nothing. The mirror cracked.

Megan dropped the torch and shot backwards, stumbling off the sofa. It was Sarah. The blonde woman was Sarah. She recognised her from her previous dream and the missing person photos and the other woman was Kerry. It was Sarah and it was Kerry without question. The lights came back on, Marc had entered the room.

'Did you ask him yet? What happened to Kerry and Sarah?' Megan rushed at Marc, breathless.

'Hush,' Marc put his finger to his lips, 'Not yet,' he said quietly, 'I'm thinking that I shouldn't doubt my mate. He wouldn't have deliberately meant for any harm to come to them.'

'So you think they've been harmed?'

'No, no, that's not what I meant-'

'So you're just going to leave it now?'

'I'm being too harsh. I've known him like forever. He wouldn't have meant for anything to happen to Sarah. If he was coming on strong with her, then I should've stepped in, not left them alone. I'm to blame too. Can't put it all at my mate's door.'

'But it pissed you off enough to get revenge on him at the

time,' Megan felt her rage burn as her hushed tone began to crescendo.

Marc put his finger to his lips again, 'What is this about? Why are you so-'

The conversation was cut dead as the others came back in laughing and singing the Ghost-busters theme tune. Sammie remained curled up on the sofa.

'Hey Sammie,' Deborah called over to her and waited for her to raise her head and murmur something back. 'Ross and I were talking; I'm going to get you on the make-up team for Ross's new film. 'What do you reckon? Do you want to?'

Sammie shot up back to life, unsteady and unaware that her dress had ridden dangerously high as she lunged at Deborah for a hug, 'Yes, yes and yes,' she slurred. 'Oh but it's Ireland isn't it? I have kids.'

'We can talk logistics tomorrow,' Deborah slurred back.

Megan gently pulled her sister away and pulled the skirt of her dress back into place and straightened her straps which had come off her shoulders.

'I've drank too much haven't I?' Sammie giggled into Megan's ear.

Megan wished that she hadn't. If only she'd kept looking into the mirror with her. Would she have seen the women too? Was it just her? She looked again and the crack was still there. No one else had noticed it yet. She didn't want to point it out, not yet. How could she explain that one, that she was having visions of the two women that were last seen at this house? It would sound accusing, wouldn't it? That wasn't one of Marc's tricks. He couldn't control what she saw in the mirror and he couldn't control her dreams. Something strange was going on in this house and she was sure that it was not what everyone was thinking.

Ross stepped over and brushed Sammie's hair away from her neck, 'Can I get you another drink?'

Something about Ross touching her sister like that suddenly made her skin crawl, 'She's had enough,' Megan said firmly. It was not long ago that Ross had tried to be a bit over affectionate with her- before he had kissed Sammie. Who did he think he was? She was glad she'd pushed him away.

'I'm fine,' Sammie grinned, 'Look at my sister looking out for me,' she continued in a patronising slur.

Marc jumped in, 'So Ouija board?'

Ian jeered and started singing the Ghost-busters theme tune again into his beer bottle and danced over to the Ouija board. Apart from Marc, the others laughed and followed suit, forming a conga line, "Let's all do a Ouija, let's all do a Ouija la, la, la," they sang out. *This is hopeless*, Megan thought. She turned back to Marc and said that this was never going to work with everyone so drunk. She felt her heart hammering against her rib cage. She felt uneasy and it felt like the walls were closing in on her. She didn't know what to think, she was confused. Deborah thought one thing, Nancy thought another and Marc had his own agenda. Two women were missing and in no way connected to nineteenth century tortured patients. She felt like she was in a mirror maze, crashing into herself at each turn. But she was more convinced than ever that she was connected to Sarah and Kerry and they were trying to tell her something. She had been too busy looking for ghosts from long ago that she was overlooking the ones here and now. Because that's what she now believed. She had a sick feeling in her stomach that both women would not be found alive.

CHAPTER
FORTY-NINE

'Right,' Megan said, 'I'm going to go elsewhere and do a lone vigil. I need the quiet, I need to meditate, I need to think.'

Marc looked at her concerned, 'You know you don't have to worry. Listen, a lone vigil won't prove anything. Ross and Deb need to see for themselves that there's no spooky goings on to believe it's all stopped.'

'But look at them,' Megan said exasperated, 'Ross was determined to make sure this house was safe and now look at him, at all of them. They're too pissed. They're not bothered. I'm not staying here another night.'

'You can leave any time Megan, no one is forcing you to-'

'I know. There's something I have to do. I'm not convinced there isn't something...' Megan tried to choose her words carefully, 'well, I experienced things each time I was alone so I just need to be sure it's all in my head. I need some space and time on my own to be sure... so I can rule stuff out.'

'You know what you're doing ghost detective, you're the expert,' Marc stepped aside, allowing her a free run.

She took a last look at her sister belly laughing and everyone singing and she bolted from the room. Halting in the hallway, she spun around trying to think where best to go. She just needed to think. She should call the police, but say what? Was she brave enough to break the Huston's confidence? She knew that Sarah was last seen here, that made her some sort of accomplice, didn't it? No, she'd be perverting the course of justice. Either way it didn't sit well with her. She needed to think. She needed to try and make contact with Sarah and Kerry. She was scared though. If they appeared to her again, it would make her fears all too real. She needed to think away from everyone, but where to go? She jogged into the kitchen and into the pantry. The last place she wanted to go was the cellar, but it was the best place, she knew she'd be alone, away from the others to think, no one would look for her in there.

With the light on, the cellar was not that bad, Megan reassured herself as she picked her way down the steps. Once at the bottom she sat on the floor and hugged her knees to her chest. It was so cold. She could no longer entertain rational thoughts. She had vivid visions of Kerry and Sarah in her dreams and they were in the mirror clear as anything. In the kitchen, that night, she'd felt their pain, just like she asked. It wasn't one of Marc's tricks and it wasn't a panic attack. It was them. The only thing to do was try to contact them. To stop ignoring them, to stop searching for patients of Doctor Holdstock. To concentrate on just them.

Megan trembled but she had to do something, 'Kkerry, Ssarah, are you here with me?' There was a scrape along the floor and Megan brought her knees tighter to her chest. 'Can I help you?'

She felt something touch her hair and a coolness brush her ear. A draught rushed around her then suddenly eased, like someone had just turned it off. Like a dripping tap stops, the draught had stopped. Megan sat motionless. She shone the torch at the light bulb hanging from the ceiling, it started to gently sway. She believed her heart would stop. A few minutes passed and she didn't move a muscle.

'Kerry? I know that you were last seen here. You too Sarah. Did you die here? What happened to both of you? I'm here to help you.' Megan buried her head into her knees.

A moment passed then she heard scratching and scuffling coming from the wall. The wall which felt deadly cold to her earlier on. She stood up to listen closer. The scuffling grew louder, she pressed her palm to the brick and quickly returned it, it felt wet and rubbery. She looked at her hand and squealed at the sight of a leech, she swept it off then spotted another on her wrist, then another and another. Her arms were covered. She jumped around, swatting and swiping at her arms. She made for the doorway, stopped and shone the torch across the floor. No leeches. Her arms were fine. No blood. No trace. Hot tears appeared as the light bulb started to sway again. She wanted to run, but fear kept her rooted.

Knock, knock, knock came from the wall. She walked back over to it. Her voice shaking, 'Please don't hurt me, just tell me where you are.'

Gentle tapping came from the bottom of the wall, she crouched down to listen closer then scurried back at speed, stumbling as she did, falling on her bottom. Hands, dark shadows of hands reached through the wall, then a head. It looked up and opened its mouth as if to scream but no noise came. The shadow was dragged back through the wall. It was gone. A loud thud sounded out and then a blood chilling scream. Megan scrambled up but her feet wouldn't move. She couldn't run. Paralysis took hold. Her lips were glued. Her mouth filled with water- acrid tasting, gritty. Her whole oral cavity was full but she couldn't spit, she was going to drown, her eyes bulged and her vision blurred. A final deep intake through her nose and her mouth opened, the contents spilling out. She spat and heaved. A dirty puddle lay at her feet mixed with leaves. She ran. She bolted out through the door and up the stairs.

None of that was in her imagination. Her niggles were no longer just that. Something terrible had happened to those two women. She'd have to make Ross and Deborah listen. She ran to the lounge but it was empty. The sitting room was empty.

'Sammie? Ross? Anyone?'

She ran up the stairs looking and calling, not a sound. Where was everyone?

CHAPTER
FIFTY

Megan ran back to the kitchen in time to see Deborah enter through the patio doors.

'Oh my goodness it's cold out there,' Deborah quickly closed the doors behind her, 'Are you okay?'

'I just wondered where you'd all gone, where's Sammie?' Megan thought that she must look like some crazy person because Deborah was looking at her with much concern.

'We wondered where you'd gone actually... well Ian and Marc went over to the woods to see if they could see any intruders and Ross has gone up to bed... and well Sammie... well she's gone up with him,' Deborah said lightly with a brief wave of her hand.

Megan was stunned by Deborah's words and didn't know how to go about replying to that. Words stuck in her throat.

'Oh it's fine. Don't look like that,' Deborah spoke instead. 'This is normal for Ross. I won't hold it against your sister. She's a darling, isn't she? Anyway so I found myself alone so I went out to join Ian and Marc but couldn't spot them. Didn't fancy walking around in the dark on my own... are you sure you're okay? You look quite pale. Honestly, all is fine.'

Megan had to do the right thing. How could she do nothing, knowing that two women were in danger or worse. She'd never live with herself. She had to do something even if she was wrong and looked a fool.

'I know about Marc's girlfriend, Sarah,' Megan gulped as Deborah's face turned stony. 'He told me about her before I found out that she was missing. I read about it online and put two and two together. She's missing too isn't she? Last seen here wasn't she?'

Deborah inhaled, 'This really isn't any business of yours, it's a matter that we as a family-'

'They've appeared to me in visions,' Megan quickly said, stunning Deborah into silence. 'Both of them, clear as anything, dressed in rags and covered in blood. I know it sounds crazy but I'm convinced something bad has happened to them. They're trying to tell me something. They've shown me their pain. It's not Victorian ghosts here, it's them.' Megan panted, her heart in her throat.

Deborah removed her coat and threw it over the back of a chair, 'So you think they're dead? That they died in this house? I'd be very careful what you are saying, what you're implying.'

'No that's not what I'm saying exactly. I feel connected to them and they are trying to tell me something. I need to tell the police. You should tell the police they were both last seen here. Their disappearances might be connected and the police will find them quicker if they have all the facts.'

Deborah relaxed her expression and sat down, inviting Megan to join her. 'We are going to the police tomorrow. Ross and I decided this earlier. You really are rushing into our business but we have it in hand. Of course we will tell the police, what kind of heartless people do you think we are?'

Megan wanted to scream they were thoughtless enough not to go to the police straight away and that they put Ross's career first over trying to find a missing woman- a woman whose family must be desperately missing her.

Deborah continued, 'All we know is that Kerry and Sarah both left here in one piece. All we are guilty of is not making sure they got home safely. You know Ian hasn't been sleeping. He's on meds, the guilt is eating him up but we can't keep living on *if only he did this or that.*' She poured a glass of wine and pushed it towards Megan and then did one for herself. 'People did die here. Those poor patients all those years ago. But you helped them find peace Megan. Their spirits have moved on, I can feel it. You truly have a gift. But you poor sweetheart, you must be under a lot of stress, your mind could be playing tricks on you. These visions...'

Megan refused the wine. How could Deborah think that she was gifted and then in the next breath suggest her mind was playing tricks on her? So she's crazy. Everyone will think she's crazy. The police will think she's crazy. Megan rubbed her face and was relieved to see Ian and Marc heading back inside.

'What on earth?' Deborah laughed and jumped up at the sight of the two men.

Marc was covered head to toe in mud and Ian's hands, knees and face took a covering too.

'Slipped down the bank didn't I,' Marc laughed

'Yeah, took me with him didn't he,' Ian sniped turning the taps on to wash his hands.

'Well?' Deborah asked.

Marc looked confused for a moment, 'Oh yes, no nothing. No one out there... Where's Ross and Sammie?'

Deborah rolled her eyes to the ceiling indicating that they were upstairs. Megan scrunched her eyes shut at the reminder.

Ian towel dried his hands and declared that he couldn't take any more excitement that night and he was getting too old for it all. He said he'd head home and bid them all goodnight. Deborah saw him to the door.

'So your sister-' Marc said.

'Just don't,' Megan said defeated.

Deborah came back in, 'Well it feels like the party's over doesn't it?' She looked tired.

'What? The night's still young,' Ross piped up, entering the room with a slight stagger.

Marc wanted Ross pissed out of his tree and he had succeeded, Megan thought. Ross had lost his composure and Megan was sure that was sick on his T-shirt. Marc turned out to be gutless though. He couldn't bring himself to confront his mate over Sarah. He couldn't carry out his plan to get to the truth. Megan was wondering what kind of man Marc really was with his childish pranks and his inability to fight for his girlfriend. How could he just let it go that Sarah was missing and Ross was the last to see her?

'Where's Sammie?' Megan asked Ross who was glugging down a glass of water.

He wiped his mouth as water gushed down his chin from his thirst. 'I don't know.'

'What, she's not still in your bed?' Deborah said with some sarcasm.

Ross looked alarmed. 'In my bed? No. Of course she's not in my bloody bed. I've had my head down the toilet for the past half hour,' Ross belched.

'What you've not been with her? You haven't seen her?' Megan jumped up.

'No,' Ross confirmed again. 'So she's not here with you?'

Megan ran from the kitchen and took the stairs two at a time. She flew into Ross's bedroom and it was empty. She threw open the en-suite door and inside smelt of sick. She suppressed a gag and hurried into the dressing room, again it was empty. She stopped to think rationally, *where was she?* The wardrobe caught her attention. It sounded like something had fallen down inside with a bump. It happened before, she remembered. The last time she was in this room. There was a noise from the wardrobe and Deborah stopped her looking inside. Megan was compelled to look and didn't hold back. She pulled open the door and was met with a row of wigs. All kinds of wigs, neatly hanging from the rail. Megan lightly ran her fingers across the array of colours and styles but there was nothing else to see. Megan all but slammed the door shut and hurried from the room.

Her room, the spare rooms, Marc's room, the bathroom were all empty of Sammie. The others had joined Megan upstairs and each one looked again in each of the rooms as if perhaps Megan didn't look properly. Sammie still wasn't there. She wasn't anywhere.

'I could've sworn she was with you,' Deborah snapped at Ross almost accusing.

'No, I haven't seen her. I came up here alone.' Ross put his hands up in protest.

'But she followed you up and didn't come back down,' Deborah swore, 'I mean it was a couple of minutes after you went up that she followed you up, I assumed, I thought, I was convinced that's where she went.'

Megan realised that Marc still had her phone and asked for it. She would just try phoning her. Marc looked sheepish and admitted that he also had Sammie's phone. Ross had taken it off her earlier in the night and slipped it to Marc to look after. It was part of Sammie's contract. Ross didn't want her taking any photo's during her stay and it was the only way to be sure that she couldn't.

'Look,' Marc said, 'I need to get out of these muddy clothes, give me a sec and I'll help you look some more.' He shut himself inside his room.

'That's it, maybe she went outside after Marc and Ian too,' Megan turned to Deborah.

'But they've not long got in, they would have seen her. Unless they crossed paths.' Deborah shrugged.

She couldn't have just vanished, Megan screamed inside her head. Where was she?

CHAPTER
FIFTY-ONE

MEGAN DIDN'T THINK, SHE JUST RAN BACK DOWN THE STAIRS, GRABBED a torch and ran out through the patio doors at the back of the kitchen. She had a bad feeling, nothing felt right. Her car was still on the driveway. Sammie wouldn't just disappear; she wouldn't just leave the company of *the Ross Huston*. She wouldn't just leave her. She was having the night of her life; she wouldn't just leave that. Megan hadn't been down the cellar that long. How can Sammie vanish in that time? No nothing felt right.

Megan jogged up the pathway until she reached the archway to the orchard. She shone her torch around the trees and called out to Sammie. Nothing. She decided to go through the small gate and try along the lake. Perhaps Sammie had slipped over like Marc had. She was so drunk, perhaps she was just lying somewhere too drunk to get up. The pathway was narrow so she gingerly picked her way along until the path widened. Megan remembered the fox that had jumped out from the bushes the last time she was at this point with Marc.

She cursed the fox under her breath and hoped not to see it again.

A sloshing sound came from the centre of the lake, like the plop of a pebble being plunged into its depths. It sounded again. Megan shone the torch slowly and methodically around the breadth of the lake. All was still.

'Sammie?' she called.

Megan's hands were now trembling with the cold. Perhaps if she went back to the house, she would find Sammie sat at the kitchen table wondering what all the fuss was about. How could she not be paranoid when two women had gone missing from this house and she was certain they were both dead? Megan moved on but came to stop for there was something blocking her path- a large black hound.

The torch fell from Megan's hand. She froze, too scared to move an inch, too scared to pick up the torch. *Don't move, don't breathe* was all she could tell herself. The hound sat there, its eyes shining red. For that moment all they did was lock eyes. Waiting for the next move. Megan ever so slowly bent down to reach for her torch, shaking the whole time. *Please go, just go.* But the hound stood, its head lowered and its teeth showing. It moved towards her. Megan backed away slowly. The hound circled her. Megan lifted her hands to her chest in defence. There was nothing she could do. She knew the dog was coming for her, she couldn't escape her fate.

Megan now had her back to the lake and the hound inched further forwards and Megan inched further back until she was very much aware that her next step would be into the murky water. There was another splash, Megan looked behind her and that's when the hound bombed at her, head butting her middle sending her tumbling back into the water. It was only shallow at the shore and Megan scrambled to her knees but as she tried to leave the water she was dragged backwards. Something had grabbed her ankle, a hand, two hands dragging her back. Megan screamed. The hands let go. She scrambled onto the bank. Through blurry waterlogged vision, she saw that the hound was no longer there. She grabbed the torch, hardly able to hold it now, her fingers cold to the bones. Shaking, she shone it at the lake, her teeth chattering hard against each other.

There was no one where she had fallen. Nothing there with hands to grab her with. But there in the centre of the lake arose a figure. A woman whose sodden gown clung around her. Her hair long and matted. She was grey and ghostly. Megan slipped as she stepped backwards. She looked on in terror as another woman arose up from the dark depths. They stood there holding each other. Both as grey as each other. Both of them in pain but no longer feeling it. Megan had found them. Kerry and Sarah. She knew it was them. One of the women nodded before they sank back down- back down to their resting place. All was still. They had vanished and the hound had too.

Megan could hardly feel her legs to move them, but she had to get back to the house. She had to get away from the house. She'd get away and call the police. Get them to search the grounds, the lake, everywhere. Her whole body shook from the cold, her clothes stuck to her skin. She moved as quickly as she could, leaving the wooded area. She saw Marc jogging towards her.

'Jesus, did you go for a swim?' Marc mocked, but he soon changed his tone when he realised Megan wasn't laughing.

She kept on walking, striding to the house, 'They're in tthere, in the llake,' Megan stammered.

'What?' Marc asked matching her pace.

'Kkerry and Ssarah.'

Marc grabbed Megan's shoulder and rubbed her arm. 'You're freezing. Let's get you in and warm and then talk to me.'

'I need my pphone,' she suddenly stopped.

Why was Marc really covered in mud? The thought struck her. Had he just fallen over or something else? Something worse? Two women were at the bottom of the lake and Sammie was missing. What had he done to them? She didn't want to think that but how could she not be suspicious.

'You can have it, c'mon let's get you inside,' he looked alarmed. The look that Megan recognised. The look that revealed she knew his secrets.

Inside, Deborah immediately jumped up in horror at the sight of Megan. Ross was slumped at the table barely able to lift his head. 'Marc get her a hot drink. Through here with me.' Deborah wrapped her arms around Megan and guided her into the second lounge where she wrapped a fleece blanket around her.

'They're in the lake. At the bottom of it. Kerry and Sarah. I saw them.' Megan blurted out, not caring about looking crazy. 'Where's my sister?'

Marc hurried in placing a mug of coffee into Megan's shaking hands.

'She's not turned up... what do you mean they are in the lake?' Deborah asked whilst rubbing Megan's arms.

'I need my sister, I have to go, we have to-'

'Marc, why don't you check all of the outside CCTV see if we can spot Sammie leaving,' Deborah ordered. 'Okay we'll find her. We need to get you sorted then tell me what you mean. Look at you? Are you hurt?'

Megan shook her head. The coffee was too unsteady in her hands so she placed it down. Marc said he'd be back in a few minutes; he'd log on to his computers in his room and check everything. Megan perched on the edge of the sofa. Thoughts raced and jumbled. If Kerry and Sarah were in the lake then they never left the property. CCTV showed them leaving the property. Did someone kill them and then bring them back to dump their bodies in the lake? Was that even possible? They never left- they couldn't have left. If it wasn't them on the CCTV then who was it? You couldn't see their faces, thinking about it, you couldn't, it was just their backs.

Then who was it? Someone else? What other women? Deborah? Only Deborah lives here. She's slim, similar build, with a wig she could look like them, both of them. Wigs- there were wigs, lots of them. With sudden realisation, Megan knew that she had been shown them- she was shown the wigs. Jumping up Megan said she had to go, she tried not to look at Deborah differently but it must have shown. The fear and realisation must have shown. Deborah blocked Megan's path. Her tone now changed to sinister.

'Oh no, you're not going anywhere,' Deborah shoved Megan down onto the floor into the centre of the room, moved the oriental vase and released the lever.

It happened so fast. No time to move. Before Megan knew it, her stomach lurched and down she fell. She dropped fast and hard and landed with a thud and a sickening crack. She screamed for she was sure her legs were broken. She looked up in blind shock to see the trap door close. The door she'd fallen through.

'Oh my god, Megan,' a voice cried.

Megan briefly saw her sister trapped in a cage before she passed out.

CHAPTER
FIFTY-TWO

MEGAN'S EYES FLICKERED OPEN; SHE HADN'T BEEN OUT COLD FOR long. She was instantly aware of a figure clamping something around her ankles, something cold and heavy. The pain was immense and she cried out. The figure grabbed her wrists as she tried to bat their hands away. She relented through the pain and the figure cuffed her wrists. Megan's eyes started to focus and she found herself looking into the face of Ian.

'What the hell,' Megan sobbed.

Ian's phone vibrated from his pocket, he checked it, smiled a wicked smile and disappeared out of the door. His footsteps could be heard running up a staircase.

'Sammie?' Megan cried, shuffling over to her sister who was cramped up in a small cage.

'I'm in so much pain,' Sammie cried. 'You have to get me out... did you know?'

'No, I don't know what the hell-'

'The keys, on the table, he's left the keys,' Sammie waved her hand through the bars.

Megan screamed out and grabbed her legs as she twisted around to look. There was a bunch of keys on the table. She didn't waste time in dragging herself over to get them. The pain was unbearable but she made it back and fumbled with the assortment of keys. The third key fit the cage lock and with a click it opened. Sammie screamed as she crawled out. They hugged each other briefly and tightly before trying the keys in the locks of Megan's chains.

'None of them fit,' Sammie cried.

'Keep trying, try again.'

'I am.'

Sammie tried frantically but none of the keys worked.

'Try the door,' Megan pushed Sammie's hands with the keys away, 'just go, get out, get help, go.'

Sammie dragged herself over to the door, reached up and tried the handle. It opened. She looked back at Megan wide-eyed.

'Go,' Megan urged.

Sammie hauled herself up the steps and met with another door but that too was open. She pushed through it and immediately screamed for help. Her whole body was barely through the door when two boots appeared at her eye level.

'I don't think so,' Ian smirked and roughly grabbed her shoulders, shoving her backwards.

Sammie tried to fight him off but once he'd shoved her to the top of the stairs he swiftly kicked and punched her, sending her tumbling down them. Megan screamed at the sight of her sister crashing back into the room in a heap. Ian emerged after her, closely followed by another person. Deborah.

'You bloody idiot,' Deborah slapped Ian across the face, 'You left the doors unlocked? Really?'

'I thought the keys were in my pocket,' Ian rubbed his cheek.

Deborah slapped the other side of his face and ordered him to chain Sammie up. Sammie screamed out and begged to be left alone but her cries were futile.

'What are you doing?' Megan shouted to Deborah.

None of this felt real, if it wasn't for the searing pain she felt, she could have sworn this was all some joke or dream or something, anything than what it actually was.

Deborah smiled, 'I've been longing for an audience. You know, I'm just going to show you a film. My work. It'll explain everything. You're both going to have to stop this crying though or you won't hear it.'

Ian pulled down a projector screen and started rolling the film. Megan and Sammie clung to each other, shaking and panting through the pain. Deborah cupped her hands under her chin and her eyes shone. She had the look of a child full of anticipation and excitement. The screen lit up and then a film clapper appeared indicating the take. Then appeared the Title-
'Blind House 1878'

Megan and Sammie looked on in horror at the opening scene, Deborah had put on a white coat resembling a doctor. There was a woman, chained, who Megan instantly recognised as Sarah. Her arms were bleeding from random incisions. Deborah started cutting away at Sarah's hair, the woman was crying and pleading for her to stop. She was then forced to dress in a white gown, screaming out the whole time. Next Deborah produced a sack and covered Sarah's head, proceeding to douse her in water.

It was Sarah. Patient Number One was Sarah. Megan remembered the Ouija board spelling out Patient Number One. *A patient but not a patient.* 'You're sick,' Megan spat. Deborah dismissed her and laughed. She winced through the following scenes as Deborah inflicted cruelty and torture on Sarah. Deborah got Ian to fast forward through some parts eager to get to the best bits- to Kerry arriving, falling through the trap-door. Megan looked away when Kerry's death played out, her throat slit. Sammie sobbed uncontrollably.

'That was genius wasn't it,' Deborah laughed and mimicked her own words from the film, *'You lose.'* I knew I had a flare for writing.

Ian nodded over to her and winked in agreement. He skipped to the end scene. Sarah fought with Deborah until Deborah plunged a knife into her stomach.

'Now that was just beautiful,' Deborah gasped. 'The perfect ending, the build-up of dramatic action, the fight and then... oh it couldn't have gone better. Sarah fuelled my script perfectly. I'd say you couldn't write that kind of action but... I did,' Deborah laughed.

'You're a fucking monster,' Megan screamed, holding her sister tighter who was excessively shaking.

'I'm not the sick one. It's everyone else,' Deborah snorted. 'You know, my parents did everything they could to prevent me from studying beauty therapy. They said I wasn't safe to work with the public. I mean who holds their child back like that? Their own fucking child. Then they moved to Australia and left me. Ross... well he holds me back too, blocking my attempts to break into acting. It's true you can only rely on yourself you know.'

Ian let out a loud cough.

'Yes, Ian has been the only one to ever support me and nurture my talents,' Deborah quickly corrected. 'Like any powerful, independent woman, I took the bull by his balls and made my own fucking movie.'

Megan couldn't believe what she was hearing; her mind whirled trying to make any sense from Deborah's madness, 'But this isn't acting, you've killed two women,' she spat.

'It's called getting into character. I was the doctor. Kerry and Sarah were my patients, they were genuinely mad. Do you think that they could sleep with my husband and that'd be okay? Women need to stop believing things will just be handed to them on a plate,' Deborah turned to Sammie, 'Did you really think you would just be handed an offer to work on a film set? No one is self-made anymore; it's always about who you fucking know. Ross relied on contacts to get him where he is today. Everyone does it. It's fucking spineless.'

'Does Ross know you're doing this, that we're down here? Does Marc?' Megan asked suddenly afraid that Deborah and Ian weren't the only insane people in the house.

Deborah laughed, 'Have I not made myself clear enough? I'm brilliant in my own right. Ross and Marc are idiots and have never suspected a thing. You know why? Because I'm a fucking good actress.'

'But two women are dead,' Megan sobbed.

'But two women are dead,' Deborah mimicked in a childish tone.

'Their spirits are-'

'There are no bloody spirits,' Deborah howled, 'I know Marc has been playing those bloody pranks. Another example of a man thinking I'm an idiot. I knew all along it was him. There was never any ghosts. Sarah and Kerry only died in the early hours of Sunday.'

Megan couldn't take it in. They were only killed the day before she arrived at the house. 'What was that all about then, finding peace for Dr Holdstock's patients?' Megan was struggling to get her words out now with the pain.

'Oh I was just winding that silly old boot up, Nancy.' Deborah burst into a laugh, the kind of laugh where a silly prank was played, like when you pull a finger and the other person trumps. Tears started to stream down her face through the fits of giggles, 'I was just messing with her. She's another sour faced cow because she didn't get what she wanted. This house should've still been in her family and she hates it. Tough. Another case where someone expects something handed to her.'

'So you were just making stuff up the whole time for fun?' Megan whimpered.

'Fun?' Deborah said, her tone changing, 'It was fun getting Nancy's back up but this is serious. This is art, this is my work. You know what this is? It's a choose your own adventure story. Dr Holdstock was actually an expert in his field, a compassionate man who treated his patients with dignity and respect. Well I chose a better ending. One with a more dramatic impact.'

Ian started unpacking a bag of props. He pulled out two white gowns, just like the ones Sarah and Kerry had worn. He held them up and said it was time for Megan and Sammie to get ready.

Sammie was the first to scream, 'Help. Ross. Help.'

Megan screamed out for Marc, Ross, anyone.

'It's no use, Ross is unconscious in bed, completely shit-faced. And I've locked Marc in the cellar. I told him you were down there,' she said looking to Megan, 'he went scurrying down there and I bolted the door. He's just the other side of the wall actually,' she pointed to the far wall, 'well there is a bit of a void between the two cellars and it's well sound-proofed. I haven't figured out what to do with him yet. He obviously didn't find anything on the CCTV showing Sammie leave and I couldn't explain where you'd gone Megan.'

Ian was shaking his head, realising things were snowballing.

'It's all fine though, we always come up with a solution, a way round things. Ross and Marc have always bought everything I've said. They don't even know what goes on under this roof, don't even know this part of the cellar exists.'

Megan shuddered knowing that she must have heard Sammie fall through the trap door when she'd hid in the cellar for those few minutes. The minutes she now regretted. But how was she ever to imagine any of this? Ian threw a gown each to Megan and Sammie saying that if they didn't dress themselves then he would do it for them with force. He waved the keys to their handcuffs until they both nodded in agreement. He unlocked the cuffs and warned them not to do anything stupid.

'I can't believe you've done this to me,' Sammie sobbed to Megan.

'I didn't,' Megan pleaded, taking Sammie's hands.

'I was stupid to trust you. You brought me here.'

Deborah gushed, 'Isn't this precious, and perfect as part of my new script. C'mon get changed.'

Megan and Sammie slowly and awkwardly slipped off their clothes and pulled on the gowns.

'Perfect,' Deborah said. 'So do you know why this house is called Blind House? Well before Dr Holdstock started using this house as a residence for the insane, he used to open it up as a home and day care centre for the blind. For respite, activities and care, that kind of thing. Again he treated his clients professionally. So I decided to write a prequel. People love a prequel don't they? Ian read a bit of my new script.'

Ian picked the script up and scanned a few pages and smirked as he settled on the passage he wanted to read, '*The Doctor pulled out a scalpel and said to Patient Number One, "You refuse to see reality for what it is. What use are your eyes if you cannot see physically or something deeper. There is more than one way to see and you have proved incapable. Your eyes are merely decoration." The doctor restrains the patient before making the first incision around her eyelid...*'

Deborah grinned, 'I think we're ready for our first take.'

CHAPTER
FIFTY-THREE

Megan clung to Sammie who had begun hyperventilating. She tried to stay holding on to her but Ian was now wrestling with her to put the chains back on. Megan closed her eyes willing for all of this to stop, that this couldn't be happening. Surely Deborah wasn't sick enough to take their eyes? She pictured Kerry and Sarah's apparitions in the lake and her heart broke.

'You're wrong you know, there are ghosts. They've been watching you all along. I know they're in the lake. I saw them. How else could I know they're there. How does that make you feel?' Megan shouted.

Deborah exaggerated a thoughtful look, 'Their bodies floated to the top? You fell in, like the stupid little clutz that you are and found them. I thought I'd weighed them down enough, ah well. No matter, we'll make sure that doesn't happen again, won't we Ian? The boat is stored in the outhouse already to take you on your final journey. Everything's set.'

Megan closed her eyes, praying that when she opened them, she'd be back in Devon sat on the dragon's back. That none of this had happened, that she never took that phone call, that she never ended up here. She opened her eyes and through blurry painful tears, she made out the shape of a large black hound in the corner of the room. Deborah was barking orders at Ian and her words now drowned out, muffled under water sounds as were Sammie's cries. The dog just sat there staring and Megan knew that this time it was finally there to take her- take her to the other side.

'Now who shall I cast as Patient Number One and which one Number Two?' Deborah's voice boomed back into clarity. 'Megan you're Number One. Ian let's get a quick take in. I'm exhausted... run the cameras.'

'Take one,' Ian smacked down the clapperboard.

Deborah had thrown on her doctor's coat and entered the scene pretending to make notes on a clipboard. She then got up close to Megan's face as if examining her eyes, 'I'm going to need a knife,' she said sternly, marching over to the table where Ian had laid out her props. She marched back holding the knife up, examining it's blade. Kneeling down to Megan's level, she held the blade to her cheek. The whole time, Megan couldn't take her focus off the hound. Sitting there, waiting for her. Waiting to take her to Kerry, to Sarah... to Christina. Her whole body shook and she felt close to passing out. Sammie screamed and begged Deborah to stop.

Deborah slowly let the knife sink into the flesh of Megan's temple, then withdrew it. She felt the trickle of blood running down her cheek. Sammie was shaking her head rapidly as Deborah turned the knife on her.

'Leave her alone,' Megan screamed.

'You have the prettier eyes,' Deborah cocked her head to the side looking at Sammie. 'I bet you're jealous of everything about your sister, aren't you?' she spoke to Megan. She suddenly raised her eyebrows, 'I haven't scripted this but I've just had a brilliant idea. Ian, did you bring the shotgun like I asked?'

Ian confirmed that he had and pulled it from its case, then handed it to her.

Deborah aimed the shotgun at Megan's head then ordered Ian to unlock her cuffs. She then forced the knife into Megan's hands.

'You take her eyes, cut out her eyes or I'll blow your brains out.'

Megan could barely hold the knife through shaking, she looked at her sister who was deadly white and covered in a film of sweat, tears and snot.

'You know you want her eyes so have them,' Deborah pointed the gun closer, like she meant business.

Megan could still see the hound. It was still there. She looked at her sister, she looked at the hound. She would die anyway, so she wouldn't harm her sister. She scrunched her eyes shut and refused to budge. She waited.

Bang, bang, bang, the knife clattered to the floor. Deborah jumped back dropping the shotgun. The room was suddenly full of police officers led by Detective Page. They'd battered through the door. Megan's eyes flew open and she sucked in a huge breath. It was a whirl of chaos, of voices and hustle. Deborah and Ian were pinned to the ground in a swift motion and Page was shouting for the keys to the chains and shouting for medics. It was all so fast, a blur. But through the action, Megan had noticed one thing, the hound had vanished.

Megan and Sammie were carefully lifted from the cellar where ambulances with stretchers were waiting for them. Whilst officers were storming the cellar, other officers had stormed the house. Marc was found hammering on the cellar door off the pantry and was let out. Ross was dragged from his alcohol induced sleep, disorientated and confused. Both Ross and Marc were handcuffed, guarded by officers out on the driveway, waiting to be taken away for questioning.

'Megan,' Marc shouted over at the sight of her being lifted onto a stretcher, 'What the hell's happened?'

Megan could hear him but didn't have the strength to shout back, to move, to do anything. She allowed the paramedics to work on her.

Once Megan and Sammie were secure in the ambulances, Deborah and Ian were marched out of the cellar in cuffs.

'Will someone tell me what the fuck is going on,' Ross growled at the sight of his wife.

Deborah clocked Ross and Marc surrounded by officers and laughed. She was being bundled into a police van but tried to resist, tried to get the last word in, 'They had nothing to do with this,' she shouted, 'They knew nothing, because I'm a fucking good actress.' She kept on laughing as an officer slammed the van door shut.

EPILOGUE

Eight Months Later

Saying goodbye to Nancy, Megan ended the call and breathed in the warm May air. She would just spend a few more minutes watching the waves crash below her from her perch on the dragon's back rock. Megan would be forever grateful to Nancy for calling the police that night at Blind House and they had stayed in contact ever since. There were ghosts, there were pranks and there was Nancy. Nancy the elusive old lady lurking in the bushes watching the house. Nancy knew that Kerry's disappearance was off, she knew Deborah Huston was somehow mad. She followed her instincts. She cared enough about her family history and that property to keep an eye out. She followed her gut, she kept saying. It paid off; she was there to witness Sammie trying to escape the cellar. She didn't know about the secret hidden door- no one did. She saw it all. Her gut wasn't wrong and she got help. Right place, right time and Megan couldn't love that woman more.

The scamper of paws and the breathy sound of panting broke Megan's thoughts. Her feet met with a small terrier wagging its tail and demanding some fuss. She bent down to tickle him under the chin and rub him behind his ear.

'Ah, I see you've got your dog under control now, he was afraid of you before,' the lady said appearing into view from around the rocks.

It was her, the same lady that she'd seen here before. The strange lady who asked her to keep her dog under control. She was wearing the same brightly coloured clothing which clashed terribly. Megan couldn't forget her, those colours and the weird thing that she'd said. She didn't have a dog then and she didn't have one now and how did the woman remember her from eight months ago?

'I don't have a dog,' Megan said.

'Ah but you do,' the lady said brightly before walking off at pace singing some tune to herself as she went.

The dog- the black hound. Megan hadn't had visions of it since Blind House. No one else saw it. Did that woman see it? Megan shuddered, that can't be what she meant. She straightened up and made her way back up the coastal path slowly. She felt accomplished, it was the first time she'd actually managed to walk out this far since moving to Mortehoe. Her recovery had been slow with two broken legs, a broken ankle and a cracked rib. But Ross had seen to it that she received the best possible care, he paid for everything- she wanted for nothing.

Sammie had received some financial compensation from Ross too, not that Megan would know how her recovery was going because Sammie had cut her off again. Wanted nothing to do with her again, believing that Megan was responsible and that she should never have trusted her or thought that she'd changed. Megan was never going to shake her past with her sister and she accepted it. If Sammie could blame her for all of this then maybe Sammie wasn't the person she thought she'd be either. Her sister had also made plenty of money selling her story to every tabloid going. Megan kept quiet and avoided all attention. Two women were murdered and Megan didn't want the story turning into some circus.

Megan reached her house and put her key in the door. It never got less exciting, turning the key inside the lock to her new home- the house Ross Huston brought for her. He insisted on making sure that she was provided for and this house- this perfect house that she could only have dreamed of was impossible to refuse. Ross had felt nothing but bewildered, stunned, disorientated, at what Deborah was capable of, what was going on under their roof without so much as an idea.

He had kept a low profile during the investigations and then moved back to the States. Besides lack of physical evidence, Deborah had maintained that he and Marc were not involved, she was too smug; admitting to have been a brilliant actress- a genius. She even paid her Uncle Ian little credit, stating he merely rolled the cameras and did a bit of editing. She demanded notoriety and films to be made about her. Ross also stepped down from his role as Inspector Dark out of respect for the victim's families and to maintain a low profile. It would be sometime before the media would die down and he could rebuild his reputation.

Marc also laid low but did check in with Megan occasionally. The odd phone call, a message to make sure she was okay. He wanted to visit but Megan wasn't ready for that. She was moving on and Marc made it all real. He tortured himself over what had happened to Sarah. Whether she blamed him up until she died, whether she believed he was in on it and did that to her. He would tell Megan that he couldn't sleep, that he just kept seeing her when he closed his eyes, blaming him, hating him. He asked a number of times if Megan could try communicating with her, talk to her. Megan couldn't bring herself to try. She believed that both Sarah and Kerry already knew. They were watching and always had been. They knew. Marc didn't have to worry. One day a cup of tea with Marc might be nice. But not yet.

Megan went straight to the bathroom and turned on the shower. She had a peaceful evening ahead of her and with such warm weather, she could have the windows thrown open and enjoy the sound of the waves. As the water drenched her, she decided that it was time to start seriously thinking about her next steps. She was back to full health and knew it was time to think about her business. She had closed down her paranormal investigations website whilst she was recovering. It was never going to be a permanent role for her, not without Christina. But things had changed hadn't they?

How the changes occurred, Megan didn't think she'd ever know or be able to explain- who could? But ghosts were real, Megan had witnessed and experienced things that she couldn't dispute, not this time. Not once had she felt sensitive to spirits, that was Christina and other people who believed. But not her. So what changed? Did the grief of losing Christina do something to her? Did her friend's energy from the other side do something to her? But Christina hadn't come through to her- why hadn't she? She connected to Sarah and Kerry hadn't she?

The thought of Sarah and Kerry being laid to rest filled Megan with comfort. They had been removed from the coldness of the lake to a better resting place where their families could mourn and remember them. The whole ordeal was terrifying but what Megan realised was that she helped uncover the truth, delivered justice. She helped the dead so they could rest in peace. It felt rewarding. It brought comfort. As Megan rinsed away the remaining soap from her hair, she decided that she would- she'd activate her website and go back into business.

She stepped from the shower and smiled at owning her own luxury towels to wrap herself in. Then the mirror caught her eye. The steamed up mirror with writing. Writing which said, "I told you so." Megan spun round, her heart beating fast. Through the doorway, there they were on the landing. Christina, a ghostly apparition of Christina- with her arm around the black hound. The two of them together. Christina was smiling and they vanished. It was quick and brief but they were there.

It told Megan all that she needed to know. Christina was watching her and was there for her. And so was the hound it seemed, a spirit guide being there for her at her every turn, every decision, every danger, letting her know that she wasn't on her own, to help guide her courage and instincts. The hound didn't want to take her to the other side, it wanted to keep her right where she was.

About the Author

Dear reader,

Thank you for choosing to read *Blind House*. It is my debut novel and if you would like to hear about future releases then I can be found on Facebook: Jamie-Lee Brooke- Author and Twitter: @Jamie_Lee Brooke. Did you enjoy *Blind House*? I would love to hear your thoughts. Why not leave an Amazon review? Reviews give independent authors a fantastic boost and are hugely appreciated. Thank you once again.

Acknowledgments

I am blessed to have numerous friends and family who have supported me and cheered me on in my quest to achieve my dreams and ambitions. I am eternally grateful for each and every one of them. Special thanks go out to my beta readers - Carla Buckley, Phil Price, Sarah Federici and Anna Wallace. Their input and encouragement have been nothing short of valuable. I'd like to thank my writing group friends who are only a message away in answering my stupid questions- John Lovell, Vanessa Morgan, Terry Walsh and Mark Wallace. Also a big huge thank you to the whole team at Spellbound Books for their hard work, having faith in me and all that they do. Lastly, I'd like to thank Ian Morgan for the loan of his laptop at times and his ongoing support.

Printed in Great Britain
by Amazon